Praise for *T...*

'Yet again the novelist convinces with a satisfying, credible police procedural. This time, William Wisting faces a major life crisis: he is himself investigated, and forced to examine his police career in a new light. His journalist daughter Line plays an important role in the book, turning the novel into both a depiction of the father-daughter relationship and a portrayal of the relationship between the police and the media.'

Riverton Prize jury's comments on *The Hunting Dogs*

'All lovers of crime fiction should read his new book. It is simply sensationally successful.'

Torbjørn Ekelund, *Dagbladet*

'Jorn Lier Horst narrates this story using the best devices of the genre, without using any easy ways out. There is a feeling that the book comes with a built-in side-shift mechanism.'

Geir Rakvaag, *Dagsavisen*

'Strikes to the very heart of the reader.'

Kjell Einar Øren, *Haugesunds Avis*

'In *The Hunting Dogs*, Jorn Lier Horst has delivered an outstanding novel – his best to date.'

Svend Einar Hansen, *Østlands-Posten*

'*The Hunting Dogs* is a book to hunt for.'

Helge Ottesen, *Varden*

Praise for *Dregs*

'Jorn Lier Horst has, right from his debut in 2004, set a sensationally good pace in his crime novels, and has today gained entry into the circle of our very best writers in that genre.'

Terje Stemland, *Aftenposten*, Norway

'Just as good are the descriptions of the characters in Jorn Lier Horst's book. They are nuanced and interesting, absolutely human. Many have known it for a long time, but now it ought to be acknowledged as a truth for all readers of crime fiction: William Wisting is one of the great investigators in Norwegian crime novels.'

Norwegian Book Club
(Book of the Month, Crime and Thrillers)

'I'm impressed once again that he has created such a sterling crime mystery as *Dregs*. For he hasn't only made use of his comprehensive knowledge, he has also done it with creative finesse.'

Marius Aronsen, Secretary of *Riverton Club*, Norway

'Once more Jorn Lier Horst has produced a sound criminal narrative with an intricate plot, an action-packed story with Chief Inspector William Wisting as a credible central character. Jorn Lier Horst has the great advantage of his own experiences as a police investigator, and is able to bring real authenticity to such aspects as investigative methodology and tactical planning.'

Svend E. Hansen, *Østlandsposten*, Norway

Jorn Lier Horst was born in 1970, in Bamble, Telemark, Norway. Between 1995 and 2013, when he turned to full time writing, he worked as a policeman in Larvik, eventually becoming head of investigations there. His William Wisting series of crime novels has been extremely successful, having sold more than 500,000 copies in Scandinavia, UK, Germany, Netherlands and Thailand. *Dregs*, sixth in the series, was published in English by Sandstone Press in 2011, and *Closed for Winter*, winner of Norway's Booksellers' Prize, in 2012. *Closed for Winter* was also shortlisted for the prestigious Riverton Prize or *The Golden Revolver*, for best Norwegian crime novel of the year. Subsequently, *The Hunting Dogs*, successor to *Closed for Winter* won both the *Golden Revolver* and *The Glass Key*, which widened the scope to best crime fiction in all the Nordic countries. Jorn Lier Horst's most recent William Wisting novel, *The Caveman*, will be published by Sandstone Press in 2015.

Anne Bruce, who lives on the Isle of Arran in Scotland, formerly worked in education and has a longstanding love of Scandinavia and Norway in particular. Having studied Norwegian and English at Glasgow University, she is the translator of Jorn Lier Horst's *Dregs* and *Closed for Winter* , and also Anne Holt's *Blessed are Those who Thirst* (2012) and *Death of the Demon* (2013), as well as Merethe Lindstrøm's Nordic Prize winning *Days in the History of Silence* (2013).

Also published by Sandstone Press

Dregs
Closed for Winter

THE HUNTING DOGS

Jorn Lier Horst

Translated by

Anne Bruce

SANDSTONEPRESS
HIGHLAND | SCOTLAND

First published in Great Britain
and the United States of America
Sandstone Press Ltd
PO Box 5725
One High Street
Dingwall
Ross-shire
IV15 9WJ
Scotland.

www.sandstonepress.com

Published in English in 2014 by Sandstone Press Ltd
English language editor: Robert Davidson

This translation has been published with the financial support of NORLA.
The publisher acknowledges support from Creative Scotland towards
publication of this volume.

ISBN: 978-1-908737-63-2
ISBNe: 978-1-908737-64-9

Cover design by Freight Design, Glasgow
Typesetting by Iolaire Typesetting, Newtonmore
Printed and bound by Totem, Poland

WILLIAM WISTING

William Wisting is a career policeman who has risen through the ranks to become Chief Inspector in the Criminal Investigation Department of Larvik Police, just like his creator, author Jorn Lier Horst. *The Hunting Dogs* is the eighth title in the series, the third to be published in English, and finds him aged fifty-two, the widowed father of grown up twins, Thomas and Line. Wisting's wife, Ingrid, went to Africa to work on a NORAD project but was killed there at the end of *The Only One*, the fifth title in the series.

Thomas serves in the military, in Afghanistan at the time of *The Hunting Dogs*. Daughter Line is an investigative journalist based in Oslo, whose career frequently intersects with that of her father. Wisting, at first apprehensive, has come to value how she is able to operate in ways that he cannot, often turning up unexpected clues and insights.

After Ingrid's death Wisting became involved with another woman, Suzanne Bjerke, a former child welfare worker who, at the beginning of *The Hunting Dogs*, has recently opened a café-bar in Stavern. However, for Wisting, Ingrid remains the absence around which all else revolves. The development of this new relationship is charted in subsequent books, including this one.

Crucial to the series are Wisting's colleagues in the police. Audun Vetti, the arrogant Assistant Chief of Police who was also the police prosecutor, came to the fore in *Dregs*, when the question of how much information to divulge to the press was bitterly contested between the two. In *Closed for Winter*, he had been promoted to the post of Deputy Chief

Constable. Wisting has more positive relationships with certain trusted colleagues: old school Nils Hammer, whose background in the Drugs Squad has made him cynical, the younger Torunn Borg whom Wisting has come to rely on thanks to her wholly professional approach and outlook, and Mortensen, the crime scene examiner who is usually first on the scene.

The setting is Vestfold county on the south-west coast of Norway, an area popular with holidaymakers, where rolling landscapes and attractive beaches make an unlikely setting for crime. The principal town of Larvik, where Wisting is based, is located 105 km (65 miles) southwest of Oslo. The wider Larvik district has 41,000 inhabitants, 23,000 of whom live in the town itself, and covers 530 square km. Larvik is noted for its natural springs, but its modern economy relies heavily on agriculture, commerce and services, light industry and transportation, as well as tourism. There is a ferry service from Larvik to Hirsthals in Denmark.

At the beginning of *The Hunting Dogs*, we learn that Wisting has added to his duties as head of CID by becoming a visiting lecturer at the recently opened Police College campus in Stavern. A lecture he had given recently had been about ethics and morality, a topic that becomes the central focus of this new novel. Jorn Lier Horst's own deep experience of police procedures and processes brings a strong sense of the novels in the William Wisting series being firmly grounded in reality.

The Hunting Dogs won the Norwegian Riverton Prize (Golden Revolver) in 2012 as well as the Scandinavian Glass Key in 2013. Jorn Lier Horst worked as a policeman in Larvik between 1995 and 2013 when he turned to full time writing.

1

Rain lashed the windowpane, streaming down the glass like rivers, the wind so strong it had the bare branches of the poplars clawing at the walls of the cafe. William Wisting sat at a window table, watching as wet autumn leaves were torn from the pavement and tossed around.

Wisting liked rain without understanding exactly why, but it seemed to help him take things easier, to relax and slow down a little. Cool jazz, mingling with the downpour, helped too. He turned towards the counter and the flickering shadows cast along the walls by the candles. Smiling at him, Suzanne Bjerke turned the music down another notch.

Three teenagers were huddled round a table at the end of the counter; otherwise they were alone. Suzanne's intimate, sophisticated café had become a favourite haunt of students from the newly established Police College campus.

He turned towards the window again, where the words *The Golden Peace* were emblazoned in a curve of reversed frosted letters: *Gallery and Coffee Bar*. He did not know how long Suzanne had nursed her dream, but one winter evening she had put down her book to tell him the story of the Hudson River ferryman who, all his life, had sailed between New York and Jersey, back and forth, forth and back. Day after day, year after year he sailed until, one day, he made his big decision to turn the boat round and set out, full speed, for the great ocean he had dreamed about all his life. The very next day, she took the plunge and bought the café premises.

When she asked him what his own dream was, he had to say that he didn't know. He liked his life just as it was. A policeman at heart, he had no wish to be anything else. His work as a detective gave him a sense of purpose and brought meaning to his life. He drew the Sunday newspaper towards him and again peered into the night.

Usually he sat further inside the café, where fewer people would notice him, but in this weather he felt he could sit undisturbed at a window table without passers-by recognising him and coming inside to engage him in conversation. Since he had reluctantly taken part in a television talk show, this was happening more frequently.

One of the boys glanced in his direction. Wisting remembered him. At the beginning of term, he had been invited to deliver a lecture about ethics and morality and the boy had been sitting in the front row.

The front page of the paper was devoted to slimming advice, warnings of more rain and intrigues on a TV reality programme. Only seldom did the Sundays contain fresh news. Canned goods were what his journalist daughter, Line, called the material lying in the editorial office for days, sometimes weeks, before being published. She had been a journalist on *Verdens Gang* for almost five years, had worked in various departments, but was currently on the crime desk, meaning that her editorial team occasionally covered cases he was working on.

Wisting managed his double role of detective and father without too much difficulty. What he disliked was the thought of Line in close proximity to the grisly side of society. He had been a police officer for thirty-one years, and his work had given him insight into most kinds of brutality and barbarism, but also many sleepless nights, something he hoped his daughter would be spared.

He leafed through the pages, skimming the news coverage,

not expecting to find anything Line had written since he knew she was on leave.

Increasingly, he valued their discussions of current news stories. Though it had not been easy for him to admit, she had altered his views on his role as a police officer. Her outsider's perspective had more than once made him reassess his fairly stale opinions of himself. As recently as his lecture to the students, when he had talked about how important it was for people's security and confidence that police officers behaved with integrity, decency and propriety, he had realised that Line's points of view had given him valuable ballast. He had tried to explain to his future colleagues the importance of these fundamental values in the role of the police within society, that it demanded impartiality and objectivity, honesty and sincerity, and an endless search for truth.

When he reached the television schedules on the back pages, the students were at the door fastening their coats. The tallest made eye contact with Wisting, who smiled and responded with a nod of recognition.

'Day off?' the lad enquired.

'That's one of the advantages when you've been on the force as long as I have,' Wisting replied. 'Working from eight till four and free every weekend.'

'Thanks for a great lecture, by the way.'

'Nice of you to say so.'

The student wanted to say something more, but was interrupted by Wisting's phone. It was Line. 'Hello, Dad. Has anyone from the newspaper phoned you?'

'No,' Wisting replied, nodding to the three students as they left. 'Why? Has something happened?'

'I'm in the editorial office now,' she explained.

'Aren't you off duty?'

'Yes, but I was at the gym and thought I would call in

briefly.' Wisting recognised much of himself in his daughter, especially her curiosity and desire always to be at the centre of events. 'There's going to be a piece about you in tomorrow's newspaper,' Line said, pausing before she continued, 'but this time you're the one they're after. You're the one they're out to get.'

2

In the following silence Line moved the cursor over the screen where the story, set and ready for print, her father's face prominently displayed, was splashed on the front page. 'It's about the Cecilia case,' she clarified.

'The Cecilia case?

It was one of the cases her father never discussed, one of the difficult and painful ones. 'Cecilia Linde,' she elaborated, though she knew her father needed no reminder. It had been one of the most sensational murders of that decade.

'What about it?'

Line glanced up from the screen as the chief editor moved away from the news desk and stepped towards the stairs and the floor above. It was time for the evening meeting, when the final threads of the next day's paper would be drawn together and a decision taken about what would make the front page. The Cecilia Linde story filled two pages, and would provide an obvious headline. Her murder would still sell newspapers, even after seventeen years.

'Haglund's lawyer has sent a petition to the Criminal Cases Review Commission,' she explained, once the chief editor had passed. The news editor shuffled a stack of papers and followed. Line skim-read the report one more time, feeling that it actually posed more questions than it answered, but appreciating that this story would run to a series, and not only in her own newspaper. 'A private detective has been working on the case.'

'What does that have to do with me?' From her father's

tone she realised he understood the seriousness of what was happening. As a young detective, he had led the investigation and had, since then, become a high-profile policeman, a well-known face who could be held responsible and used to set the news agenda.

'They think the evidence was fabricated,' Line explained.

'What kind of evidence?'

'The DNA. They believe it was planted by the police.'

'On what grounds?'

'The lawyer has had the samples re-analysed. He believes the cigarette butt on which the DNA was found had been planted.'

'That was alleged at the time.'

'The lawyer thinks they can prove it now, and says that the documentation has been transferred to the Criminal Cases Review Commission.'

'I don't understand how he can prove anything.'

'They have a new witness as well,' Line continued. 'One who can provide Haglund with an alibi.'

'Why didn't this witness come forward at the time?'

'He says he did,' Line said, swallowing. 'He says he phoned in and spoke to you, but he heard nothing further.' Her father made no sound. 'It's the evening meeting here now,' she said, 'but they'll soon contact you for comment. You ought to prepare whatever you're going to say.'

Wisting's face took up most of the space on the screen. They had used a press photograph from the talk show almost a year earlier. The studio setting was easy to recognise and acted as a kind of subtle emphasis that this was a well-known detective who was now being accused of breaking the law: a man with slightly rumpled, thick, dark hair, a strained smile, the wrinkles on his face betraying a lifetime of experience, his dark eyes gazing steadily into the camera lens.

On television he had emerged not only as the upright,

skilled policeman he actually was, but also as a caring and considerate investigator with a powerful sense of social justice. Tomorrow's caption would present him in a different light. His eyes would be perceived as cold, and the strained smile would seem false.

'Line?'

'Yes?'

'It's not true. None of what they're saying is true.'

'I know that, Dad. You don't need to tell me, but all the same it's going to appear in print tomorrow.'

3

Evening silence had fallen over the editorial offices. Pictures from foreign news channels drifted across soundless television screens, accompanied by the tapping of practised fingers racing across keyboards and occasional hushed telephone conversations.

Line was about to log off when the chief editor returned, Joakim Frost, who was only ever known as 'Frost'. They said he got the post of chief editor because he was incapable of understanding the human tragedies behind the headlines. His lack of empathy was the perfect qualification.

Frost scanned the room with a chilly expression, looking right through her. 'Apologies,' he said, taking for granted that she had seen the story. 'I was going to phone to let you know, but now you're here anyway.'

Line nodded. She knew Frost would be the driving force behind the spread but knew him too well to enter into discussion. She had no desire to listen to his usual lecture about an independent, free press and, besides, he was hardly interested in counter arguments. Frost had been in the newspaper game for almost forty years and, in his eyes, she was still an insignificant rookie.

'This is a story we can't afford to ditch,' he said. 'Have you spoken to your father?'

'Yes.'

'What's he saying?'

'He can tell you himself.'

Frost accepted this. 'He has the right of reply, of course.'

Line indulged in a wry smile. It was a waste of time furnishing a defence against accusations splashed across the front page. What's more, it was a hopeless task, responding to a story produced by the entire editorial team through a telephone enquiry made immediately before the newspaper went to press.

'Listen, Line,' Frost said. 'This story engages a great deal more than just our feelings. It is of general and national interest. I appreciate this is difficult for you but it's not easy for me either.'

Line stood up. Frost's sanctimonious arguments were window-dressing for what actually was of importance to him: circulation figures. The newspaper's integrity could be preserved without placing her father at the centre of sensational headlines, nor did the story need to be personalised. Criticism could just as easily be directed towards the police as an organisation, but that would not sell so many newspapers.

'If you need to take some time, you can have a few days off,' he said. 'You can come back when this is over.'

'No thanks.'

'I think it could have turned even uglier if we let others get hold of it.'

Line looked away. Spare me this,' she said. The thought of her father's face plastered across the front of next day's newspaper made her feel sick.

'Line!' The shout came from the news editor, who was standing beside one of the evening reporters. Ripping a sheet from her notepad, he headed across to them. 'I know you're off duty and it's probably not convenient, but can you pick up on this?'

Line replied automatically: 'What is it?'

'Murder in the Old Town in Fredrikstad. Not confirmed by the police yet, but we've received a tip-off from someone standing beside a blood-soaked corpse.'

Line felt the news fill her with vitality and yet, at the same time, deplete her energy. This was the kind of story she loved, and at which she excelled. She was expert at finding sources and exploited them to the maximum, analysing them thoroughly so that she knew what could and could not be trusted.

Frost's face broadened into a grin. 'He's phoning from the crime scene?'

'First the police, then us,' said the news editor.

'Wrong order, but we can live with that. Who can take photographs?'

'We'll have a freelancer there in ten minutes, but need a reporter.'

Joakim Frost turned to face Line. 'One way or another I think you should head off,' he said.

Line observed his retreating back, realising it would be much more comfortable for him and the others if she were to spend the next few days in Østfold County instead of here in the office.

The news editor handed her the sheet of paper with the name and phone number of the informant. 'There might be something in that,' he said, dropping his voice as he continued: 'We won't be setting the front page for another four hours.'

4

The journalist phoned Wisting just before ten o'clock. Wisting caught only that he was from *Verdens Gang*. 'We're writing about the Cecilia case tomorrow. The lawyer, Sigurd Henden, has lodged a petition at the Criminal Cases Review Commission.'

'I see.'

'We'd like your comment on being accused of faking the evidence that got Rudolf Haglund convicted.'

Wisting replied in a steady voice: 'What was your name?'

The journalist hesitated, giving Wisting a suspicion that his indistinct introduction had been deliberate. 'Eskild Berg.'

This must be an ordinary news reporter and not one of the crime reporters he usually spoke to when anything cropped up. He thought he had seen the name in print, but could not recall ever talking to him.

'What's your comment on the allegations that you falsified evidence?' the journalist repeated.

Wisting maintained his composure. 'It's difficult to comment when I don't know the allegations.'

'Henden claims he can prove that Rudolf Haglund was convicted on the basis of fabricated evidence.'

'I don't know about anything of that nature.'

'You were in charge of the investigation?'

'That's right.'

'But is it true? Was the evidence faked?' The journalist was hardly expecting to receive confirmation, but obviously aimed to provoke a reaction.

'I don't know the background to Henden's assertions,' Wisting said, so slowly the journalist had time to jot it down. 'I know absolutely nothing about any irregularities whatsoever having taken place in the course of the investigation.'

'Apparently there's a witness who wasn't given the opportunity to make a statement. A witness who wanted to testify on behalf of Haglund.'

'That's also something I know nothing about, but in that case I'm sure the Commission will give a full account of the circumstances.'

'Don't you think these are shocking allegations made against you as the person responsible, and in charge of the investigation?' The reporter was obviously attempting to goad him into voicing personal opinions.

'You can quote me on what I've just said,' Wisting responded. 'I don't wish to say anything else tonight.'

The journalist tried once or twice more before Wisting put down the phone, knowing full well that his version was not the most compelling. He had a good understanding of the role of the press as guard dog. It was their task to criticise politicians, people in positions of power, and public agencies. They had to seek out justice and expose fraud and injustice, but now it felt as though injustice was riding roughshod over him.

He stared meditatively at his reflection in the rain battered window and saw the face of a stranger.

He knew Henden, the lawyer, from a number of cases. He had not been Haglund's defence counsel seventeen years earlier, but nowadays he was an established, high profile solicitor with one of the country's largest and most reputable law firms. Added to this he had been both Under Secretary and a personal adviser in the Ministry of Justice. Whenever Wisting encountered him, he had behaved in a methodical, scrupulous manner, normally holding winning cards when initiating contact with the media, unconcerned with playing to the gallery.

Wisting had been aware that Henden was working on the case when, a couple of months earlier, the lawyer had asked for the case documentation. Occasionally journalists, private detectives or solicitors asked the police to open their archives, but it was very rare that this led to anything.

Sigurd Henden was not the type to write letters or petitions simply to please his clients. He must have discovered something that could be used to reopen the old homicide case. Wisting just did not understand what it could be, and that made him feel uneasy.

Suzanne crossed to the door where she turned the lock and reversed the sign, ensuring the information that they were closed was now facing out. Then she began to extinguish the candles. 'Are you going to help me?' she asked, starting to unload the dishwasher.

Wisting opened his mouth to tell her about Cecilia Linde, but, having no idea where to start, shut it again.

5

Rain hammered against Line's car windscreen as she drove, torrents of water pouring down the glass. For the initial few kilometres along the motorway, her thoughts were fixed on her father. She felt helpless, as though she had somehow been disloyal.

Glancing at the news editor's note on the passenger seat beside her, other thoughts took shape. She had no chance of stopping the story about her father being published, but she might manage to push it off the front page. It depended entirely on what she was able to make of this death, since the first hours of a murder case were just as important for journalists as for the police.

Pressing harder on the accelerator, she fished out her mobile phone and keyed in the number of the photographer on the scene. Erik Fjeld was a short, plump, red-haired man with thick glasses. They had worked together on a couple of previous stories.

'What do you know?' she asked, getting straight to the point.

'They've cordoned off a fairly large area now,' he explained, 'but when I arrived there was hardly anyone here.'

'Do we know who's been murdered?'

'No, I don't think the police know either.'

Line glanced at the time. Her deadline was quarter past one, just over three hours. She had delivered front-page news in less time before, but it depended more on the story than on her. Murder cases hit the headlines less and less frequently.

Their news value declined when the online editions could report so much more speedily, so there had to be something really special about the story, as well as a guaranteed unique angle.

'It's a man?' she asked, staring past the windscreen wipers.

'Aged about fifty.'

It sounded like the kind of case it would be difficult to do much with. Young women produced bigger headlines. The odds of it being some celebrity or other were not good, either. Off the top of her head, she could think of only two well-known people who came from Fredrikstad, Roald Amundsen and the film director Harald Zwart. Amundsen had been dead for almost a century, and Zwart probably no longer even lived in Norway. 'Do you have an address or car registration?'

'Sorry. Where he's lying, there are no cars or houses.'

'Is there much of a press presence?'

'Just the locals from *Demokraten* and *Fredriksstad Blad*, and a photographer who usually supplies *Scanpix*.'

'What do you have?'

'I was here early, got close up and snapped a series that's reasonably good. They've placed a blanket over the body. His dog is beside him, craning his neck. Fantastic lighting with that glow from the blue lights. Police tape and uniforms in the background.'

'Dog?'

'Yes, he must have been out walking when he was attacked.'

The information lifted Line's spirits. There were lots of dog lovers out there. 'What kind of dog?'

'Some kind of long-haired variety, a bit like *Labbetuss* on children's television. Remember him? Only not quite as large.'

Line smiled, remembering *Labbetuss*. 'Save the dog pictures until I get there,' she said, 'but send over the others.

They need something more than readers' photographs for the online edition.'

'They'll probably want photographs of the mutt,' the photographer objected. 'They're really good.'

'Wait with them,' Line repeated. If the best pictures were already on the internet the value of her own work would plummet.

Breaking off the conversation, she checked the rear-view mirror and looked into her own blue eyes. She was wearing no makeup and had not fixed her hair since her visit to the workplace gym. It felt as though everything around her had been turned upside down in the past hour. She hadn't had any plans for the evening other than finding a good film and stretching out on the settee and now was slightly over the speed limit on route E6, on her way to Østfold and a murder scene.

She changed lane after passing the exit for Vinterbro and picked up the slip of paper with the informant's number. She ought to arrange an interview, but there was no time for that. She called while driving, and the number rang for ages. The man was obviously affected, his voice trembling as he spoke.

Leaning forward, Line placed the paper in the centre of the wheel and steered with her lower arm as she jotted down key points. His story contained nothing new. He had been on his way home when he came across the dead man. 'The blood was still gushing out of him,' he explained. 'But there was nothing I could do. His face was completely smashed.' Line was disgusted, but blood gushing out was something that would look good in italicised quotes, and would help to bring the story closer to the front page. The way someone was killed was always interesting. 'Was he battered to death?' she asked, to make sure.

'Yes, yes.'

'Do you know what was used to hit him?'

'No.'

'There wasn't anything on the ground? A weapon of any kind?'

'No ... I would've noticed if there had been a baseball bat or anything. It could've been a stone or something.'

'You must have arrived right after it happened,' she suggested, thinking of the fresh blood. 'Did you see anyone?'

The man considered this. 'I was the only one there. Me and the dead man. And his dog.'

Line felt conflicting emotions as she wrapped the conversation. She was searching for bloody, bestial details in the hope that they would push her father's case off the front page. To meet her own needs, she had a sort of desire that the maximum possible suffering had been meted out to another human being.

A lorry unleashed a spray of water ahead of her. She waited until she had overtaken it before tapping in the number for Directory Enquiries.

Usually, when she was on the road, her colleagues in Editorial provided a kind of back-up service, a team that kept her informed about what the online media was reporting, checking on their own initiative but, at the moment, she did not want to speak to anyone inside the building.

A woman's sleepy voice asked how she could be of assistance. Line asked her to find the number for a petrol station in the Old Town of Fredrikstad. Rumours about what was happening in a small town had a tendency to spread fast, and she knew from past experience that late-opening petrol stations were places where most topics were discussed. She was transferred to the Statoil Østsiden station.

Line introduced herself. 'I work for *VG* and am on my way down to write about the murder in Heibergs gate,' she explained, checking the street name on the slip of paper. 'Have you heard about it?'

She could hear the girl turning the chewing gum in her mouth before replying. 'Yes, there have been a few people talking about it.'

'Has anybody said who it is?'

'No.'

'It's apparently a man out walking his dog.'

'There's plenty of people who go for walks there, you know, along the moats at the fortress.'

'He has a long-haired dog,' Line ventured. 'Looks like *Labbetuss*. Maybe he has been in the petrol station?'

'*Labbetuss?*'

Line did not bother to explain. 'The man who's been killed is about forty to fifty years old,' she added instead.

'I don't think I've seen him. Not today at least, but I can ask around.'

'Great. Can you take a note of my number and phone me if you hear anything? We pay for useful information.' Remuneration for tip-offs was not something she normally mentioned, but it could be a decisive factor in persuading people to phone back.

'That's okay,' the girl replied. 'Is it the number on the display here?' Line rattled off her number to make sure it was correct and repeated the request for her to phone. 'Strange weather to go out for a walk,' the girl commented. 'The rain's lashing down. It's been doing that all evening.'

Line agreed with the girl, but did not think to consider it further. Her next call was to the Taxi Centre. The man at the switchboard spoke in a broad, slightly nasal but charming dialect. He could not help, but connected her to a car located in Torsnesveien, in the vicinity of the crime scene.

'Have you heard anything about who it might be?' she asked once she had introduced herself.

The driver seemed eager, but could not provide any useful information. 'A lot of foreigners hang out there at night,' he explained. 'One of our drivers was robbed and threatened with a knife at Gudeberg this summer.'

'I think I read about that,' Line said, without actually recalling the story.

The taxi-driver promised to make inquiries. Line gave him her phone number and assured him that useable tip-offs would be rewarded. The clock on the dashboard read 22.19. For the time being, she had nothing to go on, and there were fewer than three hours to deadline.

6

By the time she drove over the arched bridge separating Fredrikstad town centre from the Old Town, her deadline was closer by another half hour. The GPS fastened to the windscreen guided her to Heibergs gate where, on both sides, villas were enclosed by white picket fences. The street was closed off at the entrance to a sports ground by a police patrol car, parked at an angle, and crime scene tape fluttering and twisting in the breeze. Several cars were parked close by, and a small group of people sheltered beneath an umbrella.

Driving into the pavilion car park, Line pulled up and peered into the freezing, scudding rain, absorbing her first impressions. Two strategically placed floodlights shone on the crime scene. A sizeable tent was pitched above the walkway and cycle path, running parallel to the barricaded stretch of road. Crime scene technicians in white sterile overalls walked to and fro, placing all potential evidence in plastic bags while two men in raincoats with the *NRK* TV station logo on the back were packing their equipment into a white delivery van. Line rummaged through her bag for a rain jacket, struggling to wriggle into it before clambering out to the wind and weather.

One of the other drivers flashed his lights. Line jogged over to find Erik Fjeld behind the steering wheel, and launched herself into the passenger seat. The mat was littered with empty bottles, hot dog wrappers, and other rubbish that rustled underfoot. 'Any news?' she asked.

'Nice to see you again too,' he said. He had endured a long wait.

'Can I see the photos?' she asked.

Turning his camera to display mode, Erik Fjeld showed her a better image than she had feared: the dead man covered by a pale blue blanket, only a pair of Wellington boots protruding, his dog sitting beside his head, wet, tousled coat glistening, its head tilted and a dejected, bewildered expression. She could almost hear it howl. It was a poignant photograph, and the black asphalt in the foreground could provide a perfect space for a caption and text.

'Where's the dog now?' she asked, wiping condensation from the car window with her hand.

'A Falck vehicle came to collect it.'

'From Falck, did you say?'

'They round up the abandoned dogs in this town. I think everyone was pleased when they took it away. It was awful to listen to.'

Line opened the car door again to activate the interior light. 'Where did they take it?'

'The dog?'

'Yes. Where is it now?'

'At their depot, I expect. In Tomteveien near Lisleby.' Line was out of the car before he finished speaking. 'Where are you going?'

'To have a look at the dog.'

'Do you want me with you?'

She shook her head. 'Wait here. They'll carry the body out soon. We should have photos of that. I'll call if I need you.'

Slamming the car door, she hurried back to her own vehicle and keyed *Tomteveien* into the satnav. The address, located on the opposite bank of the River Glomma, was directly outside the town centre. Eleven minutes away, according to the gadget. She got there in nine and a half.

21

A breakdown lorry was idling outside the massive building when she arrived, the driver coiling and storing a cargo strap. He glanced up as Line parked beside him. She stepped out and flashed a smile. 'Is this where stray dogs are brought?' she asked, ruffling her already dishevelled hair.

'Have you lost one?' he asked, tugging off his work gloves.

'I wondered if I could see the dog you just collected from Heibergs gate.'

The driver looked at her in the powerful light of the building's wall lamps, from the top of her blonde hair to the tips of her toes. On the return journey, his eyes lingered. 'The dog belonging to the guy who was murdered?'

Line told him who she was, where she worked and what she did. Experience told her he would either hold journalists in contempt or be one of those who read the paper avidly with a steaming coffee in his hand.

'Do you want to come in with me and say hello to it?' he asked, nodding behind him at the garage.

Line followed him into a hall with rows of bicycles suspended from the ceiling.

'Lost property,' he explained. 'Drillo's in here.' He pointed towards a door at the opposite end of the premises.

'Drillo?'

'That's what we call him,' the man confirmed. 'It's exactly the same kind of dog as Drillo's.'

It dawned on Line that he was right. The coach of the national football team owned a longhaired dog, just like the one she had seen in the photograph. He came from Fredrikstad too, if she remembered correctly. The town could claim another celebrity. Ahead of her, the man pushed open the door leading to the next room. Dimly lit, it comprised four cubicles with bars and wire mesh doors. The dog in the first cage was a heavily built Schaefer with a grey snout and vacant eyes whose head slid back down onto its paws as they passed.

Drillo was in the last cage. The dog's sombre gaze seemed to look right through them as Line approached and placed the flat of her hand on the wire mesh.

'Do you want to go inside?' the driver asked. Without waiting for an answer, he withdrew the bolt that held the mesh door closed.

Line entered and the dog sat down, watching her carefully. 'Hi, there,' she said, scratching under the dog's chin before examining under its ears. 'Do you know if it's been chipped?' she asked the driver.

'I don't think anyone's got as far as thinking about that yet, but we've got the gizmo to do that somewhere here.'

Before Line became a crime reporter she wrote an article about the ID marking of dogs. There were two methods: a tattoo inside the ear, or a microchip injected by a vet on the left side of the neck or just above the left shoulder. This electronic chip contained a registration number searchable on the internet.

'Here it is!' The driver hauled out an apparatus that resembled a barcode reader in a shop. When he moved the reader up and down the dog's neck a fifteen-digit number appeared on the display. *578097016663510.*

7

'Leave it,' Wisting said. Suzanne was about to snuff out the last candle. She looked at him in puzzlement. 'Sit down for a moment,' he said. Suzanne looked at him uncomprehendingly, but she sat down.

The flinty grey specks around the pupils of her walnut-brown eyes captured the light like quartz crystals. Wisting had to pull himself together before sitting opposite.

Wisting felt she was sailing away from him. After she opened the café it was as if she had become a different woman. For one thing, they were hardly ever together. The café had become the most important thing in her life, demanding six days a week for twelve or fourteen hours every day. She had invested most of her money after selling her own house and moving in with Wisting, but time was the most important investment. She employed some casual staff, but undertook most of the work herself, including cleaning and accounts.

When she first moved in she had filled the void Ingrid left when she died, but now that emptiness had returned. He stretched his hands across the table and entwined his fingers with hers, uncertain where to begin. The Cecilia case was still capable of giving him sleepless nights, but he rarely talked about it. 'Seventeen years ago, a girl called Cecilia Linde disappeared,' he said.

'I remember,' Suzanne interrupted. She looked around the deserted café; impatient, it seemed. 'I had just moved here. She was Johannes Linde's daughter.'

Wisting nodded. Johannes Linde had become famous

when he founded his own fashion label in the mid-eighties. Every second teenager sported a baggy *Canes* sweater at that time, and Cecilia had posed as a photographic model.

'They had a country house out at Rugland,' Wisting continued, 'where they stayed every summer. Johannes and his wife, and their children Cecilia and Casper. Cecilia was only twenty. On the afternoon of Saturday 15th July, she vanished.'

The candlelight flickered restlessly and a slender trail of wax flowed down the candlestick to form a solidified puddle on the tablecloth. Suzanne's gaze did not waver.

'She went for a run directly after two o'clock,' Wisting said. 'Just before seven her father reported her missing. We had a heat wave that summer, but Cecilia ran almost every day. She took fairly lengthy routes, but never a fixed circuit; there was a labyrinth of walking trails and gravel tracks that she liked to explore. She could be away for a couple of hours at a time, which made the search more difficult. The family thought she had sprained her ankle or fallen and hurt herself. Remember, this was before everyone had mobile phones.

'The family scoured the paths closest to home and, when they didn't find her, alerted the police. I was the first in the investigation team to meet them, and finding her became my mission.'

He closed his eyes momentarily. Seventeen years ago, he had worked closely with Frank Robekk. One year younger than Wisting, he had graduated from Police College after him. They had collaborated constructively, but something happened during the Cecilia case and Robekk withdrew. Neither Wisting nor any of the others had criticised. They knew what weighed him down and that Cecilia's disappearance must have been a source of personal agony.

'We searched long into the evening and through the

night. More and more volunteers arrived: dog handlers, civil defence forces, Red Cross, Scout groups, people from neighbouring houses, and all sorts. When daylight broke, a helicopter was deployed. Sometimes Cecilia had rounded off her run with a dip in the sea, so the search area was extended to include the water.'

'You found her a fortnight later.'

'Twelve days. She had been dumped in a ditch beside the woods at Askeskogen but, long before then, we realised that she had met with foul play.'

'How was that?'

Wisting withdrew his fingers from Suzanne's. 'No one just disappears like that.' He cleared his throat. 'Lots of people had spotted her. As the news spread, witnesses came forward. Hikers, summer cottage residents, children and farmers. First of all, she had run in a westerly direction, down to the beach at Nalumstranda. Then she followed the coastal path east and up towards Gumserød farm where all the leads came to an end.'

Wisting pictured the map that had hung on the wall in his office, covered in red dots marking the sighting locations, remembering drawing a line through them, almost like a join-the-dots puzzle in a children's book, to follow her fateful run.

'On Tuesday morning, three days after she disappeared, a man called Karsten Brekke turned up at the police station. He had read about the Cecilia case in the newspapers, just like everyone else. They used the photo for the *Canes* sweater advertisement when they reported her missing on the front pages.'

'Had he seen her?'

'No, but he saw someone who could be the murderer. Driving a tractor along the main road leading to Stavern, at the intersection where the Gumserød farm track reaches the

Helgeroa road, he spotted a rusty white Opel Rekord with its boot open and a man pacing on the gravel track.'

Wisting could still remember the description: white T-shirt and blue jeans; dark hair thick at the sides; broad face with a strong chin; eyes close set; forehead furrowed as if something was worrying him. Two simple details were of greatest significance. His nose looked as though it had been broken at some time, and a cigarette was hanging from the corner of his mouth. Sitting on the seat of the tractor, Karsten Brekke had plenty of time to study the stranger.

Wisting had sent the crime scene technicians to comb the intersection and among the items they brought back in evidence bags had been three cigarette butts.

'Something else was found as well,' Suzanne said. 'A cassette player, or something like that?'

'Her Walkman,' Wisting nodded, thinking about how greatly times had changed. At that time, people played cassette tapes. 'We collected that the same afternoon. Cecilia always listened to music while she was running, as had been mentioned in the newspapers. Two little girls found it in the ditch beside the 302 road, near to the Fritzøe house driveway.'

'That's almost the opposite side of town.'

'Not quite the opposite side, but not a logical position considering the route of her run and the Cigarette Man.'

'The Cigarette Man?'

'That's what the newspapers named him. Of course, we called him that as well.' Wisting ran his hand over the table surface. 'But, enough of that. There was no doubt it was Cecilia's Walkman.' It had contained a yellow AGFA recordable tape. 90 minutes. 'She had written her initials on it. *CL*, and the name of the programme she had recorded from the radio. *Poprush.*'

Wisting noticed that Suzanne was restless in her seat and

27

guessed she must remember the next part of the story. The newspapers had been full of it. 'The crime scene technicians still didn't have much to go on. They examined the Walkman for fingerprints, but only found Cecilia's own. The cassette player lay on my desk for three days before it dawned on me that I should play the tape.'

8

The men's overalls were pungent with oil and metal and all were as eager as Line to discover the identity of the dog's owner. She glanced at the time: 23.27, and gave herself an hour to gather information before contacting the news desk. By then she would have barely half an hour to write the story.

One of the younger men knew how to log onto an internet page listing domestic pets with ID chips. 'So,' he said. 'Have you got the number?' He used one finger to type in the digits as Line read it out. Seconds later the answer appeared.

Jonas Ravneberg
W. Blakstads gate 78
1630 Gamle Fredrikstad

There was nothing familiar about the name. Line jotted the address down before glancing again at her watch, twenty-seven minutes gone. 'Do any of you know who he is?' she asked. As the men shook their heads, her hopes of hijacking the headlines sank.

Outside again, she held her jacket above her head and raced towards the car. Soaked to the skin she flung herself behind the steering wheel, turned the ignition and keyed *W. Blakstads gate 78* into the GPS. While the device searched for satellite coverage, she googled *Jonas Ravneberg*. The only results were in the tax lists: no property; modest income.

W. Blakstads gate was located thirteen minutes away, a stone's throw from where the body had been found. She called Directory Enquiries while driving. Was there a wife, children, a live-in partner?

'Can't find anyone listed at W. Blakstads gate 78 in Fredrikstad,' the operator said.

'What about Jonas Ravneberg?'

'No Jonas Ravneberg.'

Line disconnected and located Erik Fjeld's number among her recent calls.

'Erik here.'

'Have you heard of a Jonas Ravneberg?'

Erik repeated the name and paused before answering, as though keen to be of assistance. 'No ... Entirely unfamiliar. Who is it?'

'The dog owner.'

'The murder victim?'

'Very likely. He lives in W. Blakstads gate.'

'That's close by. Are you going there?'

'I'm on my way now.' The windscreen wipers toiled against the rain. Line crouched forward, peering at the blurred road ahead, anxious to know if the police had discovered the name and address. 'What's happening at your end, Erik?' she asked.

'Nothing. Do you still want me to wait for the hearse?'

'Yes. I'll phone you if I need any photos.'

As she wound up their conversation, a text message arrived from the news editor. *When will you have the story?* This was followed by, *Have booked a room for you at the Quality Hotel in Nygata.* She had not thought of a response when he sent another message: *Everything okay with you?*

An hour. Approx., she replied, before adding another message: *Can you check out a Jonas Ravneberg? Family, job ...*

The route recommended by the GPS was still blocked by the police crime scene technicians. She backed onto the main road and drove the roundabout route to W. Blakstads. A row of white clad terraced houses lined one side of the road and an expanse of open ground stretched out to a moat running parallel with the road. Between the bare branches of the trees Line could look across to the lights at the crime scene she had just left. Number 78 was last in the row; no one from the police was here. That could mean either that she was on the wrong track, or she was ahead of the game.

She turned on a gravel area at the end of the road. Above her, on a hillside plateau, an ancient fortress was silhouetted against the night sky.

The terraced house was two-storeyed, and all the windows were lit, even the tiny ones in the basement. It seemed well maintained and tidy, with its own frame around the rubbish bins. A red Mazda was parked directly across the road. Line watched for any sign of movement as she drove slowly past, memorising the registration number. She texted it to the Vehicle Licensing Agency and the reply arrived as she returned to the patch of gravel and parked: *Jonas Ravneberg.*

She sat for a few minutes. Through one window, most of a landscape painting was visible on the living room wall; through another, parts of the kitchen. The simple wrought iron gate in the fence fronting the house swayed to and fro in the wind and the house appeared totally deserted.

As she opened the car door, a response arrived from the news editor. *Unmarried. No children. Parents deceased. In receipt of Social Security. Nothing in the text or photo archives. Murder victim?*

Unconfirmed, she replied, before leaving the car. The rain was now a fine drizzle, but the temperature had dropped. A blast of wind swept through the black, bare trees. Line shivered. The victim having no relatives simplified the story but, at the same time, she felt even more inquisitive about him. He seemed fairly insignificant. At the moment, the homicide appeared to be a random occurrence, the result of an unprovoked attack, which could provide a useful angle.

31

It crossed her mind that she needed to do three things before she started to write: take a quick look at the house, confirm the victim's identity, and talk to the neighbours.

A sign with the words *I'm on guard here* and the picture of a dog was attached to the gatepost but she entered anyway, stepping on paving slabs so uneven they were difficult to walk on. She halted at the foot of the steps. The light from the exterior lamp cast only a faint glimmer over the entrance. All the same, the signs of forced entry were obvious.

Rooted on the bottom step, she took out her mobile phone, called the police and introduced herself. 'Have you identified the dead man yet?' she asked.

'I can't comment on that.'

Line looked around before climbing the stairs to the front door. 'Wasn't he carrying a wallet or anything like that to show who he is?'

'Didn't you hear what I said? We don't have any comment on that.'

'I think I know who he is.' Silence fell. 'Jonas Ravneberg, aged forty-eight. Lives at W. Blakstads gate 78.'

'Does that mean you're at that address now?'

'Yes, but someone's beaten me to it ...'

She stopped in mid-sentence as a shadow flitted across the textured glass panel on the front door.

9

Suzanne slipped behind the serving counter. Producing a half-filled bottle of wine, she took down a glass and glanced enquiringly at Wisting. When he nodded she took down another glass.

The dark red wine sparkled as it poured in the candlelight. Wisting cradled his glass with both hands and remembered how he had pressed the play button on Cecilia Linde's Walkman, hearing it crackle as the tape stretched.

'It began in the middle of a song,' he said. Seal's *Kiss from a Rose* was in the Top Ten at the time. He still sometimes heard it on the radio and that gruff, velvety voice always took him back. 'Then the music was cut off and Cecilia's voice was speaking,'

Shutting his eyes, he remembered the raw despair in her voice although, at the same time, she sounded resourceful and clear-headed. He and Frank Robekk listened together. After that, Frank grew increasingly withdrawn.

'She said her name, where she lived, who her parents were and what day it was,' Wisting went on. 'Monday 17th July.'

'Monday?' Suzanne asked. 'Didn't she disappear on Saturday?'

'When she was found on the twelfth day, she had only been dead a few hours.'

Suzanne nodded: 'Held prisoner.'

'He may have moved her around several locations, but Cecilia somehow found a way to deliver her message.'

'What did she say?'

Wisting recalled it almost word for word. Methodically and seriously, she had explained what had happened.

'*On Saturday 15th July a man kidnapped me while I was out running. It took place at the crossroads beside Gumserød farm. He had an old white car. I'm lying inside its boot right now. It all happened so fast. I didn't manage to get a good look at him, but he had a foul smell, of smoke, though something else as well. I've seen him before. He was wearing a white T-shirt and jeans. Dark hair. Small dark eyes and bushy black eyebrows. A crooked nose.*'

Wisting pushed the wine glass back and forth between his hands without drinking. The deliberation in Cecilia's whispered voice had made the recording seem staged, almost as though she was reading from a script. Only towards the end did she break into sobs, before the recording ended, just as abruptly as it had started. An enthusiastic presenter shouted, *Hey hey hey!* and *Balalaika!* before introducing the next record.

'Was that all?'

'No. The recording lasted for one minute and forty-three seconds. You can't say very much in that time. She said the vehicle had driven around for an hour or so before stopping, but that she had been left lying in the boot for several hours. When the man finally opened it again, they were inside a cavernous, gloomy garage. His flashlight blinded her and he forced her to pull a hood over her head. Then he ordered her out of the garage, across a farmyard and into a cellar. She stayed there for two days before she was taken out in the car again. She could see his feet through an opening in the hood and believed she was on a farm.'

'How did she manage to record the message?'

'Her Walkman was in the boot and she took her chance to make the statement. We don't know where he was taking her or how she managed to drop the Walkman.'

'Had he done anything to her, down there in the cellar?'

'He only stared at her.'

'Stared?'

'The cellar she was in had white walls and a powerful light on the ceiling. There was a narrow peephole high on the wall, and he stood there looking at her.'

The candle flame flickered before the wick drowned in liquid wax. Blue smoke drifted erratically towards the ceiling. What kept Wisting awake at nights was not just the idea of what Cecilia Linde had endured in the course of those twelve days, but also the thought of the other girl, Ellen. The one who had disappeared the year before.

10

The shadow had a human shape. Line took a step back just as the front door at W. Blakstads gate 78 was thrown against her face, sending her tumbling down the steps, warm blood running from her nose. Her mobile phone slid across the paving stones.

The figure in the doorway stormed out, tripped on her legs and fell across her. Dressed entirely in black, he had a balaclava pulled over his head. Line grabbed one of his legs and held on as he desperately tried to shake her off, pummelling her with clenched fists. Line wriggled and turned so that the blows fell on her back. He hauled himself upright, dragging her with him along the path, hampered. She looked up and saw him grab a garden rake that was propped against the gable wall. He swung it over his head and brought it down on her, the prongs striking her on the thigh and buttocks. She screamed in pain and let go. Flinging the rake at her, he ran through the gate.

Line stumbled to her feet, watching him run towards the old fortifications and vanish into the darkness. Drawing herself into a crouch, she rested her arms on her knees, her heart hammering in her chest and the taste of blood in her mouth. On the ground in front of her something reflected the faint streetlight, a blue toy car with a black roof, about the same size as a matchbox, a model with moveable parts. She closed the open boot lid with her index finger and placed it in her pocket before wiping the blood from her lips with the back of her hand. A number of single-track, rational thoughts took shape.

VG journalist assaulted by presumed killer.

That was a story. A major story. If it didn't belong on the front page, all the same, they could not really print her father's story in the same edition. That would be a peculiar form of double exposure. Frost would be forced to drop his headline, perhaps for long enough.

Her mobile phone lay on the path, and she saw by the timer that her call to the police was still active. 'Hello?' she said. Police sirens were sounding in the distance.

'Are you there?' the man asked. 'What happened?'

'He was here,' Line said, beginning to shake.

'Who?'

'The murderer.'

At the same time, it dawned on her how dangerous the situation had actually been. The man who attacked her had killed another person only hours before. She glanced at the time: 23.55. Eight minutes till deadline.

11

Wisting checked the time on the clock above the counter: five to twelve. He did not know what the following day had in store, only that he needed to be well rested. On the other hand, going to bed was not such a great idea when his thoughts would keep him awake.

Suzanne was tired, but not uninterested, as she sometimes was when he was talking about his work.

'The perpetrator's name was Rudolf Haglund,' he said. 'He got the maximum sentence, twenty-one years.'

'Did he not confess?'

Wisting shook his head.

'Is he still in jail?'

'He was released on parole six months' ago and wants the case reopened.'

'On what basis?'

'He claims that the evidence against him was false, fabricated by the police. *VG* is going to cover it tomorrow,' Wisting said, and went on to tell her about Line's phone call.

Suzanne leaned back in her chair, cradling her glass in her lap. 'How was he caught? Didn't you have DNA?'

Wisting took a deep breath through his nose and exhaled slowly. 'Cecilia Linde was naked when she was found.'

'Had she been abused?'

'No signs of that nature.'

'How did she die?'

'Smothered, most probably by pressing a pillow over her face. She had acute lacerations in her mouth and eyes and fractures of the small bones in her neck. The first tip-off came in about Rudolf Haglund on the day that Cecilia was found. We had put out an alert based on the description given by Karsten Brekke, the guy on the tractor. We were looking for a Norwegian man, aged around thirty, about five foot nine tall, dark hair and with a conspicuous break in his nose, and were inundated with ninety-three names. Thirty-two of those owned a white car, and fourteen lived locally. Three of them were already known to the police.'

'What previous convictions did he have?'

'Indecent exposure. He'd been fined a year or two earlier. In addition, there were a couple of cases that hadn't been pursued, in which he was suspected of voyeurism. The other two were family men who had been convicted of theft and embezzlement. Rudolf Haglund lived on his own, had never been married and had no children. His social circle was very limited. He worked at a furniture warehouse. A loner was how people spoke of him.'

'But it wasn't it a sexually motivated murder?'

Wisting shrugged his shoulders. 'What purpose could there be for keeping a young woman prisoner for days on end, if it wasn't sexually motivated?'

'Financial blackmail?' Suzanne suggested. 'Her father was wealthy.'

'No demand for money ever arrived. That was what we were expecting. We connected a listening device to the telephone, monitored post boxes, placed surveillance on the summer house and their private residence. Nothing arrived.'

'What caught him out in the end?'

'The day after we publicised the sighting of the man and car at the intersection beside Gumserød farm, he reported his car stolen, but it was some time before we discovered that.'

'Why?'

'He reported it to the police in Telemark district. He said his car had been parked in Bjørkedalen, just on the other side of the district boundary. It was only when we received the tip-off and began to investigate that we found out.'

'Did you find the car?'

'Never. It was an old white Opel Rekord. The same type that had been spotted near Gumserød farm. Most stolen cars are found fairly quickly, if we're not talking about the expensive vehicles that are smuggled out of the country. This one wasn't.'

'Do you think he got rid of it to dispose of evidence?'

'Yes. The point is that he went to the police and reported it stolen on Wednesday 19th July. He had parked it beside an old load of timber on the afternoon of Friday 14th and had taken a rucksack, fishing rod and tent with him into the woods. When he returned on the Sunday, it was gone.'

'Why hadn't he reported it missing immediately?'

'He had to get home first, and claimed that he had walked all the way.'

'Walked?'

'He lived at Dolven, a distance not more than twenty kilometres, even less if you go through the forest. When he arrived home, he heard the news about the girl's disappearance and didn't want to bother the police. After a couple of days, he took the train to Porsgrunn and reported it there. After all, it had been in their police district that the vehicle had been stolen.'

'You believe he was lying?'

'Not one of the ten-man jury believed him.'

'But what proof did you have?'

'The grounds for his arrest were slim,' Wisting admitted. 'An old man who lived beside the level crossing in Bjørke-dalen was in the habit of walking his dog in the place where Haglund told us he had parked. He couldn't remember seeing any white car. That meant we could charge Haglund with giving false information. When the man on the tractor also recognised him in a photo lineup, we had enough to remand him.'

'You were sure it was him?'

Wisting's dead certainty had diminished with the passage of time, but he had been certain then, even prior to the positive results from the DNA examination of the cigarette butts. There was something unmistakably evil in those tiny, unfathomable, dark eyes. Also, he had a smell about him, exactly as Cecilia said on the tape. Foul cigarette smoke, yes, along with something else.

'There were aspects that pointed *against* it being Haglund,' he said. 'Cecilia said in the recording that she lay in the boot of the car for an hour before it stopped. The trip from the crime scene to Haglund's home takes fifteen to twenty minutes, but of course he didn't necessarily drive straight there. Again, Cecilia could have been mistaken about the length of time. But the most important objection was that he didn't have a cellar. Cecilia said that she was held captive in a cellar with white walls, a powerful light and a slit in the wall. There was nothing like that at Haglund's house. However, the sum total persuaded us that he had transported her to a different place, some other building.'

'Did you find any such place?'

'No. That was a loophole in the investigation, but it paled into insignificance once the analysis results came in. We found Rudolf Haglund's DNA profile in the saliva on one of the cigarette ends that the killer had discarded while waiting at the Gumserød intersection.'

Lifting his glass, he stared at the contents, recalling how great their relief had been when that telephone message arrived. There had been tremendous urgency to clear up the case. For every day that the media demanded fresh leads,

41

progress and a breakthrough, and every day they were unable to provide satisfactory answers, accusations of inefficiency, negligence and incompetence grew more intense. These allegations came not only from the press, but also from politicians. It had been liberating when the DNA result arrived from the Forensics Institute, proving not only that Rudolf Haglund was the right man, but also that the police tactics had been justified.

However, Haglund's lawyer was now maintaining he could prove the DNA evidence was faked. The clock above the counter showed past midnight. In only a few hours he would have to confront the allegations.

12

Line explained everything that had happened, but the man at the police switchboard continued to pose questions, repeating what she had said and asking again about details she had already given.

'I've got another call,' she said at length, putting him on hold as she keyed in Erik Fjeld's number. 'You have to come,' she told him. 'W. Blakstads gate 78. The killer has just been here.'

'But …'

'He attacked me. I need photos.'

'Are you okay?'

'Just come,' she said.

As she disconnected the call, the first police dog van arrived. She searched through her contacts for the news editor's direct number. He replied with a brusque question: 'Any news?'

'I have a story,' she said, wiping blood from her face. 'The murderer attacked me with an iron rake.'

She heard his chair scrape across the floor. 'What's that?' Line explained while watching a police dog handler open the tailgate of his van. A black German Shepherd leaped out. 'Are you hurt?'

'A slight nosebleed, and a few scratches,' Line played down her injuries as a patrol car pulled up. The driver headed straight for her. 'Line Wisting?'

'Give me fifteen minutes, and you'll have something in writing,' Line said into her mobile. 'Erik Fjeld is on his way with his camera, so pictures even sooner.'

'You can't write a report about yourself!'

'I'll write down what took place, and you can use that material in your own report.'

The police dog gave a couple of loud barks, but sat still as the dog handler approached her. 'Are you the one who phoned?'

'I'll phone you back when I have something written,' Line said, wrapping her conversation with the news editor. 'Ten minutes.'

'Which way did he go?' the dog handler asked.

Line pointed in the direction of the gravel where her car was parked. 'He disappeared towards the fortress.'

'*Direction of the fortress at Kongsten,*' the dog handler said down his radio transmitter. He set off until the dog halted with its snout in the air. It circled around before tugging at its lead and setting out again, this time leading its handler. Two police officers, each armed with a machine gun, accompanied.

'What happened?' the remaining officer asked.

Line repeated what she had explained by phone, aware she was losing precious time. More police arrived, surrounding the area with red and white crime scene tape. Curious neighbours were already huddled in small groups when a man with a camera forced his way through. Erik Fjeld had arrived.

'How did you find your way here?' the police officer asked Line.

She told him what had happened at the Falck depot, taking a few steps to one side so that the light from the street lamp fell directly on her face. The police officer interrogating her, the crime scene tape and the terraced house would all be included in the picture. Seeing Erik Fjeld change the lens for a close-up, she ran her hand quickly through her hair. These photographs would haunt her future as a journalist, but without them she had no story.

44

'Didn't you think to contact us before coming here?'

Line heard the sarcasm in his voice. She could have responded by asking whether anyone in the police had thought of finding the dog owner, but let it drop. She did not have time. 'I need to report to my editor,' she said, turning in the direction of her car.

The policeman blocked her path. 'What did he look like?'

'I explained all that on the phone.'

'And now you have to explain it again to me.'

Line sighed. 'I don't know. He was sort of bundled up.'

'Bundled up?'

'All in black. Trousers, sweater, shoes, gloves and balaclava. He had even taped the gap between his sweater and gloves, and his trousers were firmly taped to his socks.'

How well planned everything must have been, both the murder and the break-in. She had read about robbers who kitted themselves out like that in order to avoid being trapped by DNA evidence from hairs or skin particles.

'I really need to go now,' she said, stepping aside.

'Just wait. Our technicians need to take a look at you.'

'Why on earth?'

'Biological traces. He attacked you. You are, in actual fact, a crime scene.'

Line gave a deep sigh. She had already composed her report in her head, and was eager to get the words down before they slipped her mind. 'I don't think you'll find anything. He was well bundled up, as I said. Anyway, you have a much larger crime scene in there.' She pointed towards the house.

'This is routine,' the policeman replied. 'We're taking you in.'

'In?'

'To the police station. We need a formal interview.'

'But I've already explained myself twice!'

'They have to write it down.'

45

Line shook her head. 'That'll have to be later. I'm working just now.'

'So are we,' the police officer brushed her protestations aside. 'We're working on finding a killer.'

'At least let me take my laptop from my car,' Line pleaded.

The police officer's head moved as though to refuse her, but changed his mind when he looked into her determined eyes.

13

'Shall we go?' Wisting asked. Their glasses were empty.

''If you want,' Suzanne smiled.

After taking the glasses and bottle to the counter, Wisting held her jacket open for her before putting on his own.

Suzanne locked the door behind them. Rain was still in the air, and it was colder. A taxi pulled up, but Wisting waved it on. The stroll home to the house in Herman Wildenveys gate took no more than ten minutes, and they both liked to walk. They enjoyed the silence of the streets.

Suzanne opened a small umbrella, which he ducked under beside her. 'Have you had any contact with Cecilia's family since then?' she asked.

'A little,' he said, thinking of how a murder always had a number of faces. In Cecilia's case, there were five: her mother, father, brother, boyfriend and her own cold, blue, impassive, dead face. 'Her mother sends me a Christmas card every year.'

'What does she write?'

He shrugged, as though he was not quite sure. 'Happy Christmas.'

He was well aware of what she wrote. All the cards were lying in the bottom drawer of his desk. The same words every year: *I wish you and yours a very merry Christmas and happy new year. With gratitude, Nora Linde and family.* He had always felt this to be generous of her, but that was what she had been like. Not a single time in all their conversations during the search for Cecilia had she made a critical remark or negative comment.

'How are they doing?'

'Fine, I think. Even if they won't ever get over it, at least they've managed to move on.'

'Johannes Linde has done well for himself since then. So I've heard.'

He agreed. When Cecilia disappeared, her father had been embroiled in a conflict with a previous business partner over ownership and rights to a number of trademarks and run the risk of losing a great deal of money. The legal decision had gone in his favour, the company had grown and his son Casper had taken over at the top.

'What does her boyfriend do now?'

'Danny Flom is a photographer. That was how they met, when he took photos for the advertising campaign. Now he runs a photographic studio in Oslo. *Flomlys*, it's called.'

'Good name. Danny Flom, *Flomlys*. Did he find himself another girlfriend?'

'I think he's been married a couple of times.'

A flurry of wind blew an old newspaper towards them. Wisting drew his jacket more snugly around his neck.

'Perhaps you ought to talk to Thomas,' Suzanne suggested. 'So that he knows what it's all about. They read newspapers down there too, you know.'

Thomas was Line's twin brother who was serving for periods of six months at a time as a helicopter pilot with the Norwegian forces in Afghanistan.

'It's the middle of the night right now,' Wisting said. 'Besides, he's not so easy to get hold of. I really depend on him phoning me.'

'What about your father?'

Wisting would have to call his father. Eighty years of age and a widower for the past twenty-four, he had been a hospital doctor. He was a sprightly old man who always followed the coverage of Wisting's cases.

They walked on in silence, eyes on the ground. The sound of their footsteps combined in an uneven rhythm, hers slightly faster, shorter; his longer, heavier.

14

The dashboard clock read 00.16. Line heard fleeting messages on the radio transmitter with updates on the progress of the dog handler's team, as well as directions relayed to patrol cars. The plain-clothes police officer in the front passenger seat turned down the volume and twisted round to face her. 'Is that your blood?'

'Yes,' she replied, opening her laptop on her knee.

'Are you sure none of it came from him?'

'He would have to have injured himself.'

'We'll have a doctor take a look at you.'

The clock display changed to 00.17. 'That's not necessary,' she said. 'I can arrange that afterwards.'

'What happened?'

She glanced up from the image on her screen. 'Listen. I've explained this over the phone and then to the first patrol that turned up. After they're all done with me, I have to explain it all again to you?'

'It's important that we know exactly what took place. If I know whether he struck you in the head or the abdomen, then I'll know where to look for fibres from his gloves.'

Line logged into the newspaper's data system. 'He punched me on the back while I was holding his leg,' she said. 'After that, he walloped me with a metal rake. It's lying in front of the house.'

'What about all that blood on your face?'

'A nosebleed. The door hit me when he burst out.'

'Are you related to William Wisting?' the driver asked.

Older than his colleague, he was thickset and wore a beard.

'He's my father.'

'I seem to recall that his daughter worked for *VG*. I was at Police College with him.'

'Mhmm.'

'Tell him Jan Berger was asking for him.'

'I'll do that,' Line said, without really catching the name. She was casting about for her opening words. Only a few minutes ago, she had known how she was going to express herself. Now her mind was in chaos. Instead of beginning, she phoned the photographer.

'You look bloody awful in these photos,' he said.

'Thanks a bunch.'

'You really ought to go to Accident and Emergency.'

'Later. You need to send those pictures to the news desk. Both the one of me and the one with the dog. Tell them I'll get the text to them in ten minutes.'

She closed her eyes for a few seconds to collect her thoughts, before her fingers started moving. She began with the most dramatic element, how the presumed murderer had attacked her. Afterwards she would go back and write the introduction. The most significant and central information took only three sentences. The radio cut through her concentration.

'*We've lost the scent at the Europris central warehouse. He may have had a vehicle parked here.*'

'*Fox 3-2 take position on main highway 111 at the Torsnes exit.*'

When her phone rang she answered, cradling it between her neck and shoulder as she continued to write.

'Hi, it's Nina.'

'Who?'

'Nina Haugen, from the Statoil Østsiden service station. You phoned me earlier tonight.' The girl with her mouth full of chewing gum.

'With you,' Line said.

'I know who the man with the dog is. He comes here regularly to buy tobacco.'

'I've found out who he is as well.'

'It's a Schapendoes, a Dutch Sheepdog.'

'What's that?'

'You mentioned a *Labbetuss*, and I didn't know what that was, but it's a Schapendoes.' Concentrating on her writing, Line deleted two sentences and replaced them with one. 'It's the same kind as Drillo has.'

'I know. I've seen it.'

'It was Fredrik who realised. He's found the pictures on the CCTV camera, if that's of any interest.'

Pictures were always of interest. It wasn't anything they would publish at the moment, but maybe later when the identity had been disclosed or in connection with the court case.

'Can you send them to me?'

'Fredrik can do that.'

'Excellent,' Line passed on her email address.

'How much do you pay?'

'I'm not the one to decide, but write down your name, date of birth and bank account number and I'll pass them to the people who arrange those things.'

The laptop emitted a signal as a dialogue box popped up to warn her the battery was running out of charge.

'By the way, it's called Tiedemann.'

Line clicked away the warning.

'Who?' she asked, saving what she had written.

'The dog. I've heard him calling it Tiedemann. It's probably named after the tobacco brand. He always buys Tiedemann's Gold Mix number three and cigarette papers.'

Line peered into the night. The police car had arrived outside a yellowish-brown brick building with an enormous glass façade. Fredrikstad Police Station. 'Okay, thanks,' she said.

'Do you know what's going to happen to it?'

00.25

'No.'

'Since its owner's been killed, I mean.'

'I've no idea, Nina. I really have to go now.'

'Okay. Bye then.'

Line disconnected the call. 'Can I have quarter of an hour?' she asked, looking at the driver who knew her father.

'We have to go back,' he replied. 'We're setting up road blocks.'

'There's a technician in an examination room in there waiting for you,' the other man said. 'As soon as he's finished, he'll go back to the crime scene too.'

Line slammed the lid of her laptop shut at 00.26.

15

The examination room at the police station was cold, with bare walls and a fluorescent ceiling tube. The man waiting for her held a camera. Old and silver-haired, with heavy eyelids, he explained that he would document her injuries with photographs, and asked her to stand with her back to the wall. After each picture, he scrutinised the result on the tiny display. They followed this procedure with both profiles.

'Where did he hit you with the rake?' he asked.

'Here,' Line said, twisting her hip towards him and pointing.

The crime technician looked at the tears in her trousers where the rake tines had dug in. He crossed to a drawer and rummaged for a photo ruler. 'Can you hold this?' he asked.

Line held the ruler against her thigh as he hunkered down, placing the camera at right angles to her injuries. He took one photo that he examined closely before coming in closer and taking another. Then he straightened up. 'I wonder if we should take one without your trousers on as well,' he said.

Line set down the ruler and gazed at the man. These were photos that would be studied by investigators, defence lawyers, judges and jury when that time eventually arrived. She did not take exception to them seeing her in her underwear, but they had already taken more time than she could spare. She would not finish writing her story before the deadline, even though most of it was already inside her head. 'I have to make a phone call first.'

The digital clock on her mobile display read 00.44. She cleared it by pressing the speed dial key for the news editor. 'Did you receive Erik's photos?' she asked.

'Yep. The one with the dog is a prize winner.'

'Are we in time to use it on the front page?'

'We won't be using it, Line.'

'What do you mean? There's half an hour to go.'

'Frost has decided. The front page spread stays. We've put the murder on pages ten and eleven. The picture of the dog with its dead owner takes up most of the space. Then we'll run the story about the attack on you in the online edition right after our competitors have gone to press.'

'But ...'

'Frost has made up his mind. The front page is settled.'

She said nothing. Swallowed. It felt as if something had crumbled away, the ground beneath her feet, and disappeared. 'How does it look?'

'To be honest, Line, it looks dreadful.'

'The headline?'

'That's a quote from Rudolf Haglund's lawyer – *Planted the crucial evidence*. I can send you the whole story as a PDF file.'

A sudden rage erupted within her, a reaction to everything collapsing around her, but she managed to maintain a steady voice. 'No thanks,' she said.

'Can we do anything for you? I mean, about what has happened to *you*. We've got people you can talk to in the occupational health service.'

'No, I'm fine.'

'Go back to your hotel and try to relax,' he said. 'That photo of the dog is bloody brilliant, by the way, did I tell you? We've squeezed it in at the corner of the front page.'

'Tiedemann.'

'What?'

'Tiedemann. The dog's called Tiedemann, just like the tobacco.'

16

The coffee machine was a Christmas present from Line, hi-tech and easy to use. All he had to do was make sure there was enough water in the container, insert a capsule, and the cup filled at the touch of a button. The aroma was richer than from his old machine.

He drank a cup of coffee at seven o'clock every morning, with the local paper in front of him and the news on TV. Today it was ten past seven before the coffee had finished trickling through the machine. Suzanne was upstairs asleep. Outside, it was still dark and windy. Raindrops dripped down the windowpane.

He glanced up at the blank television screen, hesitating before lifting the remote to switch on TV2. The two presenters, one male, one female, on Good Morning Norway stood at one end of a table with a sheaf of daily newspapers before them. Wisting curled his hand around his cup without picking it up.

'*Dagbladet* features the murder in Fredrikstad where one of *VG*'s reporters was assaulted, as we heard in the news,' the female presenter said, holding up the front page, 'while *VG* runs with a different story.'

'That also has to do with a murder case,' the man explained, 'but this one is seventeen years old.'

'The Cecilia case?'

'Yes, we all remember that one. Seventeen years ago, a thirty-year-old man was convicted of kidnapping and murdering Cecilia Linde. Now the case has been referred to the Criminal Cases Review Commission on the basis of complaints that the police planted a vital piece of DNA evidence.'

He held up the newspaper's front-page spread. *Planted the crucial evidence* was emblazoned in bold letters above a picture of Wisting, together with a smaller insert of Cecilia Linde. The camera zoomed in.

He liked that photo, aware he looked good in it. It had been taken for a television programme he had been persuaded to appear on, speaking about his work as a detective and a case in which the host had been one of the suspects.

'A serious case,' the presenter concluded, before moving to one of the business papers.

Wisting was startled when he heard Suzanne's voice. 'What's up now?'

He turned. She was leaning against the doorframe in her dressing gown.

'I'm just finishing my coffee,' he said, 'and then I'll be off to work.'

'In the case, I mean.' She nodded in the direction of the TV.

Wisting wasn't sure himself. He had no idea how anyone could establish that the cigarette evidence had been planted, or how such a plant was even possible. The crime technicians who had searched the intersection at Gumserød had returned with a box full of evidence bags: empty bottles, chocolate wrappers, plastic beakers, apple cores, everything you might find at a roadside, among them three cigarette ends. Everything had been stored at the crime technology lab until Rudolf Haglund had been captured, and had been sent for analysis in conjunction with a reference sample from the accused. There hadn't been anything disquieting about the gathering or handling of the evidence. He had been responsible for the investigation, and had not even set eyes on the cigarette butts except in photographs.

'I trust the Commission. They'll get to the bottom of it all,' he said. 'They'll send us a copy of the application and ask for our comments. Then we'll have a better idea of what this is all really about.'

Suzanne moved over to the coffee machine as Wisting turned down the volume on the TV.

He had always thought of his job as difficult and demanding, but he enjoyed its challenges. At times he had felt he did not have control or an overview, and had often experienced doubt and uncertainty, but he always dealt with things from a conviction of what was right, and had always been able to defend his decisions. At the moment, he could not see what he could have done differently in the Cecilia case.

'They said something about a *VG* journalist being hurt in association with a murder in Fredrikstad,' he said.

Suzanne sat beside him. 'How did that happen?'

'I didn't catch all of it.' He grabbed the remote again and switched on the teletext function.

Accused of faking evidence was the main story. On the line underneath: *Murder in Fredrikstad*. He tapped in the accompanying number and waited as the TV picture counted its way to the right page.

A 47-year-old man was found murdered at Kongsten in Fredrikstad around nine o'clock last night. A female journalist from VG was attacked by the presumed killer when she visited the murder victim's home. Police prosecutor Eskild Hals confirms that the perpetrator had broken into the deceased's residence but had been interrupted by the journalist who arrived on the scene before the police. It is understood the journalist was not seriously injured.

'Sounds like something Line might have done,' Suzanne remarked.

59

Wisting drained his coffee. The same thought had struck him. Line was capable of discovering the address of an unidentified murder victim before the police. 'She's on leave,' he commented, but had already picked up his mobile phone. He rang her number but there was no response.

17

Line let the hot water run in the shower. At the very least, it would relax her body, loosening the tension in her shoulders. She stood in the spray for some considerable time before soaping herself and rinsing off.

The towel was damp and cold from the quick shower she had taken before going to bed for only four hours' sleep. She used it to dry her hair as she stood, naked, facing the mirror, tilting her head and studying herself from various angles. She let her hands slide over her torso. Everything looked and felt smooth and firm – arms and legs, breasts and stomach, hips and thighs.

A large bruise was forming on her right hip. She twisted first left and then right, catching sight of the marks caused by the rake, but not all of them. An idea struck her, and she lifted her mobile phone from the bedside table before standing in front of the mirror once again. The display showed an unanswered call from her father.

Opening the camera function, she took a picture of her reflection. Only then did she gain a proper overview. A couple of iron tines had punctured her skin, and small scabs formed over the wounds. Apart from that, she had escaped with a row of ten yellowy-blue roses. She put down the phone and leaned into the mirror to study her face. Her left eye was black and swollen but, thankfully, her nose looked absolutely fine.

The police had announced they would hold a press conference at ten o'clock. She would buy herself a pair of sunglasses and find some fresh clothes. Wrapping herself in a towel, she perched on the windowsill of her hotel room. Higher than the surrounding buildings, she had a view of house roofs down towards a river that seemed too diminutive to be the Glomma. The weather remained the same, wind and rain. She pressed *call* and her father answered immediately. The background noise told her he was in his car, probably on his way to his office.

'Are you all right?' she asked.

'I'm sure I'll get through it. I'm more concerned about you. You, Thomas and Suzanne, and your grandfather.'

'Don't worry about me.'

'No?' She tucked her legs underneath herself. 'You aren't by any chance in Fredrikstad?' he asked.

'I am indeed,' she answered, reading his mind and bursting into disarming laughter.

The background noise on the phone line subsided, and she guessed that he had pulled up. 'What happened?' he asked seriously.

She told him the whole story, from the time she had left the editorial office in Oslo's Akersgata until she gave her written statement at the police station.

'What are you doing now?' he asked.

'There's a press conference at ten o'clock.'

'Are you going on with the story?'

'It's my story now. I won't give it up until the police have captured him, if I don't get hold of him myself.'

Her father groaned. 'Line!'

'Okay then, okay.' It struck her that her father would be in charge of the morning meeting at the police station beginning at eight o'clock, in seven minutes according to the television clock. 'I have to go now,' she excused herself so that her father would not have to terminate their conversation. 'I'll talk to you later.'

62

'Okay, but Line?'

'Yes?'

'I look good in that photo, don't you think?'

She understood this was an attempt to stop her worrying.

'Very good.'

'There's something that doesn't add up,' he said. 'I'll work it out if I can uncover the background to these allegations.'

'You'll work it out,' she reassured him, disconnecting the call.

In the bathroom she let her towel drop to the floor and combed her blonde hair with her fingers.

She had a toilet bag and a change of clothes in the case she carried in the boot of her car. Putting on a fresh pair of jeans she remembered the toy car, retrieving it from the trousers she had been wearing the previous evening. An American car with every detail and refinement included. She should have given it to the police, she supposed, but had completely forgotten it. Perhaps the man had dropped it, but that seemed unlikely. She flipped the tiny boot lid up and down before placing it on the desk. She could use it later, an excuse to make contact with the investigating officers.

She fastened her bra and drew a turtle-necked sweater over her head. Then she lay down on the bed with her laptop by her side. The online newspapers had all written about her encounter with the killer; none had revealed her identity, but her name appeared in the bye-line on the story *VG* ran about the actual murder, and it would not be difficult to read between the lines.

Her mobile phone lit up on the window ledge. The call was from Morten P, one of her oldest colleagues in the crime section.

Crap newspaper we work for. Hope you're okay, and Wisting senior too. Phone me if you're up to talking about it.

They had worked together many times, and she had

learned a great deal from him. He had a genuine commitment to his fellow human beings, a trait reflected both in what he wrote and how he treated his colleagues. She invited him for coffee and the whole rotten story once she could manage to sit down again.

Her own paper was the only news source not to write about the fake evidence in the Cecilia case in their online edition. The other net newspapers quoted from the coverage in their paper edition. She read her father's brief comment that he had confidence in the Criminal Cases Review Commission, and apart from that there was nothing except what she already knew.

According to the article, there were two main issues in the petition from Henden, the lawyer. New analyses could prove that the cigarette end containing Rudolf Haglund's DNA profile had been planted, and they had come up with a witness who had provided an alibi. There was nothing about what types of analysis had been conducted, and Line found it impossible to understand how it could lead to such a conclusion. There was nothing about the identity of the new witness, or the alibi he had given Rudolf Haglund.

Biting her lower lip, thoughts identical to her father's ran through Line's mind. Something did not add up.

18

The conference began at eight o'clock, a joint meeting for the officers coming on dayshift to be informed about the previous day's events and given instructions for the day ahead. Last to arrive, Wisting sat at the head of the conference table. Few met his gaze. Of those present only Nils Hammer had worked in the department at the time of the Cecilia case.

'Before we begin,' he said. 'I expect you've heard what's going on in the Cecilia case. I don't know any more than is being reported. Sigurd Henden, the lawyer, made an approach two months ago, requesting case files and investigation material. They were dispatched from here that same week. Now we wait for the Criminal Cases Review Commission. It's up to them to decide whether the case should go back to law.'

One of the younger officers wanted to know what would be required for a retrial.

'New evidence has to be presented or fresh information found, capable of leading to an acquittal. Or one of the detectives working on the case might have done something illegal.'

As he clarified the situation to his colleagues it dawned on him that the defence lawyer could have a double motive; that the accusations against him would not only figure in the press, but would also lead to an internal investigation. One would follow the other.

He cleared his throat to show he was finished with that topic, and embarked on a chronological review of the previous day's operational log, dealing with routine matters: attempted burglary, car theft, stray dogs and drugs misuse.

When the meeting was over, he descended to the basement and followed the corridor to the door marked *Historical Archive*. He did not often venture here. When he occasionally required sight of an old case the girls in the criminal cases office usually helped. The fluorescent light tubes on the ceiling buzzed and flickered and the room was bathed in a blinding light.

Old case notes were stored in a huge sliding cabinet system. In some instances, the standard cardboard archive box was too small, and these cases had been placed in large portable containers stacked on shelves along the wall. There was an empty space on one of the grey shelves. Beside it was a box marked *2735/95 – Cecilia Linde. Copy transcripts, Chief Investigator*.

Lifting the box from the shelf, Wisting caught the slightly musty smell of old paper. At the top lay a blue ring binder marked *Tip-offs*. He carried it with him along the row of shelves to another cardboard box. *2694/94 – Ellen Robekk*, an even greater mystery. Eighteen-year-old Ellen Robekk had vanished into thin air, just like Cecilia, but had never been found.

Frank Robekk had been her uncle and the case had destroyed his police career. The feeling of inadequacy caused by being unable to help his own family became a wound that would not heal, that eventually became infected. The day they placed Rudolf Haglund in the cells, Frank had taken out the archive box dealing with Ellen's disappearance, reading the whole case over again, but this time with fresh eyes. Eyes that had seen Rudolf Haglund.

When he had been through everything that had been written, he started again. And then once more, and yet again. It had done something to him. The man who might have the answer to his niece's disappearance was within reach, but he could not find a link.

They had been unable to use Frank on any other investigations after he had started this remorseless reading. He had been unable to pull himself together sufficiently even to carry out simple tasks and, one month later, left the police station for the last time, without finding any suggestion of a connection. Without finding an answer he could give to his brother. Eventually, long-term sick leave was replaced by disability pension.

Wisting visited him frequently at first, but later there were lengthier and lengthier periods between visits, and at each visit Frank's decline was more pronounced. The last time had been a year ago.

His mobile phone began to ring in his pocket as he carried the cardboard box to the upper floors. He did not answer until he had set the old files down in the middle of his desk: four unanswered calls and three voicemail messages from numbers not stored in his contacts list. Journalists, he assumed, who wanted him to comment on the case.

A couple of pigeons fluttered past his office window. A grey veil of drizzle covered the fjord.

A fine layer of dust had formed on top of the cardboard box. He ran his hand across the top folder, collecting the dust into a ball he rubbed between two fingers and disposed of in the waste bin.

The blue ring binders contained details of tip-offs, while the green folders were case documents with individual divisions for witnesses, police reports and criminal technology examinations. A red binder labelled *Accused* on the spine held the interviews with Rudolf Haglund and all attendant information. In addition, there was a black ring binder containing so-called null and void documents, internal notes that did not accompany the case documents to the public prosecutor's office and were not included in the copy set forwarded to the defence team.

Wisting's notebook from the case also lay inside the cardboard box, pushed down at one side, a bound, hardback book, with his name written in the top right-hand corner. He removed it and placed the box with the remaining documents on the floor before shoving it under the desk and taking his seat.

At the front of the book was a colour A4 photograph of Cecilia Linde from a publicity campaign for one of her father's clothes collections, its white border yellowed by time. The word *CANES* was written across her chest, with *Venatici* in slightly smaller writing beneath. This image had been used with the missing person bulletin, which had been more effective than any advertising campaign. The entire collection of *Venatici* sweaters had sold out in the course of that summer, but no further production had followed.

Wisting leafed through the first few pages, revisiting his thoughts and reflections. Experienced and jotted down hurriedly, they were nevertheless clearly presented. He had spent months on this case, and the ring binders contained thousands of documents he was impatient to delve into again. Something here must form the basis of the accusations. Something still lay undetected.

19

Line had been only twelve years old when Cecilia vanished, but remembered the case well. What she recollected best was that her father was almost never at home that summer and their plans for a holiday in Denmark had come to nothing.

The search for Cecilia Linde produced 387 hits in *VG*'s text archive alone. The sheer volume of material made it difficult for her to find her bearings. She arranged the responses in chronological order, starting with the oldest.

The first news story referred to Cecilia Linde as a young girl who had been reported missing after going out for a run. Her height, build and appearance were described, and the article carried a photograph. The police encouraged members of the public who had seen her to contact them. There was no reason to believe she had been the victim of a crime, but all possibilities were open.

The next report dealt with the search, continually expanded in terms of manpower and range. The following article contained a plea to everyone present in the area on the afternoon of Saturday 15th July to come forward.

A recurrent feature of the reports was that she had disappeared without a trace. Eventually the theory that she had been abducted was launched, and the police were questioned about whether they had heard from the kidnappers, or if ransom demands had been received. Line continued to skim. Her father, participating in the daily press conferences, dismissed the idea that extortion was involved.

A longer story concerned Cecilia in personal terms. The

newspaper had spoken to her friends, a former teacher, neighbours. The daughter of one of the country's most prosperous businessmen, she worked in his fashion empire in the design department, but was also a model.

The most clear-cut clue the police possessed was a white Opel Rekord that had been parked at a crossroads Cecilia had, in all probability, run past. The driver, around thirty years of age, had been wearing a white T-shirt and jeans, had thick, black hair, a broad face, strong chin and close-set eyes. He was asked to turn himself in, but did not appear to have made contact.

One of the headlines at the end of the first week aroused her curiosity. *Desperate search for Cecilia*. The article described how police patrols throughout the whole of the Østland region visited farms and smallholdings and that even members of the Emergency Squad were called in. They had searched within a radius of up to seventy kilometres from the location of her last sighting. The picture accompanying the report showed police checking a smallholding at Rønholt in Bamble. Her father's name was mentioned in one of the final paragraphs. He would not give the reason for the large-scale search.

In an article two days later, the background was explained. *Dagbladet* broke the story. *VG* quoted them, but had obtained additional comments from a police lawyer. Cecilia Linde had somehow smuggled out a tape which described what had happened. Line recollected this as she read, not from the time when it occurred, but from conversations around the table in the *Stopp Pressen* café-bar when her older colleagues chatted about historical news items. Cecilia Linde, having taken a Walkman with her when she was out running, had recorded descriptions of the perpetrator and where she was held captive.

Line jumped back and re-read her father's dismissive

comments about what was described as a race against time, realising what had made him so taciturn. He had not wanted the information about the Walkman out. That would have been like telling the kidnapper they had a clue about where he was keeping the victim. If that went into print, they risked him attempting to move her, or worse. The papers had got wind of it anyway.

She navigated her way forward through the chronological overview. Two days later, Cecilia had been found dead.

The ancient newspaper articles had eaten up a lot of her time. Glancing at the clock, she realised she would manage neither hotel breakfast nor the purchase of sunglasses before the press conference. She closed her laptop. So much for seventeen years ago. She would spend the rest of the day hunting for details of what had happened last night.

20

Wisting concentrated on the document dealing with the cigarette end found at the Gumserød intersection and its analysis at the establishment, then called the Forensics Institute, now renamed the Institute of Public Health, Forensics Division.

Chief Inspector Finn Haber had led the investigations at the discovery site. Wisting had collaborated with him on several major cases before his retirement on full pension eight years earlier. Responsibility for the inspection of a crime scene was a critical task, involving an overview of all the material collected and the subsequent technical examinations. It required a meticulous person with a particular aptitude for organisation, exactly like Finn Haber.

The reports of the forensic tests were just as Wisting recalled Haber's work: thorough and precise. The cigarettes in question had been documented in a photograph of the crossroads with a close up image of each of the three cigarette butts, all of them rollups without filters. One of them had been trampled into the gravel, but the other two appeared to have been extinguished by being pressed between the fingers. They had been allocated individual numbers, A-1, A-2 and A-3. The folder included a sketch showing where each had been found, all within a radius of two metres.

A separate document recorded details of a reconstruction when a hired Opel Rekord had been parked at the intersection in accordance with the description given by the witness on the tractor. Frank Robekk had acted the part of the man who had been standing with a cigarette in the corner of his mouth. The cigarette ends on the gravel were found just around his feet, as if the perpetrator had been waiting there for some time.

The cigarette had been signed in for safe keeping with the initials *ESEK: Crime Lab*. A fortnight later, they had been signed out again and sent to the Forensics Institute.

The request for analysis had followed the standard formula: investigation of the enclosed material with a view to identifying epithelial cells normally found in saliva traces. The results had been reported three weeks later. On the samples tagged A-1 and A-2, no human DNA had been detected. However, on the sample marked A-3, a DNA profile had been established with the sex-typing marker determining male origin.

The next document was a report ascertaining that the trace sample A-3 was consistent with the reference sample provided by the accused Rudolf Haglund, accompanied by expert testimony in verification, and signed by the head of department.

All of this was according to normal procedures. If any objection could be made, it would be that the cigarettes had been kept at Finn Haber's laboratory for two weeks before being sent for analysis, but even that was not out of the ordinary. He shut the folder and replaced it in the box under his desk before crossing to the window where he stood deep in thought, looking out at the downpour. An idea about what might have happened with the DNA samples began to take shape, but he did not dare follow through with that notion.

As he settled back in his chair, there was a knock at the door and the deputy chief constable entered the room, dressed in a neatly pressed uniform. Closing the door behind him, he sat in the visitor's seat.

Audun Vetti had responsibility for prosecuting many of the cases Wisting had investigated, including the Cecilia case.

Their working relationship had been stressful. Vetti was rarely open to the viewpoints and contributions of others, and made himself scarce when difficult decisions had to be made. His efforts were directed towards promoting himself. Solving crime had no significance for him beyond furthering his own career. Two years earlier, his methods had paid off when he was appointed deputy chief constable and moved to an office in Tønsberg. For the past few months, he had been acting chief constable, and he had already added an extra star to his epaulettes. He loosened the buttons on his uniform jacket and placed a folder on his lap.

Wisting leaned back in his chair. 'The Cecilia case,' he said.

Audun Vetti nodded.

'Do you know something more than me?' Wisting asked.

'It was your case,' Vetti replied, shaking his head. 'Your responsibility. The irregularities that occurred are matters you are better placed to know about than I.'

Wisting did not comment on this disclaimer of liability. 'I meant, do you know anything more about the background to this petition to the Criminal Cases Review Commission?'

Audun Vetti unzipped the document folder and produced a set of papers. 'Sigurd Henden and I studied together. He's sent me a copy of the petition, obviously to give us time to prepare a defence. Soon, we'll receive it officially from the Commission seeking a response.'

'What are the grounds?'

'He has had the cigarette ends analysed again,' Vetti explained, leafing through to one of the last pages before handing Wisting the papers.

'And?'

'They've been lying in the deep freeze for seventeen years. The material has deteriorated, but analysis methods have improved. The result is the same.'

Wisting read the papers. The defence lawyer had arranged for the samples to be analysed again by a neutral, independent laboratory in Stavanger. Two of them had not contained cell material that could be used for a DNA analysis but, for the sample marked A-3, they had established a satisfactory DNA profile with ten-out-of-ten markers.

'I don't understand?' Wisting said though, in actual fact, he did.

'Didn't you consider it rather strange that in two of the samples they could not manage to find human traces, while in the last example they had extraordinary success?'

'A number of factors could account for that.'

'Three cigarette ends,' Vetti held up three fingers. 'From the same man in the same place at the same time, under exactly the same circumstances?'

'We don't know whether the other two belong to Haglund. They could be from someone else, and may have lain there for weeks.'

Vetti shook his head. 'You don't really believe that yourself.' Wisting silently agreed. 'Sigurd Henden did what you ought to have done seventeen years ago, William. He had the contents of the cigarette butts analysed.' He waved a finger to indicate that Wisting should leaf further through the papers.

Wisting skimmed the text. The three cigarette ends were examined at a Danish laboratory specialising in analytic chemistry. For each of the samples, they had listed a percentage composition of the contents. Tar and nicotine were two recognisable ingredients among a variety of chemical compounds.

'Modern cigarettes are hi-tech industrial products for which taste, nicotine content and other factors are determined during production,' Vetti said. 'There are different types of tobacco and various processing methods. Snuff, cigarettes and rolling tobacco are all pure natural products to start with. Modern tobaccos have a wide range of additives.'

Leaning forward, he pointed to the overview on the sheet of paper. 'Some of the contents here are the remnants of pesticides used in the cultivation of the tobacco plants. Some of the additives are agents to retain moisture, while others are included to adjust the taste.'

Wisting nodded. He had not read the conclusion of the investigation, but already had a good idea of what it would be.

'The point is …' Vetti said, 'that the two cigarette ends without DNA belong to a different brand from the one with DNA. The folk at the lab have even conducted a comparison analysis and can verify that the two cigarette ends that did not yield results are Tiedemann's Gold Mix number 3, while the decisive cigarette butt was Petterøe's Blue number 3.'

Wisting kept his own counsel, remembering that the initial interviews with Rudolf Haglund had been interrupted every time he demanded a cigarette break. He had sat with a pack of tobacco on his knee and rolled up before they climbed the stairs to the roof terrace where he could light up. He still had the same pack of tobacco as at the time of his arrest. When it was finished, he had been forced to scrounge from police officers. In those days, there was no thought of banning cigarettes. There had been nothing but goodwill on the part of the investigators. A cigarette was something that could keep an interview going.

'Someone,' Vetti said, raising his forefinger and pointing at Wisting. 'Someone here at the station exchanged sample A-3 for a cigarette smoked during the interviews.'

Wisting could not argue. 'What do we do now?'

'I haven't really any choice,' Vetti replied. 'You were the leader of the investigation. I don't know whether you were the one who did it, or if it was a collective initiative. That's something I have to leave to Internal Affairs to determine.'

'Internal Affairs? Isn't that premature? If anyone in the investigation team actually did what you're insinuating, then surely it's too late to prosecute now?'

'The inability to prosecute does not prevent us from finding out whether there has been a miscarriage of justice.' Vetti adjusted his tie and took back the papers. 'I hope you understand that I have no choice but to suspend you?'

Wisting opened his mouth but had to search for the right words. 'You think it was me?'

'I don't think anything, but you were in charge of the investigation.'

'And you were responsible for the prosecution.'

Audun Vetti's face flushed bright red. 'My job was to use the evidence you obtained. I trusted you to do that in an honest fashion.' Standing up, he produced a fresh sheet of paper from the folder and handed it across.

Wisting took it and read: *Temporary removal from service in accordance with the Civil Servants' Act §16,* followed by his own name.

'You have one hour to pack your personal belongings, and then you must leave the station. I shall inform Police Prosecutor Thiis in the meantime. Hand your ID badge and keys to her.'

He paused by the door, as though even he realised how brutal his instruction had been. 'It has to be this way. Until we find out what actually happened seventeen years ago.'

Wisting watched his superior officer's retreating back. This is not about what happened, he thought. This is about what we did.

21

The press conference was held in a conference room on the second floor of the police station at Gunnar Nilsens gate 25. The venue was no more than half full, and only one TV team had turned up. Line nodded and smiled at her journalist colleagues as she entered.

Erik Fjeld sat with his camera at the ready near the podium, but there was no time to speak to him or the others. She found a chair by the window and sat carefully. Her entire body felt tender. Outside, she looked down on a cemetery with old gravestones and black, naked trees.

At ten o'clock a side door opened and three police officers entered, two uniformed and one plainclothes, to take their places behind the table where handwritten placards gave their names and titles. The two in uniform were the chief superintendent and police prosecutor, while the man in civilian clothes was the leader of the investigation.

The chief superintendent opened the meeting by welcoming everyone and giving a quick summation, before handing over to the prosecutor, who spread a bundle of papers across the table and provided a more detailed account. Line sat with the tip of the pen between her lips. None of what was said was new to the journalists.

'Murder weapon?' one of them asked, before the meeting had been opened for questions.

'The murder weapon has not been found,' the prosecutor answered, as though he had just reached that point and not been interrupted.

'Do you know what it was?'

'It is also too early to say anything specific about the cause of death until we receive the preliminary report from Forensics at the Public Health Institute. The crime scene investigators describe a head injury inflicted by a blunt instrument.'

Erik Fjeld took position behind the speakers to snap the press representatives over their shoulders. He directed his lens at Line who smiled and winked to confirm her approval. He was doing exactly what she had told him to do when she phoned. He shifted to a 125 mm lens and zoomed in to photograph the police documents on the table before resuming his seat.

'The deceased has not yet been identified,' the prosecutor said, 'but we have reason to believe the person in question is a forty-eight-year-old man from here in Fredrikstad, and we are linking the murder to a burglary that took place at a residence in W. Blakstads gate yesterday evening at which a *VG* journalist was assaulted.'

Line's cheeks burned.

'Has any trace of the burglar been found?' someone asked.

'We are still working in the house. A dog patrol followed the scent to the industrial area at Øra, where the trail went cold. We have reason to believe he left there in a vehicle.'

The prosecutor now handed over to the detective, who related how many witnesses had been interviewed and encouraged members of the public who might have seen or heard something to get in touch. The meeting was opened for questions and a journalist asked how a reporter from *VG* could discover the identity of the murder victim before the police.

The prosecutor replied: 'I don't know what sources *VG* has, but in general terms I would advise the media against getting in the way of the police's work.'

Laughter broke out.

Line busied herself with her laptop, opening the email from the girl at the petrol station and clicking an attachment, a still photo from the CCTV camera at the service station. It was the murder victim as he stood at the counter, the colour image sharp and clear. The man's greying, receding blond hair was neatly parted and rather futilely combed over to camouflage his bald patch. He was fastidiously dressed, with small, close-set eyes and a penetrating gaze.

Follow-up questions concerned details and clarification of what had already been said. Most knew to keep the best questions until after the press conference. Only the least experienced reporter questioned from his earlier notes, giving the others his information free.

The next attachment was a picture of the man standing beside the dog tied to a pole outside. It was sitting at his feet staring up at him as he rolled a cigarette from his yellow tobacco pack.

One of the journalists conjured an arithmetical problem from the time of the death at just before ten o'clock and Line's attack just prior to midnight. 'Does that mean the perpetrator had been in the victim's apartment for more than two hours?'

'That's speculation,' the prosecutor responded.

An arm shot into the air. 'Was anything stolen?'

'It's too soon to say.'

'Do you know what he may have been looking for?'

An unequivocal answer: 'No.'

Line opened a third image on her laptop. The man with a cigarette in the corner of his mouth, and the dog on all fours.

'Any further questions?' the chief superintendent asked.

Line lifted her hand. 'What happens to his dog?'

The chief superintendent glanced across at the detective. 'It has been temporarily installed at Falck's stray dogs centre,' he replied, getting to his feet. The press conference was over.

22

Suspended. Wisting felt anxiety as he never had before, staring into space with the notification in his hand. The unfamiliar feeling spread from his mind through his body into his limbs.

Suffocating, confused, nauseous, he rose from his seat and left, switching off the light before closing the door behind him. On the stairwell, he mounted the stairs, past two floors, until he reached the verandah on the third. Seventeen years ago, it had been permissible to smoke in the investigators' offices and down in the cells, but this was where they had gone when Rudolf Haglund wanted a break from the interviews.

Two chairs and a table with an overfilled ashtray had taken up one corner. Rudolf Haglund sat with his back to the wall, and Wisting stood beside the railings in case the prisoner chose the quick way out.

He grasped the same railings firmly and let the cold, wet air help to clear his thoughts.

When the DNA result arrived, it had only been confirmation of what they already knew, or thought they knew, that they had arrested the right man. It was not only the DNA evidence. Rudolf Haglund fitted the description given by the witness on the tractor, and Cecilia herself on the tape. There was also the conveniently disappeared car, and his fishing trip alibi that had been shown to be worthless.

They had been certain, every single one of them. All their experience and common sense told them Rudolf Haglund was the right man, although they understood this would not be enough to secure a conviction. The question now was whether one of the investigators had tipped the burden of proof in the right direction by swapping evidence item A-3 for one of the cigarettes Rudolf Haglund had stubbed out in an ashtray here.

He released his grip on the railings and turned his back on the town, deciding it was not necessary to take his younger self for a fool. It must have happened as the front page of *VG* declared. Someone in the police station had planted the evidence. Squeezing his eyes shut, Wisting ran his hand over his face, aware of how wet he had become, but continued to stand with his eyes closed, almost afraid to gather his thoughts.

When the column supporting the chain of evidence collapsed, other possibilities opened. The DNA result had changed everything and their wide-open investigation suddenly had its focus razor sharp on one thing, one man. It went from being broad-spectrum to the narrow pursuit of one person. The time then leading to the court case had been concentrated on finding circumstantial evidence to support the indictment.

Haglund had placed personal ads in pornographic magazines. They found an old high school teacher who had caught him secretly watching girls in the shower, and unsolved incidents of indecent exposure where he fitted the description of the culprit. Nothing had been done about the possible innocence of the accused, that he did not possess a cellar like the one Cecilia had described, or that they had not found as much as a strand of Cecilia's hair in his house.

That had been Wisting's responsibility and choice. If he viewed the case from the present perspective, then his suspension was unavoidable. Through the fresh analyses, the defence counsel had tipped the balance of probability towards the DNA evidence being manufactured by the police. To retain any kind of credibility he, as leader of the investigation and accountable individual, had to be removed from his post. It was a matter of public confidence in the police.

He determined to prove himself worthy of that confidence.

Entering his office again, he removed the cardboard box with the copy documents from the Cecilia case. If he could not use his own office he would work from home. Carrying the box into the corridor, he shouldered open the door to the stairwell to find Audun Vetti standing in front of him, silent, and with his eyes fixed on the cardboard box. Then he nodded, as though satisfied that Wisting had packed and was on his way out.

The deputy chief constable moved aside to let him pass, but Wisting remained in the doorway. There was something he had wanted to say for a long time, from seventeen years before. Now he blurted it out.

'We killed her,' he said.

Audun Vetti looked unsure whether he had heard correctly.

'We killed Cecilia Linde,' Wisting repeated. 'When you approached the media and told them about the cassette you gave the murderer no alternative. He was forced to dispose of her.'

'The journalists knew about it already. I simply confirmed it.'

'That was what killed her.'

Audun Vetti's face darkened. 'He would have killed her regardless. You had come up with nothing in ten days. I know it tormented you, but I don't understand how you could bring yourself to falsify evidence.'

Wisting watched the door slide shut behind Audun Vetti as he left. Arguing would not help. He had to take action to prove his innocence.

He stowed the box in the boot of his car and replaced the luggage cover before locking the vehicle and twisting the police station key from his key ring.

A patrol car drove into the backyard, the garage door slid open and Wisting followed it inside. He walked quickly, eager to hand over his key and admittance card so that he could make a start. He would go through the entire Cecilia case with a fresh pair of eyes and the benefit of seventeen more years of experience.

Christine Thiis' office was tidy and well organised, as usual. Recently appointed to the post that Audun Vetti had vacated when he had been promoted to deputy chief constable she had, last autumn, taken responsibility for the prosecution when a dead body was discovered in a summer cottage closed for winter. Though lacking experience, she had handled both criminal proceedings and media interest with a deft and effective touch. Wisting had come to appreciate her good judgment although she had, perhaps, greater knowledge of human nature than of investigative tactics.

He placed the key and electronic admittance card on her desk, hesitating slightly before following with his service ID. It was obvious that she was as discomfited as he. 'It's okay,' he said; she could not do other than follow Audun Vetti's orders.

Christine Thiis picked up his police badge, fingered it thoughtfully and, as he headed for the door, opened the top drawer of her desk. 'I'll put it here for the time being.'

Their eyes met as he gave an answering nod and left.

Before departing the police station he wanted to speak to Nils Hammer, the detective he had worked with most closely over the years. Like Wisting, he had started in the department as a young man. They did not socialise outside working hours, and Wisting did not know much about his personal life; but, as far as work was concerned, considered him indispensable. Efficient, committed and professionally sound, he thought logically and acted deductively. Wisting stepped into his office and closed the door.

Hammer looked up. 'Good to see you,' he said. 'I have something here we ought to look at.'

'I can't ...'

'A report of a missing girl,' Nils Hammer interrupted. 'Linnea Kaupang. Seventeen years old. She's been missing since Friday.'

Wisting glanced at the photograph. A young girl with slightly crooked teeth. Her eyes were dark and bright, and her fair hair fell in loose curls around her shoulders with a little yellow bow-shaped hair clip on one side. The thought that something awful could have happened to her felt like physical pain. Thoughts of how they should approach the case were already forming in his mind.

'I can't ...' he said, as he returned the photo. 'You'll have to deal with it by yourself.'

23

Not much material to build a story, Line thought as she left the police station. Nothing new had emerged from the press conference. 'Lunch?' she suggested to Erik Fjeld.

Hooking his camera over his shoulder, he nodded. They found a café in a pedestrian street reminiscent of the café-bar Suzanne had opened at home in Stavern, a quiet place serving hot and cold lunches. She bought them each a baguette with a cola for the photographer and a foaming chai latté for herself. Erik found a spot well inside the premises where he ejected the memory card from his camera.

After placing the food on the table, Line took her laptop from her bag. Opening it, she inserted the memory card and loaded the photos from the press conference. The first was a close-up of her with makeup covering only some of the bruising around her eye, but she looked much better than in the previous evening's photos.

'Nothing at the press conference suggested an early arrest,' Erik Fjeld said.

Line agreed, but was curious whether the police really had as little to go on as they said. Clicking the next image she realised she had been luckier than she could have even hoped. The document on the screen carried the title *Deceased's mobile phone*.

She enlarged the photo. Jonas Ravneberg had owned a Nokia 6233. In addition to the phone number, the report writer had included the fifteen-digit IMEI number, followed by a chronological schedule of incoming and outgoing calls over ten days. The list was short, confirming the impression of Jonas Ravneberg as a loner.

02.10 - 14.32 hours Outgoing: 69330196 Duty lawyer, Fredrikstad

02.10 - 14.28 hours Outgoing: 1881 Directory Enquiries

02.10 - 14.17 hours Incoming: 69310167 Unregistered

01.10 - 12.33 hours Outgoing: 99691950 Astrid Solli-bakke, Gressvik

30.09 - 21.43 hours Incoming: 99691950 Astrid Solli-bakke, Gressvik

30.09 - 10.22 hours Outgoing: 46807777 Fredrikstad Blad

29.09 - 21.45 hours Outgoing: 48034284 Torgeir Roxrud, Fredrikstad

27.09 - 13.45 hours Outgoing: 93626517 Mona Husby, Fredrikstad

25.09 - 20.15 hours Outgoing: 99691950 Astrid Solli-bakke, Gressvik

Three names. Three people who might tell her more about the murder victim. Most exciting, however, were the conversations on the actual day of the murder. First an unknown caller, followed by a call to a lawyers' office.

The next image was the front page of a report from the site where the body was found. Line leaned into the screen. The report was introduced by the name of the person who had conducted the investigation and how the assignment had been given. This was followed by a description of the discovery site, the weather, the environs and the practical steps that had been taken to preserve the crime scene, as well as a paragraph about the dog and how it had been taken care of.

It continued with a description of the victim: 'male, aged

around fifty, wearing a Helly Hansen rain jacket, dark blue jeans and green Wellington boots with the Viking trademark. The deceased lay prostrate on the pedestrian and cycle path with his upper torso partly protruding from the pathway. He had major contusions on his face'.

She could not see anything else. The numbering in the top right-hand corner said page one of four.

Next was a screen printout from the National Population Register concerning Jonas Ravneberg, his eleven-digit National Insurance number and a date indicating that Ravneberg had lived at the same address for sixteen years but, apart from that, nothing that Line did not already know.

The next two photos were too fuzzy to read, but the third was the green cover of a document folder. This was useful because it contained a numbered list of the documents in police possession. The first of these was a report produced by the first patrol to arrive at the crime scene. She recognised the titles of the reports dealing with the mobile phone and the crime scene examination. Two witnesses had been interviewed: first the man who had found the body, and who had also sent the tip-off to the newspaper. The other witness was a female: Christianne Grepstad, such an unusual name that Line would easily manage to track her down.

The final image was an *Outline Report following Preliminary Examination of W. Blakstads gate 78*. This described the interior of the house: 'a terraced house of two storeys, with a basement underneath, its ground floor including a porch, kitchen and living room leading out to a little terrace, the second floor comprising a hallway, bathroom, three bedrooms and a balcony. The basement contains several storerooms and cellarage'.

Holding the baguette in one hand, she continued to eat while she read. The report writer believed the perpetrator had been in the house for a considerable period of time.

It appeared to have been searched thoroughly and systematically. Every drawer and cupboard had been opened and the contents removed. It was obvious that the perpetrator had been searching for something but impossible to know whether or not he had found it.

'Good,' she said, pointing at the screen.

'Is there something?'

'Definitely,' she nodded. 'He was looking for something.'

'Who?'

'The murderer.'

She put her food aside to drink her tea. She had a story, a follow-up. *Mysterious break-in.* The kind of thing people liked to read. She would give the police a few hours before phoning them. If she were lucky, she would succeed in getting someone to agree with her opinion that there was something mysterious about how the burglary had been executed.

'That was really risky, though,' Erik Fjeld suggested. 'Breaking into the house of somebody you've just killed. The police were certain to show up.'

'He must have been looking for something worth the risk,' Line agreed. 'Something worth killing for.'

24

Above his head a flock of migrating birds ploughed their way south, wing-to-wing in synchronised formation below low clouds. Wisting was not driving home. Instead he passed quickly through Stavern and along the main road to Helgeroa, ignoring the exits leading to the Justice Department's conference and training centre, the sports ground, the hospital and the Folk High School.

Crows flapped like dark shadows across the flanks of brown ploughed fields. He pulled into the side at a sign pointing along the gravel track to the left, Gumserød farm, and halted where the witness on the tractor had said the white Opel had been parked.

The young woman whose photograph Nils Hammer had shown him was in his mind, the one with the yellow bow in her hair. Linnea Kaupang. Somewhere, her despairing parents were waiting. Hammer knew what had to be done, but Wisting felt bad, not being able to contribute.

He forced himself to concentrate on seventeen years back in time.

Almost all murders in Norway are solved, which brings its own pressure. He was not the only one who had felt the Cecilia case heavy on his shoulders. When Rudolf Haglund appeared it felt as if a burden had been lifted from them all and Wisting experienced the satisfying feeling of success: of finally making a breakthrough, having a name, a suspect on whom the investigation could focus. But all they had achieved was the construction of their own version. They had invested their professional pride into drawing a convincing picture of Rudolf Haglund as a murderer.

Wisting had seen this before. Pressure and the demand to solve a case could lead to rash conclusions. The investigators formed their own impressions of how elements hung together based on the first evidence. After they drew their conclusions, an unconscious process had been set in motion by which they sought confirmation. They had developed tunnel vision and sought evidence to fit their theory, become like hunting dogs following the scent. All sidetracks and possible distractions were passed over. It was Rudolf Haglund they were after, and they circled round him.

Closing his eyes, he recreated his own picture of that hot summer day when Cecilia ran along the gravel track, the sunlight filtering through the leafy trees, muscles visible under her singlet, her hair pulled back in a ponytail swinging from side to side, earphones pressed close to her head, *Seal, Kiss from a Rose*, perspiration forming beads on her forehead and a veneer of moisture on her chest.

In Wisting's mind it was still Rudolf Haglund who was waiting, perched on the edge of the open car boot. White T-shirt and jeans. Small, close-set eyes, crooked nose and cigarette dangling from the corner of his mouth. When he caught sight of her, he discarded the cigarette end, glanced from side to side to ensure he was entirely alone, and positioned himself with his back half-turned. When she passed, he pounced and upended her into the boot.

For Wisting, Rudolf Haglund was still the man who had abducted Cecilia Linde but, realistically, there was doubt. He glanced in the mirror. The cardboard box on the rear seat contained thousands of documents. Several hundred names. He could not shake off the idea that it also contained an alternative name. An alternative killer.

A man with a stick and heavy rainwear came walking

along the farm track in the direction of the mailboxes. Tim Bakke, Wisting decided. A grizzled, green-eyed man with strong arms who lived in the first red house on the right-hand side of the track. He kept four hens in a chicken run behind his garage. When Wisting interviewed him he was most concerned about the fox that had snatched the fifth hen.

He put the car into gear, crunching across the rough gravel. Ten minutes later, he swung off the road again. It was almost a year since he had taken over the cottage out at Værvågen, and he had grown fond of the place. He could relax there.

Two parallel wheel ruts filled with brown muddy water stretched before him, ascending to a plateau where he could see the smooth coastal rock of the shore. The track ended at an open area surrounded by thick wild rose bushes about thirty metres from the cottage. A footpath covered the final stretch. Down on the shore a seagull posed on one of the mooring posts. Wisting parked and lifted the box of case documents out of the boot. The wind rustled the autumn leaves and waves broke against the beach. He sank his shoulders and exhaled.

Inside the cottage, he could smell the fresh paint from the final week of summer when he had been here with Line. The living room was bright and attractive with new covers on the soft furnishings as well as cushions and curtains in matching colours. The necessary female influence was his daughter's.

He set the box down in the centre of the table and removed his jacket before emptying the contents. He placed the ring binders in the centre of the table and sorted them according to colour. When he had finished, a cassette still lay at the bottom of the box: a copy, a BASF tape, marked exactly as Cecilia's. *CL*.

He looked around. Their old portable radio cassette player was still sitting underneath the windowsill. He pressed the eject button and inserted the cassette, spooling back slightly before commencing playback, and straightened up as he waited. Cecilia's voice interrupted just as abruptly as the first time he had heard her.

'*On Saturday 15th July a man kidnapped me while I was out running. It took place at the crossroads beside Gumserød farm. He had an old white car. I'm lying inside its boot right now. It all happened so fast. I didn't manage to get a good look at him, but he had a foul smell, of smoke, though something else as well. I've seen him before. He was wearing a white T-shirt and jeans. Dark hair. Small dark eyes and bushy black eyebrows. A crooked nose.*'

He listened to the entire one minute and forty-three seconds, moving his lips and repeating parts of the statement along with her. Her voice was clear and distinct, but she spoke rapidly, as though in a rush. Even though he had heard it many times before, it seemed nevertheless that there was something new there. He spooled back.

'*... he had a foul smell, of smoke, though something else as well. I've seen him before.*'

He stopped and rewound it again.

'*I've seen him before.*'

The sentence was familiar, but had taken new meaning. They had never succeeded in proving any connection between Cecilia Linde and Rudolf Haglund. Not a single one of the documents on the table suggested any point of intersection between their lives. He had thought the comment might mean she had spotted him on one of her runs, and perhaps Rudolf Haglund had even kept an eye on her as he planned the abduction. However, it might also mean that Cecilia Linde's murderer occupied a position somewhere in her social circle.

25

Among the contents of the cardboard box was an unfiled, stapled sheaf of papers, a printout from a database containing an overview of everyone involved, with each name allocated a reference. Thus it was a simple matter to find someone when the name appeared again. It also simplified the checking of named tip-offs.

There was no corresponding method for discovering which police personnel had been involved and what actions they had taken. Any one of them could have let themselves into the crime lab and exchanged evidence item A-3. If Wisting included cleaning, canteen, janitorial, civilian and other office staff, there were more than seventy people with access to the police station by means of an admittance card and personal code. All such ingress was stored in a computer system. The information would still be available but sorting would be a hopeless task. The exchange could have taken place at any time in the course of the three days Rudolf Haglund was held in custody, or it could have happened on any of the following days before Finn Haber sent the cigarette butts off for analysis.

Of the seventy members of staff, only twenty worked in the criminal investigation department. The enquiry had occurred during the general holiday period when a couple of detectives had been abroad. Of the eighteen who turned up, twelve became directly involved. If any of them had a motive to falsify the evidence it was reasonable to assume it would be someone in contact with Rudolf Haglund. Wisting was the person who had spent most time with him, but there were others.

Working methodically, he placed the red ring binder marked *Accused* in front of him. It contained everything concerning Rudolf Haglund.

At the very front was a list of personal details. Wisting himself had filled out the spaces on the standard form during the first interview. In addition to his name, date of birth, address and phone number, the report contained information about his employer, job title, income, education, qualifications, and a list of convictions.

The next document was a decision in pursuance of the Criminal Procedure Act §175 regarding the arrest of Rudolf Haglund. The actual sheet of paper was still called a blue form because, prior to the introduction of computers in police matters, the police lawyer recorded the decision on a blue sheet of paper. The document was stamped and signed by Police Prosecutor Audun Vetti and dealt with the formalities and basis for the arrest, though it did not contain any information about the actual case.

The blue form was accompanied by a separate document entitled *Report on Prisoner in Custody*. This too was a standard form containing information about the case, the time and place of the arrest, the name of the prisoner, where he was being transferred and which police lawyer had instructed that he be held in custody.

Nils Hammer and Frank Robekk were the arresting officers.

In the corner cabinet, Wisting found a writing pad and ballpoint pen. He clenched his teeth and drummed the pen on the blank sheet. His intention was to draw up a list of his colleagues who had been in direct contact with Rudolf Haglund. Clicking the pen a couple of times, he noted the first two names before leafing further through the folder.

95

The next document was a report detailing the search and seizure of belongings. The items in Haglund's possession when he was arrested were: a wallet, keys, pocketknife and tobacco. This report had been written by Nils Hammer.

There were three reports concerning the investigations carried out at Haglund's smallholding in Dolven. The first was a report about a fruitless search with dogs. The next described the crime scene technicians' unproductive examinations led by Finn Haber. The third was a tactical search led by Nils Hammer. They had seized foreign porn magazines and films with titles such as *Teenager* and *Preteens*, as well as sado-masochistic journals. These confirmed Haglund's sexual preferences and underpinned their belief that he was the right man.

There then followed the interviews that Wisting himself had written in ink, interspersed with reports about how Haglund was transported between the police station and the remand cell at the prison, and how he had been given a medical examination.

The list of names lengthened. It included retired police officers, detectives who had left the service and applied for jobs in the private sector, or had been employed in the *Økokrim* police financial branch or *Kripos*, the national criminal investigation section. Of all the names listed, only Nils Hammer was still working in the local department.

Wisting ran his eye up and down the list. They were all experienced, competent and dependable people. Many of them had been excellent role models for him and trusted colleagues, such as Frank Robekk.

Each time he came across one of the names, he placed a vertical line to its right on the pad. One name stood out: Nils Hammer. The numbers spoke for themselves. In the material, there were twenty-three intersections between Nils Hammer and Rudolf Haglund. Next on the list was himself with seventeen meetings, followed by Finn Haber with twelve.

Leaning back, he lifted his eyes to the window. Outside, the sky was even darker, and a cargo ship was journeying westwards. He trusted Nils Hammer, who had taken Frank Robekk's place. There was a certain security in having Hammer on an investigation team. Wisting could always rely on the tasks he assigned being accomplished in the fastest possible time. Again, Hammer was not an adherent of formalities. Some of his effectiveness was due to his ability to take shortcuts across the rules, and he could be extremely creative in the context of an investigation.

All the same, the list facing him was nothing more than data open to interpretation. The result could just as easily be a consequence of Nils Hammer's commitment and willingness to take on work-related tasks. He clicked his pen another couple of times before obliterating the whole list. He needed to find a different approach, but for now had no idea what that might be.

26

Around two o'clock, the rain stopped, but low clouds still hung heavy in the sky. The sea was the colour of slate and capped with waves of foam. Wisting took his phone with him onto the verandah. He could hear the steady sound of water dripping from the trees, and somewhere a bird chirping.

A long list of unanswered calls awaited. His father had phoned twice. There were unknown numbers, probably news editors. Nils Hammer's name appeared halfway down the list, and he had left a message on voicemail. Possibly news of the missing girl on what would be called the Linnea case if she did not turn up safe and well. The message was brief. He simply wanted Wisting to know that he was there for him, should he need anything. He had also spoken to their trade union leader who had offered to cover legal costs if it came to that.

He deleted the message and called his father, who could not hide his upset. The old man spoke rapidly, his pitch rising as he spoke. 'I knew it would be bad, but not as awful as this,' the old man said. 'You are being pilloried, pure and simple. Prejudged. And this Audun Vetti ...' He almost spat out the name. 'Nothing but legal procedure.'

Wisting peered indoors at the case documents spread across the coffee table as he spoke to his father, explaining the background to the newspaper headlines, confirming that someone really had faked evidence. He did not have to confirm that he was not the culprit.

Afterwards, he keyed in Suzanne's number, told her what had happened and what he thought. Suzanne seemed distant and preoccupied. He could hear her moving glasses and plates around, and the noise made by the café dishwasher. 'How are things with you?' he asked.

She explained that there were fewer customers than usual, and the way she said this made it sound as though she blamed him. They exchanged a few insignificant pleasantries until some customers approached the counter and she had to round off the conversation. Click and empty silence.

He stood motionless, with the mobile phone in his hand, recalling a conversation of last autumn.

He had guested on a talk show, discussing the discovery of a dead body in the programme host's summer cottage. The celebrity had persuaded him to say more than he had intended about things he normally did not reveal to anyone: the dangers of the job, how he had risked his life several times, even about the time he had been forced to kill someone in the line of duty. Before the camera's gaze, he described how he had already planned his own funeral, including that the service should open with the hymn *Where Roses Never Die*.

Strange to hear himself speak about such things; it had been alienating for Suzanne. 'I don't like the way you put yourself and your work above your nearest and dearest. I need to feel secure around the man I live with. Even when we're not actually together. How can I feel safe when I hear what goes on in your work? I can't relax when you're not at home. Every single night I wonder whether that will be the one you don't come home. That you've gone too far by placing a case about strangers above yourself and your family.'

Stuffing the mobile into his pocket he returned inside, sat in the armchair and drew the black ring binder towards him, the so-called null and void documents. The folder was divided into five sections, five theories for the Cecilia case that had been put aside the moment Rudolf Haglund's name cropped up.

First the ransom theory. Kidnapping and demands for money were not matters they had a great deal of experience with at the police station, but it was one of the first ideas to be discussed with Nora and Johannes Linde. One month prior to the abduction, *Finansavisen*, the financial newspaper, published an overview of Norway's wealthiest families, and the Lindes were accorded ninth place. Their business and personal lives were splashed across two pages, accompanied by a photograph of their beautiful country estate on the Vestfold coast, a feature that could have encouraged exactly this type of crime.

Both parents had been insistent that they wanted to pay if any ransom demand arrived, but agreed for the police to supervise. Every hour that passed without the kidnappers making contact, however, diminished their hopes of buying Cecilia's return.

The next theory was also linked to Johannes Linde's business activities. Linde had established the firm called *Canes* in partnership with Richard Kloster. Kloster had been bought out of the business six months before the first successful fashion collection was launched, and had taken legal proceedings against the Linde company. This had to do with ownership and rights to product names. Richard Kloster was already being investigated for tax evasion, and reports were circulating about possible money laundering. This theory had the kidnappers located in Richard Kloster's circle, and that Linde already knew what he had to do to free his daughter.

They had induced *Økokrim* to re-order their priorities in the case and draw up a charge against Kloster supplying grounds for search and seizure of his property. In conjunction with the financial investigators, they had scoured his home, his cottage, his yacht and all the other places where he spent time, without finding anything suspicious.

Frank Robekk had been responsible for the third theory: *The burglary.*

When the Linde family moved to their summerhouse at the end of June, they discovered that there had been a break-in. Frank Robekk was assigned responsibility for checking any connection between the break-in and the disappearance three weeks later.

The burglar had entered through a window in Cecilia's room, and it did not seem that he had been anywhere other than her room. An intruder alarm was installed in the public rooms of the house, but did not seem to have been activated. It did not appear that anything had been stolen. Cecilia thought a sweater might be missing, but she had so many that she could not be absolutely certain. The break-in was never cleared up.

The fourth proposal concerned Cecilia's boyfriend, the photographer Danny Flom, since violent crimes are often carried out by someone close to the victim. Nils Hammer had been assigned to this.

Wisting was never entirely able to figure out Danny Flom. Two years older than Cecilia, he had worked as a freelance photographer for a number of media bureaux. They had met two years earlier on a photoshoot for one of Linde's collections. When Wisting cast his mind back, it struck him that Danny Flom reminded him of Tommy Kvanter, Line's former boyfriend. A man who very obviously had a dark as well as a light side. Flom had years of practice in hiding his dark side, but Wisting recognised an expression that occasionally crossed his face. In general he was pleasant and forthcoming, with something almost bohemian about him that was alien to the streamlined lifestyle of the Lindes. Cecilia's parents described him as entertaining, charming and cheerful, but they had also experienced his mood swings, sides of him that Cecilia was blind to. It was obvious that Johannes Linde in particular was not especially keen on the relationship.

His record showed no previous convictions. He had been fined a couple of times for smoking hash, and one allegation of assault had been dropped after the accusation was withdrawn. They had also discovered another woman, a female photographer who had accompanied him on a work-related trip shortly after he and Cecilia met. He had confirmed the relationship when they confronted him, but maintained that it had only been a brief fling, and that Cecilia knew about it. The woman involved had given a matching explanation.

What was certain was that Danny Flom's influence on Cecilia had been enormous, and that had suggested a fourth theory: *Staging.* In other countries the police had experienced daughters of wealthy men staging their own abduction with their boyfriends to obtain money for a new life, free from her parents. This theory was never actively worked on.

The fifth theory was called the *List Project*, simply that Cecilia Linde had been abducted by person or persons unknown.

Pursuing an unknown perpetrator was one of the most demanding of all tasks, and no shortcuts could be taken. In such cases, quality of information mattered as much as quantity. They had to make a broad sweep in an effort to chart all movement along the route Cecilia had probably taken, and identify everyone then present in the vicinity. The result was an extremely long list of names that could be divided by gender and age, sorted and ranked by domicile, hair colour, clothing, sometimes vehicle, smoker/non-smoker, right-handed/left-handed.

Lists. Lengthy boring lists of things that probably would never lead anywhere but in the end, it could be statistical trains of thought that provided the solution. In the Cecilia case, the list of names was compared with the register of owners of white Opel Rekords and a list of men previously convicted of sex crimes.

It was like trailing a fishing net behind a boat, trawling the waters with no discrimination about what was caught. This was how they had found Rudolf Haglund, but the net they had used was coarse-meshed, and the likelihood that something or someone had slipped through was high.

Wisting leaned back in his seat. It might be worthwhile now, seventeen years after the events, to run through the lists again. They had already searched back in time to see if anything existed on the listed persons' records. The thinking being that the kidnapper might have done something similar *before*. Again, if they had captured the wrong man, he might have done something similar in *later* years.

He let the pages slip through his fingers. Without access to the police computer systems this was a dead end.

27

Line drew the curtains of her hotel room and pulled off her winter boots. Desperate for sleep, she sat at the desk and picked up the model car she had found outside Jonas Ravneberg's house. The plate underneath told her it was a 1955 Cadillac. The numbers 1:43 probably referred to the size ratio between the model car and the real vehicle. She opened the doors and squinted inside before replacing it on the desktop.

While in the café, she had compiled a bullet point list of actions, starting with the murder victim's mobile phone. It could have led the police to Jonas Ravneberg's house ahead of her, she thought, but she also knew that the first police patrol on the scene had concentrated on securing the site, leaving the investigation to the experienced crime scene technicians who would be called out from their homes. When they arrived, the methodical and laborious work had begun, in which the chief rule was to do nothing in a hurry.

She produced her own phone and adjusted the settings to hide caller ID before tapping in the eight-digit number listed as unregistered in the police report. The first two numbers were six and nine, indicating the subscriber's domicile as Fredrikstad. She let it ring until the line disconnected automatically.

In her experience, some people did not answer their phone if the call came from a withheld number, so she reactivated caller ID and made a fresh attempt, opening her laptop as it rang. She trusted the police report, but checked the number herself to be on the safe side. The phone rang out a second time.

It was unproblematic for the police to discover the identity of an ex-directory subscriber, but they were probably at the mercy of *Telenor*'s office hours. The report had been written at 03.40, during the night, and the officer who had checked the number had most likely chosen to leave it for others to obtain the supplementary information.

Eleven minutes after the call from the unregistered number, Jonas Ravneberg had phoned Directory Enquiries. Then he had called the duty lawyer.

Line phoned the same number. Fairly early in her career as a crime journalist she had, to her surprise, discovered that some lawyers could be extremely forthcoming, even referring to criminal case documents they had received from the police. After a while she had realised there was an expectation of returning the favour. The majority of defence lawyers and their clients, sooner or later, found themselves in the media's glare.

'Duty lawyer Anders Refsti,' said a voice.

Line introduced herself and explained where she worked. 'I'm calling about the man who was murdered yesterday, Jonas Ravneberg. I understand he contacted you only a few hours earlier.' She heard the lawyer leafing through some papers. It seemed the enquiry came as a surprise, and it astonished her that the police had not already contacted him. 'Is that correct?' she asked. 'Did he phone you?'

'I have the name recorded here, yes.'

'So you spoke to him?'

'Has it been confirmed? That he's the man who was murdered?'

'Not officially.'

'Well, at least that explains why he didn't turn up for our appointment today.'

105

'You arranged to meet?'

'He phoned yesterday afternoon,' the lawyer said. 'I don't usually make any Monday appointments. I work as a publicly appointed defence counsel in criminal cases, and Mondays are usually taken up with custody hearings, but he said it was important. We arranged for him to come at half past eight, but he didn't turn up. Now I understand why, of course.'

'What did he want to talk about?'

'He didn't say, just that it was important.'

'He must have said something, surely?'

'Yes, but I don't know if I can repeat it. Old dregs, I think he said. That there were some old dregs that had come to the surface, and he didn't know how he should react.'

Line twisted her pen between her fingers. 'No more than that?'

He hesitated, but sounded positive when he replied: 'No.'

Line let the pen slide across her notepad. 'Is it okay if I write that you confirm he sought legal advice a short time before the murder, but that you can't reveal the subject matter?'

Anders Refsti took some time before agreeing. Line had already noted the wording when he acceded to her request. She thanked him for his time and set to work on the remaining phone calls. She wanted to conduct some internet searches first though.

Astrid Sollibakke from Gressvik was the most frequent caller. Four conversations in total. On the map, Gressvik looked to be a village that had grown into Fredrikstad, only separated by a tributary of the River Glomma. Her name produced several more results than Line had expected, so she restricted her search to Norwegian pages only. That produced eight hits, five from the same website, Fredrikstad Collectors' Club. One of these led to a page where the club's

106

committee members were listed, showing Astrid Sollibakke as the treasurer. The other four results led to a collectors' forum where she had been looking for porcelain plates and vintage apothecary bottles, and wanted to sell decorated metal canisters and model cars.

One result was in the tax lists and the final two were in each of the local newspapers, *Demokraten* and the *Fredrikstad Blad*, where they reported on an Antique and Collectors' Fair held in the Rolvsøy hall. Her name appeared in the text underneath a picture of two women in front of a table decked with various items. One was slightly older and taller than the other. Treasurer Astrid Sollibakke was the younger of the two, and the other was vice-chair Mona Husby. Line leafed through her notes. Mona Husby was the other woman on the telephone list. Both were members of the same association. Perhaps Jonas Ravneberg had been a collector as well.

She made a search for Torgeir Roxrud, obtaining a result in the tax lists, but that did not really tell her anything.

It would soon be three o'clock. She sucked on her pen as she considered how to spend the rest of the day. Her father would stop work in an hour's time. She would phone him to hear how his day had gone, but first she would try to make an appointment with one of Jonas Ravneberg's three telephone contacts. As she was most curious about Torgeir Roxrud, she began by tapping in his number. A husky voice answered. Line introduced herself and was greeted by a paroxysm of coughing. 'It's about Jonas Ravneberg.'

'I've already spoken to the police,' the man said. 'I couldn't help them, and don't think I'll be able to help you either.'

Line drummed the pen on the notepad, pleased to hear the investigators were not entirely on the back foot. 'I believe you can, though,' she said. 'I just need to talk to someone who knew him.'

'Nobody knew Jonas. No one got close to him. I never understood what tormented him, but there was certainly something.'

Line moved the phone to her other ear. 'Can we meet?' she asked, glancing at the time. 'In an hour?'

28

Torgeir Roxrud was exactly the interview subject she needed. Someone acquainted with the murder victim and with the ability to express himself. Forthright and plainspoken, it had not been difficult to persuade him. She called Erik Fjeld, arranging to meet at the hotel to drive together to the man's home.

The next name on the notepad was Christianne Grepstad, the woman who, according to the list of documents belonging to the chief investigator, had been interviewed as a witness. As expected, the name was so unusual it only appeared once in the phone book. The number rang without any answer. Line made a note of the address so that she could call round after her meeting with Roxrud.

Before she left, she checked the online newspapers. The main spread was a body blow, a photo of her father accompanied by the headline *Chief Inspector Suspended*. A nasty gnawing feeling spread through her and, though she had no desire to read further, she forced herself to do so.

Acting Chief Constable Audun Vetti confirmed that experienced CID leader William Wisting had been withdrawn from duty following accusations about falsified evidence in the Cecilia case. The case had been transferred to the Norwegian Bureau for the Investigation of Police Affairs. Wisting had not been available for comment.

Her father answered at once. 'What's going on?' she asked.

Her father cleared his throat, as he did when he wanted to play for time. 'What do you mean?'

'It says here that you're suspended.'

'That happens automatically. As soon as they suspect I've falsified evidence, they are required to remove me from my post.'

'How can they think anything of the sort?'

'I've seen the new analyses, and it's not a question of *whether* evidence was interfered with, but who did it.'

'Why on earth do they suspect you?'

'I had responsibility for the case then, and have to carry the can now.'

Line shook her head. 'What about the new witness? The guy who can provide Haglund with an alibi? Do you know any more about that?'

'No, but I expect it will come out soon. Sigurd Henden is probably planning to keep the case on the boil by gradually leaking information.'

Line nodded. That was a well-known media strategy. It was not necessary to give the journalist more than just the right amount to create the headlines and, preferably, let details emerge in subsequent coverage. 'What are you doing now?' she asked.

'Trying to get to the bottom of it.'

'How are you going about that?'

Her father cleared his throat again. 'I popped down to the archive room before I left work.'

'Are you working on the case?'

'I'm trying to look at it with a fresh pair of eyes.'

Line got to her feet and crossed to the window. 'Do you think he was innocent?'

'I haven't found anything to convince me of the opposite.'

Line peered at the notes from the case she was working on. Suddenly they seemed unimportant. 'I can come and help you,' she said. It would not present any problem. She could break off and take sick leave. No one would blame her.

'It could be useful for me as well. Instructive about police methods.'

'Let me think about it,' her father said. 'How are things with you? Are you still working on the Fredrikstad case?'

'I'm staying here for a day or two.'

'Has anyone been arrested?'

Line realised he had not been following the news, and could understand why. 'No, and I think it may take a while longer. Where are you, anyway?'

'At the cottage.'

She perched on the windowsill and drew her legs up underneath her. Seeing in her mind's eye the red cabin by the coast, she longed to hear the sound of the rolling waves and screeching gulls. 'Are you sure I shouldn't come down there?'

'I'll manage. But you're always welcome.'

Line had already made up her mind. She would finish off what she had to do and request a few days off.

'Who was murdered?' her father asked.

'It's most likely a man called Jonas Ravneberg. Quite an anonymous guy. No family or job. I'm going out now to talk to someone who knew him, so we'll have the story ready when the name is released.'

'On your own?'

'I'm taking the photographer with me,' Line reassured him, understanding her father's concern. There was an unknown murderer out there, and the likelihood was strong that he would be found within the victim's social circle.

29

Erik Fjeld helped himself to coffee from the machine in the reception area. Line filled a cardboard cup for herself and was ready to go. After crossing the River Glomma, she followed the GPS instructions, travelling in an easterly direction. Soon they were surrounded by fields with black ploughed furrows and yellow corn stubble.

Fifteen minutes later, a large lake appeared on the right side of the road, and shortly afterwards, the GPS told her to take the next exit. A narrow gravel track snaked its way through the rocky, undulating landscape.

'How do you want to play it?' the photographer asked.

'Close-up. Private and personal, to reflect how well he knew the murder victim.' Torgeir Roxrud had said his dead friend was weighed down by something. Something that tormented him. 'And dark,' she added. 'Dark and shadowy.'

The track ended at a low, brown-stained house with window frames that had once been white, and green roofing felt, surrounded on all sides by rain-soaked spruce trees. The rusty gutters were speckled with moss and hung from the eaves at one side. An ancient breakdown lorry, piles of old car tyres and a wooden pallet with a car engine and spare parts, all littered the yard.

Line swung the car round to avoid a large puddle and parked in front of a makeshift carport with a ragged plastic cover, blown to tatters by the wind. "Dark and shadowy shouldn't be a problem,' Erik said.

They stepped out of the car. The cold air that greeted

them was raw and smelled of mud and rotting leaves. Line crossed the yard to knock at the front door. No reply. She tried again, a bit harder, but there was still no response.

Flowery curtains hung at either side of the nearest window. She placed a chair against the wall and perched on tiptoe to look inside at a kitchen equipped with only the barest of essentials: cupboards, worktops, cooker and fridge. A folded newspaper lay on the table beside a coffee mug. She rapped on the glass, calling out the name of the man who lived there. There was still no sign of life.

She clambered down again and turned to face the photographer. Behind him, a huge black dog came bounding out from a forest path. It stopped in the clearing and stood looking at them from a distance of twenty paces, ears cocked, tail down and head lowered. Line stood still, merely glancing towards the car. Erik Fjeld wheeled, looked in the same direction, and took a couple of tentative backward steps.

The dog did not take its eyes off them. Neither uttered a word and almost a minute passed before they heard a shrill whistle. The dog wagged its tail and approached them with a friendly expression. A man emerged from the woods behind it, wearing a black jacket, baggy trousers and a broad-brimmed hat. Erik Fjeld took a photo of him.

'Well, there you are,' the man said, reaching out as he approached. The dog sniffed Line first, licking her hand, before moving on to greet the photographer. Torgeir Roxrud tied it at the corner of the house. 'Come on in,' he said.

In the living room he invited them to sit on the settee before removing his rain jacket and draping it over an armchair. The room looked more like a workshop than a sitting room: not much space, cardboard boxes stacked along the walls, most of the furniture used to store tools and car parts. 'Can I offer you anything?' he asked. 'Coffee?'

Both shook their heads. 'I don't know how well you were

acquainted with Jonas Ravneberg,' Line said. 'But I'd like to offer my condolences.'

'Thanks,' Torgeir Roxrud replied, sitting down. 'But as I said on the phone, I don't really think there was anyone who knew him well.'

'How did you meet him?'

He sat up straight, his chest gurgling as he breathed. 'Through Max.' He cast a glance through the window at the dog.

'Beautiful dog,' Erik Fjeld remarked. 'Is it a sheepdog?'

'Yes, a Dutch Sheepdog. Every Friday I take him with me to Kongsten for a walk. We were fed up with the forests and liked to combine that with a shopping trip. We met each other when Max was a puppy; so enthusiastic and wanting to say hello to everyone. Tiedemann is a year older, but patient and playful.' He made a fist and coughed into it. 'So it was the dogs that introduced each other first, and then we started chatting.'

'What was Jonas Ravneberg like?'

'He was pleasant. Unassuming. No nonsense. He was lonely, of course. No friends or family. Just Tiedemann. What's become of the dog, by the way?'

'He's been taken to Falck's. They'll probably find a home for him. What did he talk about?'

'He had difficulty holding a conversation,' Roxrud said, lifting a spanner from the table beside him. 'He never asked about anything. I had to drag words out of him. But he could have a temper. Didn't want anyone to bother him. I think it was nerves. He was anxious in case anyone bothered him.'

He got to his feet and crossed to the window to look out at the dog. Erik Fjeld raised his camera and took another photo.

'He told me once about his father. It was between Christmas and New Year two years ago. I asked him to come here on Christmas Eve, but he didn't want to, though he came on Boxing Day and stayed over. We had a meal and went for a walk with the dogs up to the summit of Vetatoppen. We had a drink or two as the evening drew on, and he told me that his father had fallen down the cellar stairs, sustained a head injury and died. That was when he was little. And then he talked about his cars.'

'Cars?'

'He collected model cars. Classic American cars. He was keen on them. And Elvis. He liked Elvis.'

'The King,' Erik Fjeld commented.

Torgeir Roxrud headed for a cupboard at the other end of the room. 'I'm a collector myself,' he said, pulling out a folder. 'Old banknotes and stamps. Would you like to see my collection?'

Line returned his smile and accepted his offer. That would make a good photograph. Torgeir Roxrud and their common interest in collecting. 'Was he a member of the Collectors' Club?' she asked him to confirm once the stamp folder was in front of her.

'Yes, I was the one who persuaded him to go,' Roxrud answered, leafing through the album. 'I thought it would benefit him. Get him out to mix with people. Make new friends.'

He had found what he was looking for and pointed his finger at a stamp with a value of thirty øre, printed in red. Erik Fjeld adjusted his lens and snapped a couple of photographs.

'This is the jewel,' Roxrud explained, but had to break off when he was overcome by a fit of coughing. His face turned red and his bulky body was gripped with violent shaking. 'An upside-down thirty øre's,' he continued, once he regained his breath. 'In 1906, there was a shortage of stamps, and a quantity of the old seven shilling sort was overstamped with *30 øre*. Altogether 450,000 stamps were changed, and there are still a few thousand in circulation. They are worth twenty to thirty kroner each, but one of the sheets was placed upside down as it was overprinted, and those examples are worth a thousand times more.'

Line peered at a scrap of paper where the number thirty was placed upside down.

'Do you mean that this is worth thirty thousand kroner?' Erik Fjeld asked, taking a photo of the album.

Torgeir Roxrud nodded.

'How much might a model car be worth?' Line asked.

Torgeir Roxrud shrugged as he closed the album and carried it back to its rightful place. 'They're sold at the fairs for several hundreds. You can't compare that with stamps, which are a form of currency to start with, and you can build up and catalogue your collection in quite a different way from all other collectors' items.'

'Did Jonas Ravneberg have any rare examples?'

Torgeir Roxrud resumed his seat. 'Well, he had Elvis' cars, I suppose.'

'Elvis' cars?'

'Cadillacs. Elvis had at least a hundred of them, and Jonas had models of most of them.'

'Were they worth much?'

'I think he could have sold each of them for at least a thousand kroner, if he had come into contact with the right buyer. He had more than a hundred of them, you see, so it would amount to a lot of money.'

'Did he keep in touch with any of the other members of the Collectors' Club?'

'Only at meetings.'

Line riffled through her notes. 'What about Astrid Sollibakke or Mona Husby?'

'Astrid is on the nomination committee. She phoned me last week and asked me to take Mona's place on the committee. I said no thanks, but suggested that she might ask Jonas. I can't think that Jonas has had any contact with them other than that, but I know he had a girlfriend once.'

'Who was that?'

'I can't remember the name. They lived together, long ago. Before he moved here to Fredrikstad.'

Line dropped the subject and continued with her line of questioning. 'Did he ever mention that he needed a lawyer?'

'A lawyer?' No. The police asked me exactly the same question. I've no idea what that could be about.'

'Do you know why he was in contact with the local paper, the *Fredrikstad Blad*?'

Torgeir Roxrud leaned back in his chair. 'You obviously know almost more about Jonas than I do. How did you find out all this?'

Line shot him a disarming smile. 'We have our methods,' she replied, aware herself how stupid it sounded.

'He didn't get the paper delivered on a couple of days,' he explained. 'It was probably a new delivery boy, but it got sorted out after he phoned and spoke to them.'

Nodding, Line glanced through her notes. She had underlined *girlfriend* and *before Fredrikstad*. 'Where did he live previously?'

'On the other side of the fjord. In Vestfold. Down in Larvik.'

'Isn't that where you come from, Line?' the photographer asked.

Line nodded. The connection sparked her curiosity. 'Do you know why he moved here to Fredrikstad?'

Torgeir Roxrud coughed. 'I don't think he really moved *to* Fredrikstad,' he answered. 'It wasn't so important where he settled. I think it was more a case of moving away *from* something.'

30

According to the report Erik Fjeld had photographed on the sly during the press conference, Christianne Grepstad was the police's only witness in addition to the man who had stumbled on Jonas Ravneberg. She lived in a renovated timber house five hundred metres from the discovery site. She had seen the murder victim and his dog a short time before he was killed.

Line drove past her home and, noticing light in the windows, turned, drove back and parked beside the hedge.

'Do you want me to come with you?' Erik Fjeld asked, reaching for his camera. 'If not, I can sit here and edit the photos.'

'Wait here, then,' Line said. 'I'm not sure she'll want to talk to us.'

She jumped from the car and walked through the gate, the paved courtyard slick from all the rain. A Volvo was parked outside the double garage, and a bicycle lay upturned beside the gable wall, wheels in the air.

Line rang the doorbell. Part of the house interior was visible through a window beside the door. It appeared spacious, airy and inviting. A woman approached the entrance, her head tilted slightly for an advance look at the uninvited guest, a toddler trailing in her wake.

'Hello,' Line said, showing her press card. 'My name is Line Wisting and I work for *VG*. I wondered if I could talk to you about the man who was murdered yesterday.' The child clung to his mother's legs. 'I tried to phone you earlier today. I just wanted to hear what you knew about it.'

The woman nodded as though acknowledging Line's call. 'I don't know much about it,' she said.

'Do you have some time?' I can come back later if it's not convenient.'

'It's fine.' The woman stood aside to let her enter. 'My husband's on a business trip.'

Line was shown into a large kitchen with an open gas fireplace where a realistic-looking mound of imitation coal was burning cheerily. A tray of newly baked buns sat on the kitchen worktop. The enticing aroma hung in the air.

'We've just been baking,' Christianne Grepstad explained, lifting the child onto a chair. 'Would you like a taste?'

'Yes please,' Line said with a smile.

Christianne Grepstad transferred the buns to a serving plate and laid the table with some plates. She was probably around Line's age, twenty-eight, maybe slightly younger, but already settled with a husband, child and house.

Increasingly often, she met women of her own age who had advanced further in life than she had done. It did not bother her significantly. She had always thought she would like a family and children sometime in the future. For the present, she enjoyed being free, able to spend her time as she pleased, to work overtime without feeling guilt. Sometimes she felt bad that she had not met a new man since Tommy Kvanter, but the last thing she wanted was to be stuck with a man who was, quite clearly, no good for her. An older female colleague had been in a relationship with a married arts journalist for almost ten years, and Line had promised herself that she would never end up in a relationship with no future.

'What do you know about the case?' she asked, shaking off her thoughts.

'I don't really know anything, but I think I saw him. Tea?'

'That would be lovely, but who did you see?'

Christianne Grepstad filled the kettle. 'The man who died,' she said, producing a carton of teabags and a sugar bowl. 'At least I think it was him, out walking his dog. He was wearing waterproofs, just like they said. I thought I should report it. The police asked everyone who had seen him to contact them.'

The child's chubby fingers grabbed at a plastic cup.

'Where did you see him?'

The youngster banged the cup on the table before throwing it on the floor and glancing at his mother with coal black eyes.

'Down in the Old Town,' she replied, retrieving the cup. 'I'd been at a café with a couple of friends and spotted him on my way home. He was standing outside the bookshop.'

Line, unfamiliar with the area, asked the woman for more information. She had studied the map on her computer and understood that the area was situated inside the star-shaped ramparts, directly west of the location where Jonas Ravneberg was found. 'Do you know what time it was?'

'I know I left the café at half past nine. That's only a block away.'

The tip-off had been phoned in to the newspaper at ten to ten. At a rough estimate, Jonas Ravneberg had been killed ten to fifteen minutes after Christianne Grepstad had seen him. 'Was he alone?'

'Yes,' the woman answered, pouring boiling water into the cups. 'It looked as if he was waiting for someone or something.'

Line chose green tea. 'What made you think that?'

'I don't know. He was just, sort of standing there. The police asked the same thing. I've thought about it since, but can't really explain it any other way. I just had a feeling he was about to do something illegal and was waiting for the coast to be clear.'

'Something illegal? What could that be?'

Christianne Grepstad helped herself to a bun. 'It was only a feeling I had, but I think he was hiding something.'

'In what way?'

'He was standing with his hand inside his rain jacket. Exactly as if he was holding something he didn't want to get wet.'

Line stirred her tea, picturing Jonas Ravneberg waiting in the rain.

'Did you meet anyone?' she asked, drinking her tea. 'When you walked on?'

The woman considered this before shaking her head.

'Not that I can think of, but I remember him clearly. I had a bad feeling about him. He seemed to follow me with his eyes. Small, dark eyes. It's not something I've invented now just because I know he's dead. I thought it then too. I remember I turned round and looked to see if he was following me, but he just stood there watching me.' The little boy's cup fell to the floor again. This time it was left lying. 'He'll be going to bed soon.'

'Did the police ask you anything else?' Line continued. It was always interesting to hear what angle the investigators put on their questions.

'They asked the same things as you, but I had to tell them what sort of clothes I was wearing, where I had walked, who I'd been with at the café and what other people I'd seen. To map it out, they told me.'

The rain had started again by the time she left, and she scurried across the street with her head bowed. Erik Fjeld glanced at her inquisitively as she sat behind the wheel. 'Anything new?'

'Not really,' Line replied, switching on the GPS. 'She had

seen Jonas Ravneberg and his dog outside a bookshop in the Old Town.'

'What was he doing there?'

'Waiting for something or someone.'

Erik Fjeld fell into silence while Line squinted at the tiny map on the display. Once she had her bearings, she drove onto the main road and past a graveyard until a signpost indicated the direction to the Old Town. She followed the instructions and drove through an avenue of old, leafless trees. Shortly afterwards, the asphalt road was replaced by cobblestones glistening in the rain below the streetlights. The uneven surface made the vehicle shudder.

Just inside the ramparts encircling the old fortress, a large open square divided the road in two. Directly ahead was a block of four old timber houses, the largest one containing a small hairdressers' salon and a *Libris* bookshop on the ground floor. Line drew up at the kerb. A small, stout woman holding a red umbrella emerged from one side.

'What are you planning to do?' Erik Fjeld asked.

'I'm not sure.' Line looked back along the road. The ramparts blocked her view, otherwise they could have seen the spot where Jonas Ravneberg had been murdered.

The lady with the brolly glanced inside the car as she passed. Behind her came a younger man, walking with one hand inside his jacket. As he approached he brought out a thick, grey envelope, crossed over to the bookshop entrance and inserted it in a red postbox on the wall.

Line stared at his retreating back. 'He posted something,' she said.

'I saw that,' Erik Fjeld agreed.

'I don't mean him. Jonas Ravneberg. He posted something just before he was killed.'

31

It had grown dark outside without Wisting noticing, a drizzly dusk that was not actually night, but dark nevertheless. Leaning back in his chair, he closed his eyes and pinched the bridge of his nose between his thumb and forefinger. His aim was to find out which police officer could have planted the DNA evidence and, without anything specific to work on, he had decided to read all the case documents afresh. He had to acknowledge he lacked focus.

His own thoughts continually strayed to Rudolf Haglund. Could there be something they had overlooked seventeen years ago? Something he had skated over and neglected to make everything fit? So far he had not found anything pointing towards Rudolf Haglund's innocence, but neither had he found anything that supported his guilt.

He switched on the wall lamp, and its light showed his face floating indistinctly on the windowpane. His eyes looked back at him with unfamiliar emptiness. He blinked and embarked on a new document, the report of the photo lineup conducted with Karsten Brekke, the witness on the tractor.

Nils Hammer had organised the lineup in accordance with the rules laid down by the Director General of Public Prosecution. The most important of these was that the witness, who was expected to point out the wanted man, was presented with a number of choices and was not to be influenced in any particular direction.

Karsten Brekke had repeated the description he had given

of the unknown man beside the white Opel, corresponding closely to Rudolf Haglund. After this, he was shown pictures of twelve men of similar age with the same face shape and hair colour. The photos were laid out on a wall chart, divided into four rows with three pictures in each row. An A4-sized copy of the wall chart was stapled to the report. Rudolf Haglund was number two in the second row, placing him more or less in the middle of the sheet. He was the first person Wisting's eyes alighted on. That could, of course, be because Wisting was familiar with his face, but could also be because the eyes have a tendency to be drawn towards the centre.

Karsten Brekke had pointed out Haglund and his choice of words was recorded in the report. *'That's him. Number five.'* When asked how sure he was, he had replied: *'As sure as it's possible to be.'*

After the identification there had been a break in the interview before Karsten Brekke had been called in again and shown the same pictures, this time in a different order. On this occasion, Rudolf Haglund was number eleven in the lineup. Karsten Brekke was equally sure.

The next document in the case was an *Arrest Warrant*, signed and stamped by Audun Vetti.

The photo lineup had been the basis of their case against Haglund, a crucial step and, strictly speaking, a more critical breakthrough than the DNA result. If Karsten Brekke had not recognised Rudolf Haglund, they would not have had the opportunity to collect a reference sample from him for comparison with the analysis result from the cigarette butts.

The photo used was acquired from the police's own criminal records, taken in connection with the indecent exposure complaints made against him two years before. His appearance was almost unchanged.

Wisting re-read the report. It was difficult for someone

who had not been in the same room to judge how far Karsten Brekke might have been influenced in any way. The position of the pictures was random, according to Nils Hammer, and there was no reason to believe that the central placing of the suspect was intentional. Nonetheless, it was a weakness that Nils Hammer had been alone during the process. The guidelines stated that a photo lineup ought to be arranged and conducted by a senior police officer accompanied by at least one assistant.

He laid aside the report, suddenly aware that he was hungry. It dawned on him that he had not eaten all day. He crossed to the kitchen worktop and poured a glass of water. It was eight o'clock and he decided to sit for another hour before going home.

The report of the photo lineup lay open on the settee. Wisting drank half the water before refilling the glass and bringing it back with him. He resumed his seat and held up the wall chart with the photos to the light. The eleven other men were an arbitrary selection who, judging by appearances, had been drawn from the photo records. They were pictured in profile as well as full face. Wisting did not know any of them.

He flicked through to where Hammer described how the lineup had been conducted. No reference was made of bringing to Karsten Brekke's attention that the wanted man was not necessarily among the twelve photographs. This point was intended to relieve the witness of pressure, and eliminate a possible source of mistaken identification. Hammer might have mentioned it without it being recorded, but it was striking that it had not been included when the report was otherwise so painfully exact with, for example, Karsten Brekke's statements in quotation marks.

He leafed back to the photos. The sheet was a third of the size of the original wall chart, and moreover it was a black and white copy, making the details difficult to distinguish. All the men had similar features, but it looked as though only Rudolf Haglund had a crooked nose.

Wisting took the sheet with him to the kitchen worktop to study more closely in the harsh light. The men were around the same age and had identically shaped faces, but the position of the eyes and the nose structure were inconsistent, with Rudolf Haglund quite distinctive thanks to the deep depression on his nasal bone. His nose was not flat, like a boxer's, but looked as if it had been smashed in at one time, which was how Karsten Brekke had described the unknown man at the initial interview.

Wisting riffled back through the papers and re-read the description. A Norwegian man, aged around thirty. About five foot nine, with dark hair and a conspicuous break in his nose. This was the description they had released that had triggered the list project. They had gathered ninety-three tip-offs about men fitting that description. Ninety-two of them had been filtered out, leaving them with Rudolf Haglund.

In advance of the photo lineup, Karsten Brekke had repeated his description of the man. Wisting read it again: about thirty years of age, dark hair, broad face, strong chin and dark, close-set eyes. The description of the nose was left out. This could have been an oversight, but Wisting had difficulty believing that. Such individual characteristics were valuable to investigators. It was this kind of detail that had contributed to Wisting's conviction that Haglund was the right man.

He could not shake off the suspicion that Nils Hammer might have withheld that detail to make it more difficult for anyone who read the report to notice that the witness' attention could have been drawn to one person in particular, rather than equally focused on all the pictures.

32

Two questions had been central in the Cecilia case: who had done it, and why?

When they knew, or thought they knew, the answer to *who*, the question *why* had been overshadowed. It had never been answered. It was easy to guess that the abduction had been sexually motivated, and the murder committed to cover up the original crime. However, Cecilia had not been sexually abused. She was naked when she was found, but that was the only aspect to suggest a sexual motive. No semen residue or other traces of the perpetrator had been discovered on her body.

Forensic science had made tremendous progress in seventeen years. At that time, the laboratories were almost completely dependent on recovering saliva, blood or semen in order to isolate DNA. Now, it was sufficient for the perpetrator to be in contact with an object or person.

The folder of illustrations showed the naked corpse on the autopsy table. The skin was paler at her bust and crotch as though she had been sunbathing in a bikini. Her waist and hips were slender, and her pubic hair was fair and trimmed. Her breasts were small, round and firm with dark nipples. A red graze ran from her waist down to her pelvic bone, thought by the pathologists to have been sustained when she rolled down the gravel verge where her body was found. Apart from that, her skin was smooth, with no birthmarks or scars. She had small hands and feet, fingernails varnished red, and a border had grown close to her cuticles. Her face was impassive and her complexion bluish white. Her eyes were half-closed, but there were tiny specks of blood on the whites, and pupils with grey, glistening splinters that drew him into the picture. A vacant gaze somewhere between fear and oblivion.

Her nakedness might have been meant to lead the investigators astray. The actual motive might have been something different, but it was perplexing to imagine what on earth that might have been – at least, with Rudolf Haglund as the perpetrator.

The judicial observations were included as document number fifty-eight in the red folder, giving a deeper insight into Haglund's personality than had the interviews. The purpose of a psychiatric examination is to determine diminished responsibility, or otherwise. Examination was dependent on the prisoner being willing to participate in discussions with two specialists. This made interesting reading, in which his family, upbringing, schooldays, working life, health and sex life were described from a different point of view from that of the strictly professional police officer.

Haglund had been born and brought up in Skien, and described his early childhood years as happy. An only child, his parents had been of mature years when he was born. His father worked in the postal service, while his mother had a part-time job in a shoe shop. When he was eight years old, his father contracted stomach cancer that spread to other organs in his body. He was treated with chemotherapy and lived with the cancer for five years. However, his illness changed him. He became irritable and angry, and Rudolf Haglund was on the receiving end of frequent blows. At the same time, his mother suffered from nervous problems. As far as the boy was concerned, his whole life was knocked out of kilter. Among other things, he became a bed-wetter, and was alienated from everyone and everything. He was bullied at school, but was tall and robust for his age and retaliated. He could also assert himself by violent means in other situations and was regularly suspended following violence against teachers. Violence directed at his mother was also mentioned.

He had not managed to cope in theoretical subjects and halfway through his eighth year of schooling was transferred to a special needs school. After junior high, he obtained a place at a technical college but felt out of place and dropped out. His aggressive impulses isolated him, and he was found to be unfit for military service.

His mother committed suicide on his twentieth birthday, leaving him without family ties. With the money he inherited, he severed his connection to his hometown and moved to Larvik, where he bought a house in the rural location of Dolven.

Through the employment office, he obtained a position at a furniture warehouse, where he coped well and, after a probationary period, was offered a permanent post, a post he still held at the time of his arrest.

Emotionally, he had difficulty distinguishing between feelings of unhappiness, disappointment and anger. Insignificant things, such as not being able to tie his shoelace, could rouse his temper. He felt solitary, but not that his existence was empty. He was content on his own and enjoyed going for long walks in the forests and fields, most especially going fishing.

A separate paragraph was devoted to his sex life. His sexual debut had taken place at the age of sixteen, with a girl of the same age, but they had not become a couple. After he moved to Larvik, he entered a relationship with a woman in the neighbourhood. She was thirteen years older and the liaison ended when she moved to western Norway. After this, he had only casual sex with partners found via personal ads in specialist magazines. He had frankly admitted to being sexually stimulated by sadism and domination of his sexual partner.

The conclusion of the experts had been that Haglund did not have any symptoms or behavioural traits indicative of a psychotic condition. The strength of his mental faculties had not been so simple to establish. His intelligence quotient lay well within the normal range, but he appeared to have deficiencies in personality development, especially in his ability to control his aggressive impulses. Despite his intellectual capacity being insufficiently developed, it was estimated that he was not permanently impaired. He was considered criminally liable and able to be prosecuted according to the law.

As far as the investigators were concerned, the legal psychiatric declaration was further confirmation that Rudolf Haglund was Cecilia's murderer: a man who committed violent crimes against women.

Wisting checked his mobile phone. The list of unanswered calls had lengthened, but there were none from either Line or Suzanne. It was nearly ten o'clock, later than he had anticipated. He left the papers and his own notes lying, but closed the curtains before pulling on his jacket and going out, locking the door behind him.

The cold air that hit him full force was filled with the raw salt tang of the sea. Inhaling deeply, he stood for a moment while his eyes adjusted to the darkness, before heading along the path to the parking area. The downpour had made the little patch of grass fronting the cottage quite muddy, and he walked in a sweeping curve to avoid the worst of the puddles.

When he started the engine, the radio station was in the midst of a news bulletin, reporting a politician charged with sexual abuse of underage boys. He was about to switch off when the newsreader announced that the police had reported seventeen-year-old Linnea Kaupang from Larvik missing. She had been gone since Friday, and they had not ruled out the possibility that she was the victim of a crime. After providing a short description, an appeal was made for anyone who had sighted her to contact the police.

Wisting switched off the radio and drove though the silent darkness, deep in thought. He should have been at the police station so that he could be entirely certain everything possible was being done to find the missing girl and whoever had probably violated her.

33

Alone in her hotel room, Line lay half undressed on her stomach on the wide bed with her laptop in front of her. The police had confirmed the identity of the murder victim, clearing the way for her to write about the homicide.

The story had four elements. She used the mysterious break-in to whet the reader's interest, following it up with the lawyer's appointment that was never kept. The third element was a pen portrait of the dead man, based on her meeting with Torgeir Roxrud and the final section was of the *'this is where the murder victim was last seen'* type. She was convinced she had more material than anyone else, but found it difficult to get the words down on paper. Her thoughts strayed to her father and his astonishing ability to accept his predicament and view it from the outside. He had seemed so calm and collected.

There were two ways to clear his name, she reasoned. One was finding who had planted the cigarette evidence. The other was finding something fresh in the wider Cecilia case. Both seemed hopeless, at least for one man working on his own.

She decided to visit him the following day, helping him at the same time as following the leads on Jonas Ravneberg, who had been in a relationship and lived in Larvik before moving to Fredrikstad. She wrote an email to one of the researchers at the newspaper, asking if they could locate something from the deeds registry or historic address data from the National Population Register.

Moving to a sitting position, she made an effort to focus on the story again. The news editor wanted a whole page spread, which meant 3,500 characters. She had no problem filling the space. On the contrary, she had to squeeze the maximum information into the minimum space, making it concise and succinct. She was usually good at that, but now everything was drifting in all directions.

The detective who had interviewed her about the assault outside Jonas Ravneberg's house had asked her to phone if she remembered anything else. She glanced at the model car. Elvis Presley's Cadillac. She had stored the number on her mobile. Now she took it out and called. 'I thought of something,' she said, after introducing herself. 'Something I found outside Jonas Ravneberg's house.'

'What was that?'

Line rose from the bed and crossed to the window. 'A little car. I thought at first that it was a toy belonging to one of the children in the neighbourhood. But it seems that it might be a valuable model car, the kind people collect. It's old and in good condition.'

'So?'

'Do you know if Ravneberg collected such things?'

The investigator hesitated. 'There are several of them in his living room,' he said.

'Have you discovered what the killer took?'

'Do you have the car in your possession?'

'Yes. Do you think that's what he was looking for?' Line drew the curtains and picked up the model car.

The man was again hesitant. 'No,' he replied.

'Do you know why he took it with him, then?'

The policeman declined to answer. 'I'll come and collect it. Where are you?'

She gave him the name of her hotel.

'I can be there in half an hour.'

'Okay, but there's something else.'

'Fire away.'

Line flipped the boot of the model car up and down. 'Have you checked the mail?' She made the question as challenging as possible.

'The mail?'

'We're writing in the paper tomorrow that Jonas Ravneberg was last seen in the square at the entrance to the Old Town. That's correct, isn't it?'

'Yes.'

'There's a postbox there. Do you think he might have posted something?'

Yet again there was silence at the other end of the line. 'That would be mere speculation. I'll come and collect that model car.'

Line stretched out on the bed once the conversation was over, feeling she had done well. She had presented her inadvertent removal of a possible piece of evidence and drawn his attention to the postbox without expressing it as a report. It was probably too late all the same. The mail was more than likely already uplifted.

Half an hour later she finished her story.

She put on her trousers again and straightened the bed cover, crossing her fingers that the policeman would turn up soon. She had caught little sleep in the past twenty-four hours, and had to make an effort to restore her strength.

Slumping in the chair, she flicked through the channels without finding anything of interest, got to her feet again and pulled the curtains aside. The unremitting rain formed beads of water on the glass, drawing a veil over the outside world. An ambulance, blue light flashing, passed on the street below as someone knocked. She picked up the model car en route to the door. When she opened she quickly took a step back. It was not the police officer, but Tommy.

She had not set eyes on him for almost three months. They had been together for more than two years, but last autumn had separated in a mutual understanding that it was for the best. However, it had been more difficult for her to move on than she had appreciated. After Tommy, she continually measured all others against him.

He was exactly her type: laidback, intellectual and interested in culture. He was fearless and radiated the sort of cool craziness that shouted out danger and gallantry, but his impulsive and inconsiderate side made her feel insecure.

Their chemistry was impossible to ignore. Line had never before experienced such a strong physical attraction, and it both mesmerised and appalled her. Now here he was with his hands in his pockets and his head tilted quizzically to one side.

'How are you doing?' he asked.

She did not invite him in, but embraced him out in the corridor, revelling in his body's closeness.

'What are you doing here?' she whispered.

'I had to know how you were.'

'How did you find me?'

'It said in the newspaper that you were in Fredrikstad. There aren't too many hotels here.'

She returned his smile, taking several paces back into the room. He followed her, closing the door behind them. 'How are you?' he repeated.

"My head's a bit chaotic, but I'm fine, really.'

Tommy took hold of both her wrists and stared at her, searchingly. 'You were attacked by the killer. Have you talked to anybody about it?'

'I'm fine,' she repeated. 'I've spoken to the police and the newspaper. They've offered me crisis intervention and all that stuff, but that's not my style.'

'I know,' he answered, without letting go. 'What about your father? Have you spoken to him?'

135

It struck her that the calm she felt since the attack must have been inherited from her father, the ability to create a distance from what had happened and not to allow the emotional response to gain the upper hand.

'It's good to see you,' he said, pulling her towards him.

She could feel the muscles in his chest and one hand found its way up to his neck, where his soft, dark hair curled over his shirt collar. She twisted it round her fingers.

Pushing her away, he smiled slowly, leaned down and kissed her on the forehead. 'What have you got there?' he asked.

She held up the model car. 'Piece of evidence.'

There was a knock at the door. One of the staff from the hotel restaurant was standing outside, holding a tray with fruit, cheese and biscuits, and a bottle of wine. She wheeled round to face Tommy.

'Put it down here,' he said.

As the waiter passed she suddenly realised that she was wide-awake. Tommy took the bottle of wine and handed over a hundred kroner tip.

They tucked into the food sitting on the bed where she told him about her experience and what she thought about the accusations against her father. 'I'm going home tomorrow,' she added.

'Would it be all right if I come with you?'

Someone rapped on the door again. 'I'm actually expecting a visitor.' He looked at her in surprise as she picked up the model car and took it with her to the door.

'Sorry I'm late.'

'Quite all right,' Line said, handing the policeman the car and glancing back into the room behind her. 'I wasn't thinking of sleeping for a while yet anyway.'

136

34

William Wisting moved from sleep into full wakefulness. He ran his hand through his tangled hair, but his first coherent thought was of Linnea Kaupang and whether the night had brought any news of the girl with the yellow bow in her hair. He could not shake off the thought that, had he been on duty, he could have made a positive contribution.

He turned towards Suzanne, studying her sleeping face and speculating whether she understood that he could not have done what he was accused of. She had entered his life three years earlier, filling an immense void. He and Ingrid had known each other since primary school and shared nearly forty good years. He was confident she would have stood by him, and hoped Suzanne would too.

He followed his usual morning routine: showered, dressed, fetched the newspaper and sat at the kitchen table with a cup of coffee. Today, however, he left the TV switched off. The front page of the local paper was devoted to his suspension. He read the story, conceding that it was factually correct, including the information that William Wisting had not been available for comment.

The newspaper covered the latest disappearance as well, including a portrait of Linnea Kaupang, describing the search conducted by volunteers in a wooded area close to where she lived. Several of her school friends had taken part, and they had tied yellow ribbons, like the one Linnea had worn in her hair in the photograph, to their jackets.

He folded the newspaper, but sat thinking about how it

was about to happen again. Yet another disappearance rocking the local community. Ellen Robekk, Cecilia Linde and now Linnea Kaupang. In those days, seventeen and eighteen years earlier, he had spent almost every waking hour searching for Ellen and Cecilia. He prepared to leave. Ingrid would have had an equally restless night and been downstairs by now.

He decided to let Suzanne sleep, scribbling a note to let her know that he had gone to the cottage. Leaving the house allowed him to retain part of his routine, although it felt strange heading out towards the coast instead of towards the town.

He tried to think what he might have done differently in the Cecilia case. The only thing that struck him was that he should have kept a closer eye on the critical tasks in the investigation. Instead, he had relied on his colleagues: in his experience, the best results did not come from micro-management.

The surrounding landscape vanished in a dusty grey, swirling mist. As he drove to the cluster of cottages, he spotted a roe deer at the edge of the track, its head raised and ears pricked. As though frozen in time, it followed him with big, brown eyes, before dashing between the trees.

As he parked, he regretted not bringing any food, but decided to purchase something in the course of the day. He planned to visit Finn Haber, who had been responsible for the forensic procedures at the time of Cecilia's disappearance.

He slipped and almost fell on the muddy path. With the air so raw and damp, he should probably light a fire at the cottage.

The key was sticky in the lock. As he forced it round he thought about buying something to grease it. There were other things to do: putty the old windows, maybe replace them, renew the fascia boards, and change a couple of broken roof tiles. He actually had time to do that now, and it was what Ingrid would have suggested. It would do him good to disengage completely.

The case documents piled on the coffee table attracted his immediate attention. He flung his jacket onto a chair in his haste to sit down. His notepad was still lying open at the last page. He drew it towards him, glancing through what he had written. For anyone other than himself, it appeared no more than an intricate mind map, key words and ideas that had struck him as he read. Names either underlined or circled, connected with arrows and lines, but nothing of real substance.

The red folder was slightly farther away than the others. He pushed it into line with his forefinger, noticing the yellow post-it note marking how far he had progressed. Something was amiss. It was intuition, pure and simple, more fundamental than the senses of smell and sight, and it made his flesh crawl. Someone had been here.

He could not say what made him so certain. It was simply an uncomfortable feeling that things were not as they had been when he left them. He crossed to the door and tried the lock. From the inside, the knob turned easily, but the key on the outside turned only with difficulty.

Outside, he let his eyes roam. Deserted rocky shoreline and empty grassy slopes. The sea was steel grey, and he could only just discern the farthest islands in the dank mist. A seagull took flight from one of the mooring posts on the jetty, screeches like mocking laughter.

On the floor of the timber verandah, he could see not only his own damp footprints, but also several lumps of clay that he had not brought with him. He moved to the top of the broad staircase. The ground below was waterlogged, with small puddles scattered across the patch of grass. From where he stood, he could see two prints in the mud with a different sole pattern from his own. He padded out to the side of the path and hunkered down. The prints showed a waffle pattern crossed by rough zigzagging lines. From the mid-point, the impression narrowed towards the heel. A heavy boot print, only a few hours old. He found his own prints from the previous evening. The weather had spoiled them more.

He followed the prints to see if any were more distinct than others, and found one at the side of a muddy puddle. He could make out a circle in front of the heel, with something inside it. Squinting, he wondered if it could be the shoe size, but decided it was probably the letter A. This was a print that could identify the brand of boot. The length could also indicate the size.

He used his mobile phone to take photos from various angles. They were not very good, but it was easy to see the pattern.

The deep blast of a ship's foghorn sounded from sea, followed by a feebler response from another vessel.

Back at the cottage, he lingered in the doorway. Now he could also distinguish a number of dried mud stains on the floor inside. He scanned the room to ascertain whether anything had been removed, pausing at the table where the case documents lay. They were numbered and arranged according to a particular system. Anything missing would be easily identified, but he felt reasonably certain that nothing had been stolen. He was probably the focus of interest. Someone had been here to find out what he was up to.

Not many people knew he was here, or what he was doing. He had told Suzanne and Line, and mentioned it in a text message to Nils Hammer. He trusted all three, but only one of them was a genuine candidate. Within the police station, rumours about where he was and what he was doing had very likely spread like ripples in water. Hammer was not the only one who knew about the cottage. The thought that pushed itself to the front, regardless, was that one of his own colleagues had been here.

Instinctively, he began to pursue other theories. Several people might like to take a look at his cards. He had made himself unavailable to the press and everyone else. The cottage was no secret; he had even allowed himself to be interviewed here by a free newspaper. If anyone wanted to find him, this was a logical place to call.

Crossing to the table, he leafed haphazardly through a folder. Whoever knew the truth about Cecilia Linde's killer would obviously also be interested in what he was doing.

That someone was peeking at his cards ignited a fresh spark in him, the hope of finding new answers in the old investigation material. He had to go through it with a fine tooth comb, scrutinise every single item and search for something out of the ordinary. Not now though.

Setting aside the papers, he stepped over to the kitchen drawers and rummaged for a ruler to measure the boot prints on the path, but could not find one. Instead he brought a plastic basin to cover the print, protecting it as best he could from the weather, with a stone on top to hold it in place. He stood mutely with his face towards the sea, struggling to keep paranoid thoughts at bay. He could not shake off the idea someone wished him harm.

Another long drawn out, mournful wail from a ship's foghorn broke the silence.

35

Finn Haber lived in an old pilot station in Nevlunghavn, one of the furthermost outposts overlooking the Skagerrak. The final stretch of track down to the weather-beaten location was narrow and winding, in some parts cresting over the shiny surfaces of rocky hills. The former crime scene technician had always been fond of the sea and fishing. When he retired, he had settled as close as possible.

Wisting parked where the track ended, in front of a detached garage, and stepped from his car. A squall had blown up, sweeping the mist out to sea. The dark surface of the water was broken by white horses, and invigorating sea spray crashed against the pebbles. Below the white-painted house lay a jetty and boathouse. A fishing boat rocked at its moorings. The boathouse door opened and suddenly Haber stood in the doorway, gazing at him, dressed in a chunky woollen sweater and a shiny brimmed cap. He looked older, his grey hair thinner, the features on his narrow face even sharper. They shook hands.

'Coffee?'

'Sounds good.'

Haber led the way to the house with lumbering, toiling steps. He pulled off his Wellington boots and set them aside on the cellar trapdoor beside the staircase before venturing inside. Wisting was about to do the same, but was stopped. 'Keep them on,' Haber insisted, hanging his peaked cap in the porch.

Finn Haber lived on his own, but the house possessed the

same order and tidiness that had been the hallmark of his work. The kitchen was kitted out with linoleum, Formica and pine cupboards. A small television sat on the worktop, the news on but the sound turned off. Linnea Kaupang's face filled the screen. People in her neighbourhood had tied yellow ribbons in front of their homes as a sign of sympathy. Scenes from the organised search followed, then the symbol for the sports news.

'You never get used to it,' Haber said, switching off.

'What's that?'

'Not being part of it. I've been retired for eight years, but long to be back every time I see pictures of a crime scene. Just to be sure nothing is overlooked.'

He filled the coffeepot with water as Wisting took a seat at the table in front of the window, directly opposite what was obviously Haber's place, since a coffee cup sat on the table beside the daily paper and an empty ashtray.

'We caught the right man that time,' Haber said, setting the coffeepot on the stove. 'Rudolf Haglund killed Cecilia Linde.'

Wisting would have liked to be equally certain. 'I think so too, but I would like us to be able to prove it beyond all reasonable doubt.'

He explained to Haber about the new analyses of the three cigarette butts from Gumserød crossroads. The old crime scene technician listened without interrupting. By the time Wisting finished the water was boiling. Haber took the pot from the hotplate, measuring out five spoonfuls of ground coffee from a tin and produced a cup for Wisting.

He stood with his back to the worktop while he waited for the coffee to brew.

'So the third butt was exchanged for one from a cigarette smoked during the interviews?'

'Petterøe's Blue number 3.'

143

'Have you drawn up a list?'

'What do you mean?'

'You know what I mean! A list of everyone who worked on the case.'

'I have a list,' Wisting admitted.

'Divided into smokers and non-smokers?'

'I've no idea who smoked or didn't smoke. Far less who smoked Petterøe's. What's more, that doesn't necessarily have anything to do with the case. Anyone at all could have picked up a cigarette butt after him.'

Haber carried the coffeepot over to the table. 'You have to start somewhere,' he said, pouring. 'Do you have it with you?'

'The names are in my head.'

Haber replaced the coffeepot on the stove and sat down. 'You can begin with me,' he said, drawing the curtain to one side and lifting a packet of tobacco that lay on the windowsill. Petterøe's Blue number 3.

'I think Kai Skodde smoked the same brand, and Magne Berger. Thore Akre and Ola Kiste as well. He scrounged off me now and again. Håkon Mørk smoked a pipe, Eivind Larsen had his cigarillos. Vidar Bronebakk used Eventyrblanding tobacco, Svein Teigen always smoked ready-rolled cigarettes with filter tips, and Frank Robekk preferred Tiedemann's Gold. He smoked Tiedemann's Gold and sucked Fisherman's Friend lozenges.'

Finn Haber opened his tobacco pack as he spoke and spread some tobacco on the fine paper. 'Good people, all of them,' he went on, rolling the cigarette.

'How were the cigarette butts stored?' Wisting asked.

Haber licked the paper. 'In the refrigerator.'

'Weren't the evidence bags sealed?'

'Not while they lay there. They weren't sealed until they were put in the mail, when the request for laboratory examination was written and sent to Forensics. In principle, anyone at all could have come in and swapped the cigarette ends.'

Wisting corrected him. 'Only one of us.'

Finn Haber fell silent. He placed his cigarette in the corner of his mouth, produced his lighter from the window ledge and lit up. His gaze slid out to the restless sea. A sound reached them, like a door banging in the wind.

Wisting lifted his cup to taste the coffee. 'I've had a break-in,' he said. 'At my cottage.'

'Is that where you're staying?'

Wisting took out his mobile phone. 'Someone's showing an interest in what I've found.' He showed him the photograph of the boot print.

Haber took a deep drag of his cigarette before pinching it between thumb and forefinger and setting it down on the edge of the ashtray. He took the phone and produced a pair of glasses from his breast pocket. 'One of us.'

'Maybe.'

Haber shook his head. 'No. This is one of us. I've seen this footprint before.'

Wisting leaned forward across the table. Haber was holding the phone so they could both inspect the image. 'Many times before.'

'Whereabouts?'

'Various crime scenes.' His finger tapped the screen. 'This is an Alfa M77 field boot. Issued by the Police Supply Service.'

Wisting slumped back. He owned a pair of those boots himself, inside his locker in the police station basement.

'Did you find any distinctive marks?'

Wisting understood what he meant. Distinctive wear marks or an accidental tear in the sole from a sharp stone to distinguish it from every other boot of the same brand and size. 'I didn't study the print so closely. I just covered it.'

Haber returned the phone. 'Do you have plaster and equipment for making a cast?'

'No.'

Haber stood up. 'I'll see what I've got.'

Crossing to the door, he gestured for Wisting to follow. They snaked along a narrow corridor and passed the living room doorway. The broad wooden floor planks creaked. Haber halted in front of the farthest door, where he opened up and entered a workroom with tall bookshelves crammed with books, ring binders and archive files. An old large-screen computer sat on a broad work table in front of the window.

Haber approached a cupboard behind the door. Two shelves inside were full of forensic equipment, jars of finger-print powder in different colours and tools for plastic casts. Moving a few cartons aside, he removed a white bag with blue writing.

'Do you know how to do it?'

'I haven't done it since Police College.'

The old forensics technician scrutinised him. 'I'll come with you,' he decided.

'You don't have to ...'

'We'll go now,' Haber closed the cupboard door. 'Before the print is spoiled by the rain.'

He stowed the equipment he had gathered in a carrier bag and crossed to the door. Wisting followed mutely. On the stairs outside, Haber handed him the bag as he pulled on his boots. 'I can take the blame,' he said, locking the door.

Wisting did not understand what he meant.

'It was my fault,' Haber said, taking back the bag of equip-ment. 'I shouldn't have left the evidence lying unsealed. It should have been sent in immediately. I can take the blame. Say I was the one who swapped the third cigarette end.'

Wisting opened his mouth to say something, but merely stood transfixed, staring at the old man.

146

'I've nothing to lose by it. No family to consider. It will bring the whole case into the open. You still have a number of working years left. You can do a great deal of good. You can find this other girl. Linnea Kaupang.'

'That's not how it works,' Wisting said. 'Not for me, at least. Two wrongs don't make a right.'

Haber tugged his jacket more snugly round his neck before hunching his shoulders and heading for the car.

Wisting was left gazing at his retreating back, unsure whether the retired policeman had meant what he said, or if the offer he had made was said to test him, a tactical move. Letting Haber take the responsibility would be just as wrong as switching the DNA evidence at that time, a fraud, a deception.

The old forensics technician turned round and looked at him. Wisting took a first step to follow, unsure whether he really knew the man ahead of him.

36

Line was overcome by a strange but increasingly familiar feeling of contentment tinged with regret. Regret because every hour and night she spent with Tommy made it more difficult to move on with her life. Contentment because she craved and longed for intimacy. They were among the last guests at breakfast.

Tommy helped himself from the breakfast table for a second time. Line picked up a copy of *VG*. The main spread described a new low carbohydrate diet, but at the top of the front page was a headline about the Cecilia case: *The Witness who was never Heard.*

She leafed further through the paper. Her own story was just as she had envisaged. They had used the photo of the dog again, as a kind of reminder. Then there was a picture of the row of houses where Jonas Ravneberg had lived, with police crime scene tape stretched round the white picket fence. Both images complemented the headline about a mysterious break-in where nothing seemed to have been stolen. The article was shorter than she had reckoned, but that was fine. She had placed the most significant information first.

Tommy resumed his seat at the table as Line was confronted by a photo of her father. The newspaper had obviously not let him off the hook.

Another picture was of the reconstruction at the crossroads beside Gumserød farm, with a white car in the centre of the photograph. A man was leaning against the boot while several investigators huddled in discussion. Line recognised the skinny crime scene technician and several other police officers, now retired. The main photo was of the witness whose testimony had not been heard: Aksel Presthus, a tall man in his fifties with dark brown, curly hair. He wore an Icelandic sweater and a black cotton scarf round his neck.

Like Rudolf Haglund, Aksel Presthus liked to go fishing. Every weekend, he tried fishing waters, recording his catches in a special diary, which he had retained and showed to the *VG* photographer. On Saturday 15th July, he had written *Damtjenn, 20.45 hours: Trout 132 grams. 21.15 hours: Trout 94 grams. 21.35 hours: Trout 168 grams.*

Damtjenn was the fishing lake where Rudolf Haglund claimed to be on the weekend Cecilia was abducted. The witness recalled seeing people on the other side of the lake. He had arrived at the lake relatively late in the evening, and it had taken almost an hour for him to catch his first fish. He had left his car parked behind a rather old white Opel Rekord, and when he had returned the next day, the other vehicle was gone.

Aksel Presthus had followed the Cecilia story in the newspapers, and when he read about Rudolf Haglund's alibi, realised he ought to talk to the police. When he phoned the central switchboard he had been transferred to describe what he had seen. The person in charge of the enquiry thanked him for the information and promised to call back if his observations were of interest to the case. He heard nothing more.

Haglund's defence lawyer said he had sifted through all the investigation material without finding any mention of Aksel Presthus. The police, therefore, had been selective in their use of information.

Chief Inspector William Wisting had not been available for comment, but Deputy Chief Constable Audun Vetti said that the case had been referred to the Bureau for the

Investigation of Police Affairs, and that the investigation leader had been suspended.

She put down the newspaper.

'What are your plans?' Tommy asked.

'I'm going to follow up some information in the murder case.'

'What sort of information?'

'About Jonas Ravneberg. He lived in Larvik before he moved here to Fredrikstad.'

Tommy speared the last piece of bacon with his fork. 'Are you going home?'

Line glanced down at the newspaper photo of her father. 'Yes, I'm going home,' she said.

37

When they turned off the main road, Haber took out his pack of tobacco and rolled a cigarette. Another larger and heavier vehicle had left deep wheel ruts on the muddy track, which was shared by approximately fifteen cottages. Farther along, it divided in two, but the wheel ruts led to the right, the track leading to Wisting's cottage.

The car tossed from side to side as it lurched forward, tyres spinning up the last incline before the track sloped down to the parking area, where an unfamiliar car was parked, an expensive Mercedes with splashes of mud along the side panels. The driver was standing on the verandah outside the cottage.

'Other visitors?' Haber speculated.

'Uninvited,' Wisting said. He parked the car.

The man at the cottage stood facing them, wearing an ankle-length coat and with a document folder in his hands. He was too distant to be recognised.

Haber placed the cigarette he had rolled in his mouth and lit up. 'I'll follow you,' he said.

Wisting trudged along the path, recognising the waiting man before he had reached halfway. Sigurd Henden, the lawyer. Rudolf Haglund's new defence counsel gave him a nod, but did not offer his hand.

Wisting nodded in return. 'We probably shouldn't talk to each other,' he said.

'Probably not.' The light drizzle had coated the lawyer's dark grey hair with a film of moisture. 'I'm sorry about the consequences all this has had for you personally,' he said.

Wisting turned to stand at the lawyer's side, with his face towards the sea. A cargo ship was heading west. 'How did you find your way here?' he asked, glancing at the plastic basin on the path.

'Your partner told me.'

Wisting looked at him in surprise. 'Suzanne?'

'Apologies. I tried to phone you, but when you didn't answer, I tried a roundabout route. She said you were here.'

'When did you speak to her?'

'Yesterday evening. I wouldn't have called her if it wasn't important.'

The nearest trees swayed, raindrops sprinkling from the branches in a sudden gust of wind. Brown leaves were tossed along the ground at the front of the cottage. Suzanne had not mentioned it.

Ingrid would never have given out that information. Though not exactly risky it was unnecessary all the same. Sigurd Henden was a professional participant in current events, but who else might Suzanne have spoken to? Ingrid would have limited herself to taking a message and passing it on. He ran his hand across his rain-soaked face. Haber had left the car and walked over to the birch thicket, where it seemed he was breaking off a few twigs. 'What's so important?' he asked.

Sigurd Henden cleared his throat noisily. 'He doesn't believe it was you.'

Wisting turned round to face him. 'What do you mean?'

'Rudolf Haglund. He doesn't believe you were the one who planted the DNA evidence.'

Wisting fixed his eyes on a seagull flapping its wings to catch the air currents. What Rudolf Haglund believed was of no significance. The defence lawyer had not come all the way out here to tell him that. There must be something more. 'What do you both want?' he asked.

152

'Justice.'

'That makes three of us, but for your information I still believe he did it. That your client abducted and murdered Cecilia Linde.'

The lawyer ignored that. 'He knows who it was,' he said.

The seagull broke off its gliding motion, launching itself into a breakneck dive towards the surface of the sea. Wisting opened his mouth, closed it and then opened it again. 'Knows who did what?'

'Who planted the DNA evidence.'

'Who was it then?'

'I don't know. He didn't want to tell me.'

'How can he know?'

The defence lawyer shook his head. 'I don't know.'

Stepping forward, Wisting raised his hand to pull his jacket more snugly round his neck. 'So what do you want right now?' he repeated.

'He wants to meet you. He wants to give you what you need to clear your name.'

38

Settling behind the steering wheel, the lawyer switched on the ignition before lowering the electric side window to offer a newspaper. 'Take this.'

Wisting approached the vehicle and took the paper.

'Read that,' the lawyer continued, pointing his finger at a headline on the front page: *The Witness who was never Heard.* 'I don't think it was you. Not then either.'

Wisting watched the car disappear over the brow of the hill. It felt as if he had been left behind, and wondered at what he had agreed to. When Rudolf Haglund had been led from the courtroom seventeen years earlier, he had hoped never to clap eyes on him again. Now he had agreed to a meeting tomorrow, twelve o'clock, at Henden's office in Oslo.

Haber approached him, blowing a cloud of cigarette smoke after the enormous Mercedes. 'What did he want?' he asked.

'I don't really know.'

Haber regarded him through narrowed eyes, before pressing his cigarette between thumb and forefinger and lobbing it away. 'Shall we make a start?'

Wisting opened the car boot. Haber lifted out the equipment and walked off in the direction of the plastic basin. 'I need some water and a container to mix the plaster in.'

Wisting fetched a bucket and a large jug of water. When he returned, Haber was shaking an aerosol can of hair lacquer.

'Lift off the plastic basin,' Haber said. 'Hold it above the print so the rain doesn't touch it.'

Haber produced a leather strap he drew around the footprint like a kind of casting frame, crouched down and sprayed the impression with lacquer. He angled the aerosol from a distance, not to damage minute details in the print. He did this twice. When the print was fully prepared, he mixed the plaster.

'I assume you're not planning to report the burglary,' he said.

Wisting shook his head.

Haber poured the thin, white liquid carefully into the mould, placing fresh birch twigs in a criss-cross pattern, for reinforcement, before pouring in the rest. ' 'Now, it has to be left for an hour. Coffee?'

Wisting invited Haber inside. He found a half-empty glass jar of instant coffee and a packet of biscuits in the kitchen cupboard, took out both and put a kettle of water on to boil.

Finn Haber unfolded the newspaper on the kitchen table. 'There are pictures of us both.'

Wisting leaned over and saw the inset photo of himself. Haber was in an archive photo at Gumserød crossroads, during the reconstruction, gesticulating among a group of detectives. Nearly all of them were present, except Wisting. Kai Skodde, Magne Berger, Thore Akre, Ola Kiste, Vidar Bronebakk and Svein Teigen. Frank Robekk was in white T-shirt and jeans like the perpetrator, but with his own thick glasses. He was leaning against the boot of the white Opel, rolling a cigarette.

'This doesn't give him an alibi,' Finn Haber asserted, placing his finger on the picture of the witness whose statement had not been recorded. 'He saw the white Opel around eight o'clock in the evening when Cecilia had been missing for almost six hours.'

A pair of icy blue eyes stared out of a rough-hewn, weather-beaten face. His hair was curly and dishevelled.

'What kind of person abducts a young girl, locks her up and goes off fishing?'

"A person such as Rudolf Haglund,' Haber said.

Wisting removed the kettle from the hob. 'That's not the point, though,' he said. 'He was never interviewed. His tip-off was never followed up.'

Haber read on in silence.

'He doesn't say he spoke to you,' Haber continued, taking the cup Wisting handed to him. 'He's quoted as saying he asked to speak to the person in charge of the case.'

'I was in charge.'

'Did you speak to him, then?'

Wisting shook his head.

'I would have remembered that.'

'Not only remembered, you would have brought him into the interview room. All tip-offs were directed to Frank Robekk's office, the only use we could put him to.'

Wisting nodded. Frank Robekk had dropped out almost entirely, but had been taking care of tip-offs received by phone. All enquiries directed to the central switchboard were transferred to his office. Even if callers had asked to speak to the person in charge, they would have been connected in the first instance to the tip-off reception centre that also filtered requests aimed at the investigation leader.

'He didn't even manage that,' Haber groaned. 'There was always something odd about Robekk.'

'He was a competent police officer.'

'Until he went crazy, but there was always something odd about him.'

Wisting had known Frank Robekk as a strong-willed and stubborn investigator, a determined tactician with a strategy for everything he did. Right up until everything unravelled.

156

However, there may have been something else about him, on a different plane from the professional interests he and Wisting shared.

'I remember wondering if he was homosexual,' Haber said. 'He never had a girlfriend and never took part in any social events. Never a beer on a Friday or a trip into town.'

Wisting looked at Frank's picture with fresh eyes. He ran his gaze over the other policemen before returning to Robekk. He would go and speak to him.

39

The plaster cast was perfect, and Finn Haber smiled for the first time that day. He brushed the white print clean, revealing an identical copy of the bootprint on the path. 'It looks little used,' he said. 'No signs of wear. A clean, intact sole. It might be difficult to link it to a particular boot.'

Wisting still did not know how to use the cast, but hoped to connect someone to the break-in.

'The earth here is saline,' Haber said, turning to face the sea. 'If you find the man who's been here, you should take samples from his boots. A comparative analysis would be supporting evidence.'

Wrapping the plaster cast in a rag, Wisting placed it in the boot. Haber brought the spray can of hair lacquer and the bag containing the rest of the plaster, and they both sat in the car. 'Is he on your list?' Haber asked when they were halfway back to the pilot station.

'Who?'

'Frank Robekk.'

'He's on the list of people I want to talk to, yes.'

No more was said until Wisting stopped his car in front of the garage at the end of the track. 'Thanks for your help,' he said.

Haber opened the car door, but remained seated. 'I've something for you.'

'What's that?'

'Something that might be of interest. You should really come in.'

Wisting followed him down to the main building, where Haber set his boots on the cellar trapdoor as before. Wisting kept his on. They entered the workroom where Haber had stored the plaster.

'Over there,' Haber said, pointing to a tall cupboard at the far end of the room.

Wisting advanced a few steps. Behind him, Haber replaced the equipment he had used for the plaster cast. 'I saw you had copies of all the other material in the Cecilia case out at your cottage.'

He opened the cupboard. The contents looked no different from what sat on the shelves all around. Ring binders, books and journal folders, a number of shallow, but broad, cardboard boxes located on the two top shelves. Haber lifted one down and carried it across to the desk. 'I don't have any use for it,' he said.

'What is it?'

'Surplus photographs from the Cecilia case.'

He opened the box and Wisting peered inside. Several hundred photos had been placed edge-to-edge, in three rows, separated by dividers marked with date and location.

'They should have been shredded when I left,' Haber said 'but I couldn't bring myself to do it. It's as if my whole life is in these boxes. Everything I've been involved in is documented. I even considered writing a book and using the photos as illustrations, but nothing came of it.'

Wisting let his fingers run across the rows of pictures, drawing out a random selection from the section marked *Clinical Examination 30/7*, pictures of Rudolf Haglund in an examination room at the hospital to record wounds possibly inflicted by Cecilia Linde. Scratches, bites or suchlike. The examination had been fruitless. Perhaps that was why Wisting had not seen the pictures before, but only read the doctor's report.

Rudolf Haglund stood with his upper torso bare. He was pale, but appeared muscular and sinewy. His face had the same blank expression Wisting recalled. The other photos were close-ups of hands, arms and other body parts.

'What's this?' he asked, pointing at a photo of an old scar on Haglund's inner thigh.

'An operation scar. He had three from having a number of moles removed. They were cancerous.'

This was news to Wisting. He could not remember hearing that Rudolf Haglund had suffered from cancer, but the scar seemed old, and health status information was not something normally included in the investigation of a crime.

In what were probably test photographs to measure the light, the two investigators who accompanied Rudolf Haglund to the examination appeared in the picture: Nils Hammer and Frank Robekk. The flash was reflected on one of Robekk's glasses, and Wisting thought he could see in his eyes the emptiness that eventually stopped him. Nils Hammer was different, almost triumphant, his eyes shone like a well-trained hunting dog delivering its prey.

'Take them with you, if you think you can use them,' said Haber.

40

Finn Haber accompanied Wisting to his car. Though the weather had cleared, the temperature had dropped.

Behind the wheel, Wisting's thoughts turned to Suzanne. He felt he had unintentionally embarrassed her, and that it was time to talk, to ask her frankly what she felt for him. At the same time, however, he realised this was not the moment. Instead he drove towards Brekke, turning off for Ruglandstrand and the Linde family's summer house. A gate closed off the last stretch leading to the property. Wisting parked and walked the rest.

He had been here every day in the weeks following Cecilia's disappearance, if only to say there was no news. It seemed to have grown even quieter and more desolate, rain-sodden and dull. The estate held several buildings. The main house was a white two-storey sea captain's house with green window shutters, a hipped roof, protruding dormers, and faded red roof tiles. Roses and wild ivy climbed along the walls.

A flock of crows took flight from one of the nearby trees, cackling as they flew towards him. The stone path was overgrown with weeds, and what had once been a well kept garden was now autumnal brown grass. A circular patio table lay upside down, surrounded by high stinging nettles. In the middle of the courtyard, a flagpole stood with the tattered remains of a blue pennant flapping at the top, the cord whipping against the pole in the wind. A faded letter C from the company name *Canes* was barely legible on the blue background.

The once magnificent summer estate was not only empty, but also completely abandoned. The Linde family could not have been here since that summer seventeen years ago.

He placed his hands on the glass of a grubby window. The window ledge was covered in cobwebs and dead flies lay spread-eagled, wings down and legs in the air. The faded curtains were closed, but through a gap he saw the past: massive pine furniture with close-weave covers in traditional colours and patterns, wainscoting and mahogany-coloured walls.

Cecilia's room was located on the east gable wall. He could see the traces left by the burglary on her windowsill. How really strange that the place had been left untouched, even by thieves.

Here, too, a chink in the curtains allowed him a glimpse inside: a wide bed with a pink blanket at the footboard, a large cassette player on a chest of drawers, and on the shelves above, her music cassettes arrayed with ornaments, little plush teddy bears and other items.

Wisting advanced onto the south-facing terrace and stared out across the ocean, listening to the pounding waves in the cove below.

On the beach a man was walking a black Labrador, the dog scampering freely at his side. When he caught sight of Wisting he called the dog and attached its lead. Wisting thought there was something familiar about him, but he had reached halfway before he knew who it was. Danny Flom, the photographer who had been Cecilia Linde's boyfriend. Still retaining some of his bohemian style, he was dressed in jeans full of holes, a black polo-neck sweater and a well-worn windproof jacket. His clear brown eyes were overshadowed by the stiff brim of an old-fashioned cloth cap.

'It's been ages since I've seen anyone here,' he said, holding out his hand to Wisting.

'It's ages since I've been here,' Wisting replied. 'Seventeen, to be exact.'

'Do you recognise me? It was another detective I had most contact with. Hammer. Is he with you these days?'

Wisting confirmed his recollection and that Nils Hammer still worked at the police station. The black dog sniffed round his ankles. He crouched down to scratch behind its ears.

'I'm here a lot,' Danny Flom said. 'Not exactly here at the Linde place, but I have a cottage on the other side of the headland.' He pointed in the direction he had come. 'We bought it four years ago. Despite everything that happened I always longed to come back. My life took quite a different direction from what I had expected that summer, of course, but I moved on. Onwards and upwards.'

'*Flomlys*,' Wisting said.

Danny Flom looked surprised.

'I read about you in a newspaper a few years ago,' Wisting said. 'You'd won an award.'

'*Flomlys* was an idea Cecilia and I had. She was brilliant in front of a camera, but even better behind it. I managed to get it up and running all the same. It just took a bit longer, and with another guy as my partner.'

He unclipped the dog's lead and it shuffled off in the direction of the huge glass doors of the main house. Virginia creeper had spread across the walls and its fronds had spread over the cracked glass.

'I read about you in the newspaper as well,' Danny Flom said. Wisting did not reply. He walked over to the railings, spattered with dried bird droppings. 'I'm not bothered how you managed to catch him. I'm just happy you did. I told Hammer that at the time. Just get him caught. What pains me is that he's out again. He took Cecilia from us forever, but now he's out and has the nerve to claim he's innocent.'

163

Danny Flom had been the special project assigned to Nils Hammer. His financial difficulties and strained relationship with Cecilia's father had meant that they had considered the theory that the abduction had been arranged by the lovers.

'Do you have any contact with her family?' Wisting asked.

'Not now. Her mother sent me Christmas cards for a few years, and I phoned her a couple of times, but I had to move on with my life, you see. I got married four years later, if you didn't know. Then I got divorced and remarried. I put the Cecilia business behind me.' He called to the dog, though it did not respond. 'Now it's happened again.'

'What do you mean?'

'The girl who's missing. Linnea Kaupang. Haven't you considered that someone may have taken her?'

Wisting had indeed considered that. It overshadowed everything else.

41

On the way back to the cottage Wisting stopped at the *Meny* supermarket in Søndersrød, but didn't get out of the car. Too many familiar faces, and as he preferred to avoid the questions, comments and looks, he had driven on.

He put Haber's box on the coffee table and picked up the newspaper still lying open at the Cecilia story.

Haber was right. The amateur fisherman who gave a statement to *VG* was not an alibi witness. He might have seen Haglund at the lake, but Haglund could have managed to fit in a fishing trip while Cecilia was in the cellar. He checked himself. This was exactly the kind of thinking that led to Haglund's prosecution when they had found means of explaining away all objections.

He leafed through to the story Line was covering in Fredrikstad and a large picture of Jonas Ravneberg's house. His name had been released. A smaller photo showed the crime scene with the contours of his body visible underneath a blanket. The most dramatic aspect of the image was his dog sitting with big dark eyes at the foot of the stretcher.

The break-in at his home was described as 'mysterious'. The break-in at the Linde family's country estate had been too. Mysterious. Again, nothing had been stolen.

He read the remainder of the story before folding away the newspaper. Line wrote well, he thought, uncomfortable that she was close to something so dangerous.

From Haber's box he took out the picture of Rudolf Haglund stripped to the waist at the hospital. *Unsullied* was the first word that had come to him in Haber's workroom. Again the word seemed appropriate. He could not imagine how to interpret it but knew of psychological tests with ink stains where patients were invited to say the first word that entered their head.

On the wall at the other side of the room there was an old framed maritime map of the Oslo fjord. He unhooked it and pushed Rudolf Haglund's picture onto the nail, piercing his taut ribcage, and taped Cecilia's picture beside it.

Seductive was the first word that came to mind. Several other pictures followed: alluring, teasing, was probably the desired effect. Danny Flom had said she was brilliant in front of the camera. This image had been used in an advertising campaign for that sweater. Her breasts lifted the letters of the word, *Canes.*

Canes was the fashion collection and each garment was given a supplementary name. The sweater in the picture was called *Venatici. Canes Venatici.*

Wisting said the words aloud, *Canes Venatici* the constellation known as the Hunting Dogs. Johannes Linde had pointed it out to him one evening at his estate, an almost insignificant group of stars situated below the Plough.

He turned his mind to Rudolf Haglund. 'The Hunting Dogs,' he said, into empty space.

That was what they had been, he and his colleagues. A pack of dogs pursuing a murderer. Rudolf Haglund was the man they had caught but, like any other hunting dogs, they had followed the warmest scent without further thought.

In Haber's box, behind the divider marked *Reconstruction 20/7,* he found several photos of the Gumserød reconstruction, with the investigators gathered out at the intersection, not in a huddle, as in the newspaper, but spread out. Frank Robekk still stood alone with a cigarette in his mouth, peering over his glasses at the others. Audun Vetti and Nils Hammer seemed to be discussing something. Wisting selected one to hang on the wall.

He stared at the three photographs with the curious feeling that something he had seen or read recently was significant, and struggled to reconstruct his actions of that day in his mind. Footsteps on the verandah fronting the cottage brought him back. Light steps, almost inaudible, stopping outside the door. Journalists, he thought, his heart beating faster as the door creaked open. He grabbed a log of firewood to use as a weapon.

'Hello?' It was Line, greeting him with a broad smile. 'Lovely to see you.'

'You too.'

'It's cold in here,' she said.

'I was just about to light the fire.' He threw the log in the open hearth and stacked kindling around it.

'I've tried to phone you,' Line said, examining the three photographs.

'It's on silent. I keep forgetting to check.'

'Is that him?' she asked, pointing at Haglund's photograph. 'Yes.'

'Why is his chest bare?'

The fire caught the dry firewood and the flames cast a reddish-gold glow across the room. 'It was taken at the hospital. He was being examined for wounds possibly inflicted by Cecilia when he abducted her or smothered her.'

Line leaned closer to the picture. 'Did you find any?'

'No.'

'Isn't that rather odd? I'd have done all I could to get free. Kicked and scratched.'

'We're all different,' Wisting said. 'Many rapists don't sustain any injuries.'

'Was she raped?'

'No.'

'Isn't that rather odd too? I mean, why else would he take her?'

It struck Wisting how acute Line was, but asking questions was her job.

She carried her shopping bags to the kitchen worktop. 'I brought some food.' Ten minutes later, they were sitting on opposite sides of the coffee table, eating freshly buttered bread rolls. 'What are you looking for?'

Wisting hardly knew himself. 'Inconsistencies,' he said. 'Insignificant snags or exceptions that I didn't notice seventeen years ago, or that I thought had nothing to do with the case.'

Line picked up one of the police reports. 'Can I help you? I'm good at that kind of thing.'

Wisting by now understood the task was too extensive for one man. Line would be an asset. As a journalist, she had an inbuilt mistrust of everything in public reports. She was accustomed to attacking the establishment. 'You can't use any of it in the newspaper,' he said.

'I'm not here as a journalist. I'm here because you're my father.'

He cleared the dishes before explaining the case and how the documents were organised: the lists, the projects and the fresh analysis, the break-in at the Linde estate, the footprint, and Haber's offer to take the blame, the encounter with Danny Flom, and the appointment he had with Rudolf Haglund at the lawyer's office the next day. It had grown to quite a list.

'What are you actually looking for?' she asked.

'What do you mean?'

'Are you looking for the colleague who planted the DNA evidence, or something to support your belief that you arrested the right man?'

'Both,' he said. 'I think they'll both be found here.'

Line got up and examined the three photographs, looking at them for some time. 'So you think a policeman planted the DNA evidence to make sure the murderer didn't go free?'

'Yes.'

'What if that wasn't what happened at all?' she asked.

'What then?'

'What if a policeman abducted her and planted evidence to give somebody else the blame?'

42

Wisting was minded to dismiss Line's theory, but then he looked at the picture of the investigators again. In all probability, one of them had falsified the evidence. Possibly the same officer had committed other crimes. He had to admit that Line's suggestion was plausible. More than anything else, it reassured him that Line was the right person to go through the case documents. If he had overlooked anything, she would home in on it.

He added a couple more logs to the fire. 'I need to do something,' he said, lifting his jacket.

Line was engrossed in the first ring binder. 'What's that?'

'Pay Frank Robekk a visit. Frank fielded the tip-offs in the Cecilia case.'

'The witness who was never heard! The phone call was probably transferred to him rather than you.'

Wisting tucked the newspaper under his arm. 'I didn't have any direct contact with callers of that kind. Will you lock the door behind me?'

'Switch on your mobile, then,' she said. 'So I can get hold of you.'

She stood up and went out with him. The leaden sky was heavy with low, scudding rain clouds, and a bitterly cold wind came sweeping in from the southwest.

His mobile rang before he sat in the car. An unknown number, it was not already listed in unanswered calls. The voice sounded officious, introducing itself as Chief Inspector

Terje Nordbo of the Bureau for the Investigation of Police Affairs.

'This concerns your handling of the Cecilia Linde murder,' he said. 'Acting Chief Constable Audun Vetti has sent the documentation received from the defence lawyer, Sigurd Henden, with regard to possible irregularities in the collection of evidence. We have decided to initiate an investigation and would like to conduct a preliminary interview with you.'

Wisting opened the car door. 'Is this an investigation of me directly?'

'Your status is that of a suspect. We are treating the case as gross negligence of duty. That gives you the right to be accompanied by a defence lawyer.'

'When were you thinking of?' Wisting settled into the driving seat.

'As soon as possible. Preferably as early as tomorrow.'

'Where?'

'We're based in Hamar, but also have offices in Oslo.'

Wisting started the car. 'What time tomorrow?'

'Shall we say twelve o'clock?'

'I've another appointment then. It'll have to be two.'

Wisting thought about what he would say as he drove. A great deal would be dependent on what Rudolf Haglund said in his lawyer's office.

He would have preferred the meeting after he had made further inroads, but perhaps it was just as well to endure it and get it done with.

When they had both embarked on a career in the police, Frank Robekk had lived on a smallholding in Kleppaker with his parents. Now they were both dead, he lived there on his own.

Wisting parked in the yard at the end of a long avenue of birch trees. Comprising twelve acres of cultivated land and a similar area of grazing, the place provided Frank with a good

171

rental income in addition to his modest disability pension, as he had once confided to Wisting.

His elder brother Alf lived on the other side of the fields, in a house built on a separate, hived off plot where Ellen Robekk vanished the summer before Cecilia's disappearance.

The breeze carried the scent of a bonfire, and a plume of smoke rose behind the old barn. Taking the newspaper with him, Wisting found Frank Robekk leaning on a stick, smoking and gazing into flames that leapt from a rusty oil drum. Tiny flecks of ash hung in the air.

Wisting was beside Robekk before the man noticed him, startled, as if he had been lost in his own thoughts.

'On your own?' Robekk poked the stick into the drum to revive the flames. Sparks shot a metre into the air. 'What brings you here?' he asked, flicking his cigarette end into the blaze.

'I'm looking for answers.'

Robekk produced a paper bag from his jacket pocket and popped a couple of lozenges into his mouth to cover the smell of cigarette smoke, as he had always done. 'Who isn't?'

'Have you read the newspapers?' Wisting asked, holding up that day's edition of *VG*.

'Not today, but I've caught what they're saying about Rudolf Haglund's DNA profile.'

'Did you hear anything about it at the time?' Did anyone mention doing something like that?'

'Never, and I don't believe any of it. I don't think any of the boys would have done that.'

'It had to be someone.'

'Some other explanation? What if one of the cigarette butts out at Gumserød really belonged to Haglund, and the other two had been dropped there earlier?'

'Tiedemann's Gold was the brand he used.'

'I do too, but if they're sold out I'll take another.'

172

Everything could be explained and dismissed, Wisting thought, if you did not wish to believe anyone on the force had tampered with the evidence.

'It could have been done more convincingly, don't you think?' Robekk said. 'To be certain, you could have planted a more decisive piece of evidence, a strand of Cecilia's hair, for example, a more direct connection between victim and killer.'

The smoke gusted at them and they moved to the other side of the blaze. No matter where they stood, the smoke found them. Robekk removed his thick glasses to rub his eyes. He had worn the same frames for as long as Wisting could remember; without them he became a stranger.

Wisting handed him the newspaper. 'Pages eight and nine.'

Frank Robekk took the paper and put his glasses back on. 'A witness says he phoned in a tip-off that would have provided Rudolf Haglund with an alibi.'

'That's me,' Frank said, pointing at the archive photo the newspaper had used.

'Have you heard about this before?' Wisting asked. 'That somebody phoned and said they had seen Haglund on a fishing trip?'

Frank read the whole article before shaking his head. 'I would have remembered that. Besides, all the tip-offs were recorded and allocated a number. They were passed on to you.' He handed the paper back. 'Have you checked him out? To see if he's some guy Haglund met in jail that he's persuaded to fool you?'

'That's up to the Criminal Cases Review Commission to discover,' Wisting said. Silence settled round them. The flames in the oil drum crackled. 'I went to the Linde family's estate today. They haven't been back there since. It looks completely abandoned.'

'I know. I was out there this summer.'

173

'Why did you go?'

'Just a whim. I've been there a few times. Walked the paths Cecilia used when she was out running.'

'You were there before the kidnapping too,' Wisting said. 'Remember the burglary?'

Robekk pushed the stick into the drum again, rooting around in the embers. 'Did you ever see Cecilia alive?' Wisting asked.

'She was there.'

'You spoke to her?'

Robekk shook his head. 'No. She returned from a run just as I left. A fortnight after that, she disappeared.'

Neither spoke for some time. The fire in the drum was dwindling, a cold wind sweeping over the agricultural landscape. Wisting drew his jacket more tightly round his neck.

Robekk leaned the stick against the wall of the barn. 'If you've come to talk about the old days,' he said, 'we could just as well go inside and have a cup of coffee?'

43

Line had been immersed in the investigation material, but now stood up, crossed to the fireplace and placed the last log from the firewood basket on the embers.

She was astonished to see how painstakingly the work had been accomplished. How meticulously the investigation machinery had operated. The documents were organised in such a way that manoeuvring through the information was straightforward, aided by the alphabetical list.

A total of 792 interviews were conducted. All the witnesses explained where they had been, what they had done, described their own appearance and clothing, retold their stories. Each and every movement was charted, with the most crucial information plotted on a map. Line unfolded it and carried it to the wall where the pictures of Cecilia Linde, Rudolf Haglund and the detectives were displayed. She hung it up and stood back, proud that her father had led this demanding effort.

She continued reading, soon realising that those who came forward had to do so on their own initiative. Others may have had something to hide. Several had seen a red car on a side road, a highly polished sports car. One thought it was a Toyota MR2. Some witnesses had seen the car there previously, though it had no connection to the nearby cottages. Accounts varied on whether there had been one or two persons inside the vehicle. The driver was described as tall and dark, but Line could not find him among the people who had come forward.

She thought she remembered something about a red sports car in the text archive, and logged on to her computer. The search word produced two results linked to the Cecilia case. It was obvious that the red car had raised her father's interest. It had been mentioned at the press conference.

In an article two days later, there was simply a brief mention that the red sports car had been ruled out of the case.

Line did not discover the explanation until half an hour had passed. A woman on a camping holiday with her family at Blokkebukta cove had made contact. She explained that the car belonged to a married man from Bærum who was staying in a neighbouring caravan. They had met each other repeatedly in the grove of trees where the car had been observed for what was described as 'intimate relations'.

Everyday secrets put spokes in the investigators' wheels and stole their time.

A motorcyclist dressed in black had halted at a bus stop and entered the woods. The witness who had seen him thought he was carrying something while another witness had not noticed that. A methodical search with sniffer dogs had been conducted and a drugs drop discovered. So, the biker was explained if not identified.

So far, Line had noted three people not included on the chart. A number of witnesses had seen a man with a camera in various places along the coastal path. It looked as though he had been on the route Cecilia had chosen for her run. Until now, she had not found any witnesses who fitted that description. There was also a man in a black singlet who was mentioned in several accounts and a silver goods van at Gumserød farm around the time Cecilia had set out.

The flames in the hearth had consumed the last log, and only a bed of embers was left. She carried the firewood basket outside. Reading so much had made her sluggish, and it was invigorating to breathe fresh air. A few chinks of light appeared in the cloud cover above and, for the first time in days, she could make out a hint of blue sky.

In the woodshed she filled the basket and was carrying it out again when a text arrived. It was from Tommy, wanting to spend more time with her. She replied that she had appreciated his visit to Fredrikstad but did not know what else to say.

Looking at her phone she remembered the unregistered number that had called Jonas Ravneberg only a few hours before his death, prompting him to make contact with a lawyer. She tried it at regular intervals but had never received an answer. Once again it rang without anyone picking up.

Inside, she placed a couple of logs on the fire and resumed her seat to check the online newspapers and her emails. An email had come in from one of the researchers in the fact-checking department. The subject was Jonas Ravneberg: a short list of key points with no information other than exactly what she had requested.

They had found the house at W. Blakstads gate 78 in Fredrikstad in the deeds registry, registered to Jonas Ravneberg, as well as a property in Larvik that was simply listed with a farm registration number and a title number. The historic overview of previous addresses showed he had lived at the unregistered address for many years before staying at Minnehallveien 28 in Stavern for about two years. After that, he had moved to Fredrikstad.

She looked up the address in Minnehallveien and found four mobile subscriptions registered there. From the names, a family.

She returned a short email of thanks and asked them if anyone else was listed at the address at the same time as Jonas Ravneberg.

She entered the series of maps on the council's website to key in the farm and title numbers. The segment that appeared was in the area known as Manvik. The blue marker was just beside a river. At a larger scale she homed more closely into the property, two large buildings and one smaller. A winding road led some considerable distance to the nearest neighbour.

An aerial photograph of the area revealed an agricultural landscape, with the river dividing the picture in two. Fields of varying hues made a patchwork of the terrain. The marker was surrounded by densely growing woodland and a small, barely visible cluster of houses among the trees. Jonas Ravneberg was still listed as the owner, though he had moved from Larvik seventeen years earlier.

Line moved to the map view again and clicked out to an overview picture. The property was situated five kilometres as the crow flies from the spot where Cecilia was last seen. The distance to the place where her body was found was even shorter.

44

The smell of the bonfire still hung about his clothes as Wisting aired his jacket on a hook beside the door, acrid smoke still in his hair.

Darkness was closing in around the cottage.

Line had taken his place on the settee, settled with her laptop in front of her. The documents lay spread across the table and settee cushions, several of them marked with yellow post-it notes. On the wall where he had hung three pictures, she had added a map and a number of extracts from the document folder including the transcript of Cecilia's tape message.

'Have you discovered anything?' he asked.

'Nothing decisive, but I can't get away from the fact that Rudolf Haglund had no injuries.' She pointed at the photo of the reconstruction. 'The guy was wearing only a T-shirt, but Haglund didn't have as much as a scratch on his arms.'

'He was arrested a fortnight after the abduction. Scratch marks can heal in that time.'

'Cecilia must have put up some sort of resistance. When her body was found, she had only been dead for a few hours, hadn't she? That was two days before you picked him up.'

'She may have been weak and exhausted.'

'She got food,' Line said, waving the post mortem report. 'Her stomach contents are listed as undigested remains of potatoes, red fish and wheat grains.'

No good explanation. 'He liked to fish,' Wisting said. 'Maybe he served her trout he had caught himself.'

Line recognised a desperate joke. 'You had a project focused on her boyfriend,' she said.

'It was in two parts. We were looking into the possibility that Cecilia and Danny were in cahoots and arranged the kidnapping, or that he did it on his own.'

'Did you check his background?'

'Of course.'

'What did you find?'

'It's all in the folder. A few black marks on his credit record and he had been fined for use and possession of hash. There was also a report of assault, I think.'

'Other women?'

'There was a story, almost two years old. A photographer colleague he had been travelling with right after he met Cecilia. She started in another job immediately afterwards.'

Line picked up the black ring binder and leafed through to a page where she had attached a yellow note. 'Tone Berg?'

'I don't remember. We spoke to her.'

Line returned the ring binder to its place. 'Did you know Danny Flom has a son who'll turn sixteen in two days' time?'

Wisting was surprised. 'He's been married twice.' He counted the months in his head.

'Born fifteen months after Cecilia disappeared, meaning that before six months had passed, Danny Flom had embarked on a relationship with a new girlfriend and got her pregnant.'

'Where did you get that?'

'Facebook.'

'Facebook?'

Line regarded him. 'Don't you use that in the police?'

'It wasn't invented seventeen years ago. The internet had hardly been invented. Anyway, there's nothing to suggest he has anything to do with the case. We have Cecilia's own account.'

Line turned to the transcript. 'I'm just pointing out some inconsistencies.' She removed the sheet of paper from the wall. 'Wasn't that what you called it? Snags you can get caught up in.'

Wisting let her continue.

'I haven't listened to the tape, but what she says seems a bit contrived.'

'There's a copy tape in the cassette player,' Wisting said, indicating the old travel radio on the shelf underneath the window. 'Just rewind it slightly.'

Line was unsure whether this was something she really wanted to hear, but she did as he said, and for one minute and forty-three seconds, Cecilia Linde's voice filled the room, eventually breaking into sobs.

'All the same,' Line said, stopping the tape. 'In addition to the factual information there's a couple of interesting things. She says he smelled foul. Like smoke, but also something else. Didn't you get anywhere with that?'

'Rudolf Haglund stank,' Wisting answered. 'Just as she said. He smelled of smoke, but also something else. He had some kind of unpleasant body odour.'

'When she says smoke, does she mean cigarette smoke or smoke from a bonfire?'

'I've always thought of it as cigarette smoke.'

Line nodded. 'You had already found the cigarette butts on the ground at Grumserød crossroads when you played the tape.'

Wisting realised that they had been prejudiced.

'Did Cecilia smoke?' Line continued.

'No.'

'Her boyfriend or parents?'

'Her father smoked, and her brother. I don't think Danny did.'

'So she was used to cigarette smoke?'

181

'I don't think this is leading anywhere,' Wisting said. 'If she had meant smoke from a bonfire, then we could discuss why she didn't say more specifically that he smelled of bonfire smoke.'

'Fine,' Line said. 'But what is really interesting is the sentence, *I have seen him before.*' Wisting agreed. Those five words had tormented him. 'Do you know if Cecilia and Rudolf Haglund had ever met?'

'No,' he said, 'but the abduction seemed planned. We know he was waiting for her. It's not unlikely they had bumped into each other, or at least seen each other, and that he planned it on that basis. Perhaps even stalked her.'

Line returned the transcript to the wall and Wisting returned to his seat, understanding that he had fallen into the same trap as all the investigators on the case. Instead of probing what might prove the suspect's innocence, all such information had been ignored or explained away, a psychological mechanism that made it possible for innocent people to be convicted.

It was the task of the court to draw conclusions about guilt, but it was difficult for suspicious investigators to retain an objective viewpoint. Through the investigation they had cultivated their own convictions and the question of guilt was decided before the case came before the court.

He still felt sure that Rudolf Haglund was the right man, but he felt himself wavering. He was not quite as certain as he had been seventeen years earlier.

45

'I'm going out for a walk,' Line said.

'Now?' Wisting asked, peering outside. Only the reflection from the fire in the hearth could be seen on the dark windowpane.

'Just a short walk.'

Wisting glanced at the time: not long after seven o'clock. 'Are you coming back here or going home?'

Line pulled on her jacket. 'How long were you planning to stay?'

'A couple of hours at least. Suzanne's at the café.'

'Have you spoken to her today?'

He shook his head.

'You ought to pop in to see her on your way home.'

Wisting looked at her. 'Maybe I will.'

They stepped out onto the verandah. Pale moonlight shimmered through breaks in the clouds. She gave him a hug and at that moment his mobile phone rang inside the house. He waved her off.

He found it in the gap between the seat cushion and the chair back. It must have slid from his trouser pocket while he was sitting on the chair. As he fumbled to retrieve it, he touched the keys so that he accepted the call involuntarily, before he had checked the caller's identity. 'Hello?'

The gruff voice at the other end sounded elderly. Wisting moved the phone away from his face and saw from the display that this was an unknown number. 'Yes?'

'This is Steinar Kvalsvik. I'm a senior consultant, now

retired, at the psychiatric department of the Central Hospital in Akershus.'

Wisting knew who the man was. He had been chiefly responsible for the forensic psychiatric examination of Rudolf Haglund. At the time, they had entered into a number of brief, professional discussions. He had been employed in more recent cases.

'It's about Rudolf Haglund. I don't have anything to do with it any longer, but I'm worried.'

'You know I'm suspended?'

'Formalities,' the man snorted. 'I can't think of anyone to contact other than you.'

Wisting crossed over to the window, where he saw his own reflection, but could also make out the sea and a sliver of moonlight. 'What's this about?'

'I have conducted hundreds of psychiatric evaluations over the years, but encountered very few like Rudolf Haglund.'

'How's that?'

'It may not have emerged very clearly from the paperwork, and it's difficult to put into words. Our remit was to decide whether he was criminally sane, and he was, almost on the border of the calculations. Nevertheless, there was something about him that I felt was terrifying.'

'How so?'

'We used a newly developed method of analysis to judge the risk of future violent behaviour. The method comprised variables that assessed relevant past, present and future circumstances. Historic, or constant, factors are allocated equal weight as the combination of existing clinical and future risk management variables.'

'What conclusion did you reach?'

'Rudolf Haglund scored extremely high. He had an early introduction to violence, lacks empathy, is socially

184

maladjusted, holds negative attitudes, is emotionally unstable and devoid of self-knowledge.'

'What does that mean?'

'Often the risk of future violent conduct is weighed against the likelihood of landing in dangerous situations. For example, if someone is a drug addict with unstable relationships, the risk factor is increased, but Haglund appeared to be more methodical in his actions.'

'I see.'

'I'll spare you all the jargon,' the doctor concluded. 'I haven't dealt with serial killers before, but I'm afraid that he might do something similar again, now that he's out.'

Wisting watched a dark cloud drift across the moon. 'Meaning he might abduct someone and kill again?'

'Rudolf Haglund is the type to repeat his actions. He has been inside for almost seventeen years. He is probably extremely vulnerable to the desires that have driven him to commit murder before.'

'My God ... are you sure about this?'

'Psychiatry is not an exact science, and I wouldn't have got in touch if it hadn't been for the girl who has disappeared. Linnea Kaupang.'

'What about his actions in the past? Could he have done something like this before?'

'The murder of Cecilia Linde was hardly the act of a beginner. He has probably used extreme violence before.'

Wisting suddenly realised how urgent this was. 'I'm going to ask the officer in charge of the Linnea case to contact you. You must tell him everything you've told me.'

'Of course,' the psychiatrist agreed, 'but, as a matter of form, this bleak prognosis presupposes that it really was Rudolf Haglund who killed Cecilia Linde. There are other confused and dangerous people out there, apart from him.'

185

46

Line turned at a layby, drove back and parked at the turn-off before the dirt track, her headlights lighting up a rusty old mailbox on a telephone pole. She stepped from the car and peered at the lid, at a white plaque on which the names Ingvald and Anne Marie Ravneberg were engraved. Underneath, it looked like there had once been another name.

Jonas, she thought. This was his childhood home.

She drove on, dense vegetation beating the sides of the car, until she noticed vehicle tracks in the soft ground ahead. It could be a police patrol car, here in connection with the murder in Fredrikstad, but she doubted that. She reversed out, turned onto the main road and parked in a layby, an estimated six or seven hundred metres from the smallholding by the river. She changed into a pair of boots and took her camera from her bag. It had an ISO setting of up to 25600, and could take photographs in almost total darkness.

The forest had grown close to the narrow track, so that overhanging branches formed a sort of tunnel. She set off on foot, the river thundering somewhere to her left behind the trees, in spate after many days of heavy rain. The sky was sprinkled with pale stars.

Soon her eyes became accustomed to the darkness but she stepped cautiously down the slope. The farther she ventured along the track, the quieter it became. And darker. She was wondering whether she should turn and come back in daylight when she saw a light between the trees. Soon the little cluster of buildings came into sight.

She approached more closely.

The red farmhouse had white borders and latticed windows but darkness hid anything that might be seen as pastoral charm. At one corner a solitary light bulb cast a yellowy-grey glimmer. It was a dying house, suffering rot, paint flaking from the walls and a broken porch. Two collapsed, grey outhouses were situated on the opposite side of the yard with, between them, an old car with weeds growing round it. No chance it was the vehicle that had made the fresh ruts on the track. Slightly farther away was a weather-beaten barn with its roof sagged into the shape of a saddle.

A grassy hill sloped down towards the river and another building, a low structure with a turf roof and a tall, narrow chimney.

The place looked abandoned, but the electricity was still connected, and the tyre tracks meant that someone had been here not too long ago. Partly eroded by the weather, it was difficult to tell how old they were. Probably a day or two.

She climbed the grey concrete steps of the main building and put her hands on the door; locked. There was a window, but it was too dark to see inside. She took out her mobile phone and used the flashlight function as a torch. Two paintings hung on a wall, and a rug was spread on the wooden floor, with a pair of clogs on it.

She waded through the long grass to the next window, which was draped with white curtains and a crocheted valance. She used her mobile phone again and this time pressed her forehead against the glass. It was an old kitchen: enamel stove with three rings, a deep kitchen sink, slop sink, worktop and wall cabinets. A table with a grey top stood directly beside the window and, in the centre of the table, a vase sat on a patterned cloth.

She placed her phone on the windowpane again. There

were flowers in the vase, red roses. A petal had fallen; apart from that, they were quite fresh.

She turned and let her eyes roam. The trees at the edge of the forest creaked as they swayed in the breeze. Pearly moonlight cast moving shadows. The sound of something scraping against something else. Where? Close. From inside the house. She stepped forward and the sound vanished, but returned with the next gust of wind. It was the branches of a tree scratching against the roof tiles.

Fear was irrational, but it felt like a clammy hand running down her back. The house should have been empty for seventeen years, but someone had been here a short time ago. A light drifted through the trees, headlights moving slowly along the track. The low rumble of an engine followed.

She hid behind a tree as the car drove past. The headlights had robbed her of her night vision, and she could not see anything more than the driver's profile. The vehicle stopped in front of the farmhouse, bathing the derelict yard in light. The driver remained seated with the engine idling.

Line crossed quickly to the other side, in among the trees again, and took a couple of photos of the car and its surroundings. She zoomed in on the number plate.

Five minutes later the car drove towards the two shacks and switched to full beam. The wrecked car was a Saab, its dull red paint speckled with rust and the rubber on its tyres rotted. Two minutes later the car reversed out again.

Line pressed against a mossy boulder and, as she heard the car drive past, took a photo of the driver, a man around the same age as her father. He wore glasses and had dark hair flecked with silver at the sides. There was something familiar about him but, whoever he was, his behaviour was very strange.

47

Re-reading the forensic psychiatrists' report, Wisting was brought up short by a paragraph dealing with Rudolf Haglund's health. The subject was reported to be in good physical condition. He had not been treated for any serious illnesses and had never been an in-patient at any hospital in Norway or abroad. No hereditary conditions existed in his family and he was not prescribed any kind of medication.

He looked at the photo of the scar where Haglund had been operated on to remove a mole. The psychiatrists had been thorough but the incidence of skin cancer was not mentioned. An operation could have been carried out at day surgery, and might have been on benign skin tumours, but it was strange that it was ignored.

Wisting called the senior consultant, now retired. 'Do you know whether Rudolf Haglund had an operation for skin cancer?'

The man smacked his lips, as though his mouth was dry. 'Why are you asking that?'

'I've been reading through your report. It stays that Haglund had never been in hospital or treated for serious illness. We have photos showing three small scars which he said were from the removal of moles.'

'I can't recall that the subject ever came up,' the psychiatrist said. 'Information about physical health comes from the subject. All the same, it's peculiar that he didn't mention it. His father had suffered from cancer, and his illness was

189

a turning point in Haglund's life. We talked about it a great deal, but he never told me this.'

'Isn't that rather odd?'

'Yes, but, when all's said and done, he's a typical candidate for malignant skin lesions. I remember his skin was extremely pale and, of course, it's hereditary.'

Wisting leafed through the other pictures. Haglund also had a scar below his left shoulder blade and another high on his neck.

'Is it important?' the psychiatrist asked.

Wisting heard footsteps on the verandah and set the photographs aside. 'Probably not. I just thought it strange that he should withhold such information when, for example, he was open about his predilection for sadomasochism.'

Line entered, her boots covered in mud. She pulled them off. Wisting moved his lips in a silent *hello*.

'That admission came after he was shown the pornographic material you found,' said the psychiatrist. 'You must remember that Rudolf Haglund is a complex character. Understanding his motives for sharing his thoughts is hardly simple, far less understanding his actions.'

'He's not mad?'

'No, but he's something of a psychological puzzle.'

Line settled on the settee, opening her laptop and clicking through photos on her camera as she waited for the computer to start. Drawing his conversation to a close, Wisting sat opposite her.

'Who was that?' she asked.

'One of the forensic psychiatrists who examined Rudolf Haglund. The one who called, concerned that Rudolf Haglund might be involved in Linnea Kaupang's disappearance.'

Line slumped back on the settee. 'My God,' she groaned. 'He really must speak to the people working on the case.'

'I've told Nils Hammer.'

'What did he say?'

'I sent him a text.'

'A text? When an experienced psychiatrist puts forward the opinion that a previous killer may have abducted another girl?'

Wisting did not want to say that Nils Hammer was at the top of his list of colleagues who might have planted the DNA evidence.

'Did he answer?' Line asked.

'He wrote that they would look into it. They had a couple of other interesting leads.'

He knew the Haglund theory would be at the bottom of the list. When it came to the crunch, it was no more than conjecture.

'They'll not follow it up,' Line said. 'As things stand, they won't dare go after Rudolf Haglund.'

Wisting agreed. Further investigation of Rudolf Haglund would require the approval of the prosecuting authorities and, with no more than the suppositions of a retired psychiatrist, Audun Vetti would certainly apply the brakes.

Line stood up, crossed to the fireplace and placed the last log on the fire. 'Are you meeting Haglund tomorrow?' she asked.

'Twelve o'clock at Henden's office. Then I can feel my way forward. Find out how things stand.'

She picked up the poker, prodding the log she had added to the embers. 'We could follow him,' she said. 'The meeting gives us our starting point. We can follow him from there.'

'I don't know ...' Wisting said.

'It's the only opportunity,' Line said obstinately. 'If he's holding her, it's the only chance of finding her.'

'That's a job for the police.'

'Do you think they'll do that?' Line asked.

Following Rudolf Haglund could lead to something, but he did not believe that Nils Hammer would set up an extensive surveillance procedure. The justification was too slight.

'I have another appointment afterwards,' Wisting said. 'I have to give a statement to Internal Affairs at two o'clock.'

'We'll do it without you. He might recognise you anyway.'

'Who are *we*?'

'I'll bring someone from work.'

'It's not just a matter of tagging along,' Wisting said. 'Surveillance demands training and practice. It's a special skill.'

'It's part of our work too,' Line reminded him. 'Following the police to see who they contact in a major case is always interesting. You've probably had crime journalists on your tail several times without noticing.'

'You can't write about this. We agreed on that.'

'I won't write about the Cecilia case.' Line pointed to the coffee table piled with notes. 'But if Rudolf Haglund leads us to Linnea Kaupang, that's another case entirely.'

48

They sat at the table again. 'Have you spoken to Suzanne?'
Line asked. Wisting shook his head. 'Don't you think you
should have?'

'Yes,' Wisting admitted. 'Where have you been?'

'At Jonas Ravneberg's.'

'The man who was murdered in Fredrikstad?'

'He grew up on a smallholding out at Manvik. He still
owns it.'

'What were you doing there?'

'I wanted to have a look. He moved away the autumn after
Cecilia's murder. The place is deserted, but somebody had
been there. There were wheel ruts on the track all the way,
and a bunch of red roses on the kitchen table.'

'Perhaps someone looks after the place,' Wisting said, 'and
when they heard he died, they took flowers. A final goodbye.'

Line gave him a doubtful look. 'A car arrived while I was
there as well,' she said, picking up her camera.

'Who was it?'

'A guy who just sat in his car. I thought I should check
the registration.'

Wisting looked at the display on the back of the camera.
'You could have saved yourself the trouble. I know who it
is. I spoke to him earlier today: Frank Robekk.'

'The policeman?'

'He quit after the Cecilia case. It all became too much for
him. His niece had vanished the same way as Cecilia, one
year earlier.'

'What was he doing out at Ravneberg's?'

'I guess he's picked up where he left off all those years ago. The question is how he made the connection.'

A possibility had opened up, like a door slightly ajar. Wisting crossed to the box marked *Cecilia case* and took out the alphabetical list of names. Under *R* he found *RAVNBERG, Jonas*. The name was referred to in document 6.43.

Ravneberg without an E between 'Ravn' and 'berg'. It could be due to something as simple as a typing error.

'What is it?' Line asked.

'Jonas Ravneberg is mentioned in the Cecilia case.'

He located the ring binder marked with a large number 6, the witness statements. Document number forty-three was an interview with Hogne Slettevoll, one of the five members of staff at the furniture store where Rudolf Haglund was a warehouseman. He was a character witness.

The interview had been conducted by Nils Hammer, the main substance of which was a complaint by a female customer after Haglund offered to assemble a double bed and help her test it. He had also explained that the headboard was suitable for attaching handcuffs. This episode had been almost ten years earlier. Just prior to the interview, a similar incident had taken place when the witness took a complaint about a defective bed base. Haglund had made insinuations about the reason the bed gave way.

Half a page dealt with Rudolf Haglund's temperament, how trivial events made him explode with rage: goods not in the right place, delivery notes not completed, packaged items difficult to open.

Towards the end, Wisting came across the name Jonas Ravnberg, without an E. He read the paragraph aloud to Line:

'*The witness does not socialise with the accused other than in connection with work. He does not know his circle of*

194

friends or his hobbies, but is aware that he collects things, for example Matchbox cars. He does not exactly recall how the subject came up, but the witness had a box of these model cars that had belonged to his father and that he wanted to sell. The accused bought three of the cars and had a possible buyer for the others. They arranged a meeting down at the furniture warehouse. This might have been about two or three years previously. The buyer's name was Jonas Ravnberg. The witness received fifty kroner per car, and the total amount came to 1,150 kroner, which the buyer paid by cheque.'

'Jonas Ravneberg collected model cars,' Line said, telling Wisting about Elvis Presley's miniature Cadillac outside his house in Fredrikstad. 'It must be the same man.'

Wisting put his head in his hands in an attempt to gather his thoughts. A connection had appeared between Rudolf Haglund and a murder victim who had moved from the town at the same time that Haglund was convicted. The link had seemed insignificant then and he did not know whether it was any more significant now. In the midst of all this, Frank Robekk had turned up.

Line took hold of the folder of witness statements. 'Why wasn't Jonas Ravneberg interviewed at the time?' she asked.

Wisting did not have a good answer. Early in the investigation, each new name became a focus for further examination. As the case progressed, peripheral characters became of less interest. By this stage they had more than enough on Rudolf Haglund. From the moment he was arrested, that was all that mattered. Finding enough evidence to convict him.

49

At ten o'clock, Line buttered herself a bread roll and asked her father what he wanted to eat.

'Nothing thanks,' he said, moving to the window. '7.4 degrees,' he reported, after looking at the thermometer. 'Shall we call it a day?'

'I want to stay a bit longer,' she said.

'Are you sure? You can take the folder home.'

'Everything's sort of connected. I read something in one place and have to cross check somewhere else. Here is best. You go ahead. I'll be fine on my own.'

She knew he did not like to leave her alone, but she had stayed here by herself the previous autumn and both knew she would manage.

'I don't want you to spend the night here,' he said. His tone did not leave any room for discussion.

'Okay, I'll get home before midnight.'

'Fine. I'll go to see Suzanne at the café.'

As soon as Wisting was gone, Line turned to the dull, dark window. The darkness seemed impenetrable, as though built in layers. She looked up the online *VG* newspaper. The most recent article was written by Morten P and Harald Skoglund.

She had been too preoccupied with her own concerns to pay attention to the rest of the news. She had heard about the missing teenager, but knew little more.

The last definite sighting of seventeen-year-old Linnea Kaupang had been made by the bus driver on route 01. The girl was in her final year at high school, and on Friday, 2nd

October, had been at school until ten past two. Half an hour later, she caught the bus in Torstrand. The route followed the main route 303 through Tjøllingvollen to Sandefjord, and Linnea Kaupang had alighted at ten to three at the Lindhjemveien intersection. No one had seen her since.

Linnea Kaupang lived with her father about eight hundred metres from the bus stop. Three neighbouring houses were situated between her home and the main road, and only one person, a retired sailor, had been at home. He had often seen her walking home from the bus, but not that day.

Morten P and Harald had talked to Linnea's school friends who described her as conscientious and reliable. Nils Hammer had refused to exclude the possibility that the missing girl had been the victim of a crime. She phoned Morten P.

'How're you doing?' he asked.

'I've still got a pain in my backside, but I'm off that story now, at least almost.'

'Almost?'

She explained how she had followed a thread from the Fredrikstad murder victim's past, and how it had led to the Cecilia case. 'I don't really like it. I'm wondering whether there might be a connection.'

'Coincidences happen all the time. That's why the word exists.'

She conceded the point. 'I'm actually phoning about the Linnea case.'

'Bloody peculiar case,' Morten P said. 'Until yesterday evening, the signal from her mobile phone was traced to near the High School in Vestfold.'

'That's almost at Horten, in the far north of the county.'

'That's what's so damn strange.'

'Could it have been left on the bus when she got off? The number 01 route goes through the whole county, all the way to Horten.'

197

'That's a possibility, but then it must have got off the bus at Bakkenteigen by itself.'

'What do the police say?'

'Nothing. We have photos of them searching along the main road from Åsgårdstrand to Borre. They won't make any comment.'

'I have a theory about who might have taken her,' Line said.

'A theory from the police?'

'No, and it's possible this will make me sound desperate, but it doesn't come from me or my father. It comes from a chief consultant psychiatrist.'

'Interesting.'

'He believes Rudolf Haglund may be behind it.'

She visualised Morton P sitting behind his desk fiddling with a ballpoint pen and wondering how on earth, as gently as possible, he could dismiss her idea. 'I know it's far-fetched.'

Morten P cleared his throat. 'Something has happened to her,' he said. 'I've spoken to her friends who don't believe she has disappeared of her own free will. It's likely someone has taken her and more than likely he has done something similar before.'

'The psychiatrist believes the spell in prison has built up internal pressures in him,' Line said.

'Are the police thinking along the same lines?'

'I don't know what they're thinking, only that there aren't sufficient grounds to place him under surveillance.'

'Does anybody know where he is now?' Morten P was becoming enthusiastic.

'Not right now, but I know where he'll be tomorrow at twelve o'clock.'

Morten P laughed, realising she was thinking the same as him. 'Harald and I can watch from our cars,' he said. 'But we need one more, in addition to you.'

198

'I can arrange that.'

'I have to finish this story; we'll take this further tomorrow.'

Line located Tommy Kvanter's number, it was her turn to surprise him. *I need you*, she tapped into the phone, and pressed *send*.

That done, she called the unknown Fredrikstad number again, the unregistered subscriber who had triggered a chain reaction when he phoned Jonas Ravneberg. It rang for the same length of time, and she was about to disconnect the call when someone answered with a simple *Hello?* The voice sounded like that of a young man.

'Who am I speaking to?'

'Who do you want to speak to?'

'My name is Line Wisting,' she said. 'Who am I speaking to?'

The person disconnected. Line swore and called the number again. This time, no one answered, but the phone pinged in a text.

When and where?

50

A yellow ribbon was tied to the railings on the staircase leading to *The Golden Peace*. A picture of Linnea Kaupang hung on the door. The word *Missing* was emblazoned above and underneath was a description of her, stating what she had been wearing and where she had last been seen. Wisting could not shake off the notion that he could have made a difference if only he had been on duty. If it hadn't been for Audun Vetti.

The little bell pealed above the door as the café fell silent and all the customers turned towards him. Wisting nodded to right and left as he walked to the bar. The pleasant atmosphere he was used to was missing.

Suzanne smiled from behind the counter. 'Lovely to see you. Do you want anything?'

'Coffee, please.'

'Sit down,' she said, nodding towards his usual table. 'I'll bring it to you.'

Wisting hung his jacket over the back of the chair. Suzanne arrived with coffee and a slice of cake. He invited her to sit with him. 'Still busy?' he asked.

'Not as many customers as usual, but how are things with you?'

'Line has arrived.'

'That's nice,' she said.

'Did someone phone asking for me?'

'Why do you ask?'

'I had a visit from Rudolf Haglund's defence lawyer. He said you had told him I was at the cottage.'

'Shouldn't I have done that?'

'Someone else has been there too,' he said, describing the break-in.

'It would be easier if you answered the phone when people called,' Suzanne threw a glance at the counter as a customer approached. 'Then I wouldn't be bothered all the time.'

'You're right,' he said.

Suzanne left to serve the customer from the coffee machine, before coming back to the table.

'I just wanted to know who you had spoken to. There weren't many people who knew where I was.'

'There have been journalists phoning constantly. I told them you were at the cottage.'

There was no point in pursuing the subject. Neither of them spoke. Suzanne got to her feet again and walked around the café, collecting empty glasses and dirty plates.

It astonished him how little she seemed to care. When he needed someone to speak to he felt she was accusing him. The café was perhaps not the right place to talk, but could she not take at least some time out?

Their relationship had begun suddenly, three years earlier, only two years after Ingrid's death when Wisting had not even considered finding someone else. As time passed though, he grew to appreciate how well they got on and their relationship came to mean a great deal to him. He felt they had been happy over the past three years, but now Suzanne was preoccupied and distant and he felt she was slipping away.

He understood her need to feel secure. She had experienced a lot, and assurance was important to her. It was important to him too, but he probably defined it differently. For him it was not so much physical presence. He was used to being on his own. It was everything to do with not having to weigh his words too carefully, secure in the knowledge that the other person would construe everything for the best. With a feeling of closeness, even if the other person was at work, or in another country, as he and Ingrid had achieved.

She had been employed as an aid worker with NORAD and, although he had missed her at times, they never lost that feeling of closeness. With Suzanne it was more difficult when they both worked such long hours. He watched her manoeuvring between the tables, thinking there was something different in her eyes. Something slightly cold and suspicious, maybe even frightened. They had become strangers.

It was visible now, he thought, even though it had been present for a while. A distance had opened between them. At the beginning he had sat up waiting at night, but more often these nights he went to bed before she came home – and was away before she wakened in the morning. He had to come here to spend time with her.

He sat for a while longer, finishing his coffee, before getting to his feet, picking up his jacket and making his exit.

51

The house in Herman Wildenveys gate lay empty and silent. Wisting parked among yellow autumn leaves in the court-yard. When Suzanne had moved in, she had filled the space left by Ingrid. Scared she would erase all traces, he had kept her slightly at a distance but soon realised that he had missed having someone to come home to.

So, perhaps Suzanne had felt like a replacement. He slammed the car door behind him.

Line was not home; which suited, he thought. From his bedroom wardrobe he took a black cap, a pair of leather gloves, a black polo-neck sweater, and dark jeans.

After changing his clothes, he posed in front of the mirror. He was unshaven and red-eyed, but the outfit was right, even if he couldn't look himself in the eye. The plan had taken shape after his first call from the forensic psychiatrist, prompting the notion that whoever abducted Cecilia had also taken Ellen Robekk.

One of the older detectives had responsibility for the Ellen enquiry, and Wisting had never been given a complete overview. When Cecilia vanished the following year, Frank Robekk took it on himself to go through it all again. He would have been thorough and painstaking, but now Wist-ing needed to check it all himself, and that meant he had to get into the historical archives at the station without a key or admittance card.

Letting himself out, he pressed himself against the hedge bordering his neighbour's garden, where there was a trampoline in the centre of the extensive lawn. A tricycle lay toppled beside a children's playhouse, and a skipping rope lay where it had been thrown. He found what he was looking for in the rose bed, a football, took it to his car and reversed out of the courtyard to head for the station. He had driven this same route almost every day for thirty years, and could probably do so with his eyes closed.

He turned off at the old fire station and drove to the car park at Bøkkerfjellet. From this vantage point, he had a clear view of the fifty metres along Linneagate to the vehicle and staff entries. It was 23.04. The night shift had just come on and the evening shift was probably in the locker room.

Three minutes later, one of the oldest members of the uniform branch trundled out, pushing a bicycle. He stopped to put on his helmet and cycled off. The door opened again, and two men and a woman emerged. Wisting knew them all. Three cars drove out in turn from the car park in the back yard, none choosing his direction. When the lights had gone, he stepped out of the car, carrying the football.

The building next door was what was left of the Brynje hosiery factory, demolished to make way for the new police station. Wisting crept beside its old brick walls to a winter grit container. The back yard was dark, the only light from a streetlamp above the parking area. Through a crack between the container and the wall he had a clear view to the vehicle gate but could not, himself, be seen.

The entire police station seemed to be asleep. His own office was in darkness but a light shone in Nils Hammer's. Nothing else suggested work was being done on the Linnea Kaupang case. From experience he knew that, by now, there would not be much more for the investigators to do. Four days had passed; most of the witnesses had been interviewed and the relevant places searched. Without anything more specific all they could do was wait.

The sky was filled with stars. He found the Plough, with *Canes Venatici* in pursuit. The Hunting Dogs. The air felt very cold and damp.

The new group would spend half an hour or so preparing for their shift, the senior officer running through the list of assignments, going over what had happened since they were last in. They updated themselves on planned and expected events, produced lists of stolen vehicles and wanted persons and checked over their equipment. Soon they would drive out from the basement garage and the gate would remain open behind them for about fifteen seconds.

A star fell through the darkness, leaving behind a slim, milky white trail. Looking up at the stars was like looking backwards in time. For all he knew, the hunting dogs could have died up there, disappeared from the heavens long ago.

Not until almost an hour later did the gate begin to clatter, sliding up as a patrol car rolled out. Wisting recognised the driver: Frank Kvastmo, one of the oldest and most experienced officers in the uniformed branch. At his side sat a student from the Police College, meaning there was at least one more officer still inside the station. The car stopped with its engine idling, waiting for the gate to begin its downward slide before setting out.

With the car gone and the gate about one and a half metres from the ground, Wisting threw the ball. It landed close to the opening, bounced on the asphalt and broke the optical beam installed to prevent crushing injuries. The gate stopped with a judder, slid up again and the ball rolled inside to stop in front of the washing bay. Wisting, head down, ran inside, where the strong ceiling light made him screw up his eyes.

The air was raw and damp, and the white walls spotted with black patches of mould. A CCTV camera was mounted on the ceiling. The last time they had made use of the video film was three years earlier when someone had placed a suspicious suitcase in front of the main entrance. The video footage was of such poor quality it had been difficult to identify the man who left it. They had talked about installing new CCTV equipment, but still had not found enough money. There were ten cameras in total at the police station. Wisting knew where they were located and that it would be difficult to avoid them all. This was a risk he had to take. If no one suspected a break-in the recording would be erased in seven days.

Two doors in the garage led into the station, one through the cells, no longer in use after the establishment of a central jail at the police station in Tønsberg. The other was the main door to the stairwell. Both were locked and he did not have a keycard although the code was in his head. His footsteps echoed off the concrete walls as he approached the locked main door, the sound hollow and cold.

The lock made a buzzing sound and the colour on the card reader changed from red to green. He crouched behind one of the unmarked police cars.

A uniformed officer shouldered his way out, carrying a large bag of equipment. A student followed. The door clicked shut behind them and they stepped across to the nearest police car, placed their bags on the rear seat and rummaged through the boot. Assured they had all they required, the student sat behind the wheel and eased the vehicle towards the gate. He lowered the side window and tugged at a cord hanging from the roof. The gate slid open and they drove into the night.

Wisting waited until the gate was fully closed again before he stood up. He stared at the stairwell door. Expecting it to be closed, he had worked out a plan. There were spare cards that could be used by staff who had forgotten their own, visiting investigators from out of town or workmen needing access. Sometimes these cards were left in the police cars.

206

Inside the nearest car he searched through the centre console, behind the sun visor, and in the glove compartment without finding anything other than a petrol card and an empty snuffbox. He was luckier in the next, where a card lay beside the logbook in the glove compartment. He took it to the door, drew the card through the reader and keyed in the code. The green diode flashed as the lock buzzed and Wisting stepped through.

The historical archive where the Ellen case was stored was located at the end of the corridor and locked with a cylinder lock, but he knew the duty officer kept a master key in his office on the floor above. He climbed the stairs, emerging into the public area, and let himself into the duty officer's office with his borrowed admittance card.

Pictures from the CCTV rolled across the screen of a dusty monitor. He had been alone in the station during the late night hours many times before, but this time he felt like a stranger: worse, like an outsider.

The master key hung in the cupboard where the performance and contingency plans were stored in suspended files. He almost dropped it when a gruff voice from the radio broke the silence.

'*Fox 3-0 answering.*'

'*Drive along main road 40 to Bjerke. Report of someone driving off the road. Single vehicle off the road. No passengers reported injured.*'

'*Message received.*'

Wisting returned to the basement, walked along the corridor to the historical archives and was soon inside. The fluorescent tubes on the ceiling made a humming noise, blinked, and went on.

The box of documents from the Ellen investigation was sitting in the same place. He lifted it down and carried it to a separate area of the archive. Intended as a workroom it actually stored Christmas decorations, old orderly books, driving licence papers, enforcement books and journals, all waiting until they were old enough to be destroyed or transferred to the Regional State Archive.

He placed the box on the desk and looked at the contents. There were fewer documents than in the Cecilia Linde case, because they had never found a crime scene, a body or a suspect. The case consisted almost exclusively of witness statements given by people who knew Ellen Robekk or who were around Kleppaker when she disappeared.

Seventeen-year-old Ellen Robekk had vanished on a Sunday. She was still in bed when her parents came to her bedroom at twelve noon to say they were going for a walk in the woods. When they returned, she was gone.

Wisting left the details of the disappearance lying and took out the list of people, running his eyes over the names. He recalled some, but others were unfamiliar. Almost halfway down one of the sheets he spotted a name with an asterisk beside it. *RAVNEBERG, Jonas.* He was the subject of two documents. In one, he was interviewed as a witness; the other was a special report from one of the detectives.

He placed the printout on top of the box and lifted it, but put it back down again. There was a computer on the worktable. Wisting pushed the mouse across the tabletop, and the login image appeared on the screen.

He glanced from the computer screen to the box and back again. Then he abruptly made a decision and keyed in his own user name and password. He had obviously not been removed from data access, since he soon gained entry, and regretted it at once since it would be possible to trace when and where he had logged in. But there was no reason for anyone to check his data log unless they became suspicious.

He had seventeen unread emails, the majority group emails, and he did not bother reading those. Instead he clicked into the database for investigation of criminal cases and looked up the name Linnea Kaupang. The name appeared as the victim in case 11828923 – *Missing woman under 18 years of age.*

The documents were listed in chronological order. Wisting opened the document that had begun the enquiry. Linnea Kaupang was reported missing by her father on Saturday at quarter to one in the afternoon. By then, she had been missing for almost twenty-four hours.

The missing girl's mother had died twelve years earlier, and her father had sole responsibility for his daughter. He had explained that she had not been at home when he came back from work on Friday. During the course of the evening, he had contacted her classmates and other acquaintances but no one had known where she was. She had not gone missing before and was not depressed or in any kind of dispute with her father.

The three final pieces of information were enough for the police to begin working on the case. The assumption could reasonably be made that something had happened to her, rather than leaving the matter in abeyance as with other runaway teenagers.

Two classmates said that Linnea had boarded the service bus between Larvik and Sandefjord. The driver was interviewed. He remembered her and was certain he had let her off at Snippen.

Wisting skipped over the search reports and instead read one summarising the door to door questioning in the neighbourhood. This strengthened the picture of Linnea Kaupang as a sociable, cheerful and positive girl, but no one had seen her.

The report concerning the trace on Linnea Kaupang's mobile phone surprised Wisting. The last phone call was logged three hours before she disappeared. She had phoned a friend about schoolwork. The phone had been located in an area of coverage that included the Thor Heyerdahl High School. What was unusual was that when the phone was traced in real time, it was located in an area near Bakkenteigen between Horten and Tønsberg.

It was impossible to trace the route of travel to that point. On Monday evening, the signal had disappeared when the phone's battery ran out. The investigators had thought as Wisting had, that it had been thrown from a car. Searches were conducted along the ditches bordering route 19 and, at the turn off leading to Berg Prison, they had found Linnea's Sony Ericsson Xperia. The discovery provided no further answers, and the enquiry remained open.

As far as he knew, the discovery of the mobile phone had not been mentioned in the media. He could not understand why. If he had been in charge he would have gone public, hoping for fresh information to be presented. So far the disappearance remained a local case, but if residents of the Horten area learned this it would lead to further tip-offs and observations.

A sudden noise startled Wisting out of his thoughts. A fire door slammed shut somewhere in the building, echoing through the basement. He listened but, as he heard nothing further, turned back to the computer.

Two people had been set aside for special attention. One was a retired sailor who lived in the nearest house. He was described as a recluse and alcoholic. Other neighbours had seen him sitting up late at nights watching pornographic films on TV. He was interviewed twice and had no alibi for the time frame of Linnea's disappearance.

Beside the stop where Linnea left the bus, was a shared house for people with mental illnesses. The residents and staff members were interviewed, many noting that Rolf Tangen, a former drug addict who had been convicted of rape, had been out that afternoon. He had returned about half past six in the evening, sweaty and upset. Tangen himself gave no explanation other than that he had been walking in the woods.

Wisting logged out of the computer and carried the box of documents towards the door. By his own lights this was not theft, though to authority it certainly would be, and he would have serious problems if caught. Shouldering the door open tentatively, he looked out and listened: nothing. He walked towards the garage.

The enormous basement space was in total darkness until the movement sensors switched on the power. He set the box on the floor beside the bin frame, and returned to the duty office with the key. From the interference on the police radio, he understood that both patrol cars were busy investigating a burglar alarm at the *Farris* factory.

In his peripheral vision he caught sight of a movement on the CCTV monitor. Someone was walking through the empty jail section. The screen switched to the garage and Nils Hammer on a shortcut used frequently by investigators on their way home. He stopped at the bin where Wisting had placed the box, to throw something away. The screen switched again to show the deserted entrance area.

Wisting waited until the screen rolled over all the cameras and returned to the empty garage. The distance to the bin frame was too far and the image too indistinct to be sure that the box was still there. He lingered for a few more minutes before going down to the garage.

The case files were sitting where he left them. He replaced the borrowed card in the glove compartment of the unmarked police car before picking up the box and tugging on the gate cord. As it closed behind him, it dawned on him that he had forgotten the ball.

52

Wisting got home at seven minutes to two. Suzanne's car was parked at the top of the driveway, in front of Line's Golf, but they must both be in bed by now. He parked and took the box inside knowing it would be impossible to sleep with all these thoughts whirling in his head.

The house was silent; he could hear only the sounds he was so used to that they barely registered: the hum of the heat pump, ticking of the kitchen clock, hissing through a water pipe, the fridge switching itself off. He set the box on the kitchen table and skimmed through the introductory reports on Ellen.

Frank Robekk had called the police. As uncle of the missing girl, his brother had contacted him when they began to worry. She had slept late on the day of her disappearance, but there was nothing unusual in that, since it was the weekend. Her parents had gone for a walk in the woods while she was still in bed.

When they returned there was water on the floor of the shower cabinet. Her mother said that she was wearing a pair of jeans and a plain yellow T-shirt. They thought she might have gone to her uncle's farm where she had a horse stabled, but the horse was still in its stall and it had not been cleaned out.

That day's interview with Jonas Ravneberg was relatively short. Most of the time was spent explaining the reason he had been called for interview. A witness had observed a red Saab 900 parked at the side of the road not far from the turn-off leading to Ellen Robekk's house. This witness worked as a salesman at the local Saab dealership, and checked the number plate to see if it was a car he had sold. He could therefore remember that it was a car from out of town with the letters ND at the beginning of the registration number.

His professional knowledge led him to believe it was a car from 1987 or later, as the model had been given a facelift involving new bumpers and radiator grille that year. In 1993, the model went out of production, and the police had the names of all owners of ND-registered red Saab 900s from those years. There were no more than seventy-four in the entire country. Jonas Ravneberg was one of four in the area, and the first to be interviewed.

He had an alibi. He had been in Sweden with a girlfriend and visited her family in Malmø. They had used her car and been away for a week. Accompanying the interview report was a copy of their ferry tickets. His girlfriend's name was Maud Torell and she confirmed the explanation by phone.

The car idea was shelved after the salesman was re-interviewed. He was no longer certain that the letter combination ND was correct, and could only exclude the possibility that the car had been registered locally, which would have meant the LS combination. Nor was he still sure that he had spotted the car on the day Ellen vanished. He was on holiday at the time and could not quite distinguish one day from another.

Wisting read Jonas Ravneberg's statement again, noticing that he and Maud Torell were listed at the same address: Minnehallveien 28 in Stavern. So, she had been more than a girlfriend. They were living together.

The actual statement was simple and verifiable, but a number of questions had not been posed. Did anyone else have use of his car? How many sets of car keys did he possess, and where were they located? The phone interview with his girlfriend seemed to have been undertaken to dismiss Jonas

Ravneberg from the enquiry. Close family members were never satisfactory alibi witnesses. When they were not even required to attend a face-to-face interview their testimony was worth little.

The relationship between them must have ended the following year, when Jonas Ravneberg had moved to Fredrikstad. In the reports about his murder, he had been described as a man who lived on his own. Wisting replaced the papers in the box. The connection between Jonas Ravneberg and Rudolf Haglund had existed for seventeen years without being spotted.

He slumped back in his chair with a sense of being faced with an unfinished work of art: a landscape already in its frame, the main features in place, the subject sketched out, but the details missing. For the moment, the outline was so indistinct he could not imagine how it would look when it was complete.

53

Suzanne was not asleep. 'Hello,' he whispered.

She replied with *Mhmm*.

Under the quilt, he lay on his back staring at the ceiling.

'Do you think it's worth it?' she asked.

'What?'

'Your job in the police. No one ever thanks you. You risk your life and health. Wallowing in other people's misery. Hundreds of hours of overtime you don't get paid for, phone calls at home at all hours. Demands and expectations and now your own boss has laid a charge against you. Do you think it's worth it?'

He had no answer. His job involved burdens of many kinds, but he had not chosen it to have a quiet life. He had trained himself to face resistance and enormous pressure.

Suzanne turned over.

Wisting closed his eyes, but it made no difference in the dark room. The picture of Linnea Kaupang was imprinted on his retina.

'It's my job,' he said. If he could work on the new missing person case, it would all be worth it. To kindle hope that she was alive would outweigh everything else. 'You hung up a yellow ribbon.'

'The flat above the café is vacant,' Suzanne said. 'It's for sale.'

An unpleasant sensation spread through his body, as though something cold had crept under the quilt. 'What are you getting at?'

'It would be practical,' she said.

It felt as if Suzanne had raised the stakes, like a poker player who had thrown a high-value card on the table, but what they had together was no game. 'You're talking about moving out?'

'I'm down there all the time anyway. And you're at work most of the time. We have the same address, but we don't really live together.'

It's not fair, he thought. That she should come out with that now.

He had always considered himself independent, but after Ingrid died he had felt an increasingly powerful anxiety for the people he loved, terrified to lose them. It would be linked to his work. Too many times he had witnessed meaningless loss.

He had not only bound himself to Suzanne as a person, he had also become dependent on her as a life partner. Perspiration lay like a cold cloth on his skin. He tried to say something, but the words stuck in his throat. Instead he ran his hand over her black, wiry hair, struggling to control his breathing. 'I don't need any ribbons outside the door. I need to act. That's my way of handling things.'

'I wish I could demand less of you,' she said, 'but we are the way we are, both of us.'

They lay without speaking, and eventually fell asleep. Suzanne's face turned to the wall, Wisting on his back.

54

The first grey light of day had barely filtered into the room when Wisting woke. Suzanne was still asleep by his side, even more beautiful with her eyelashes resting on her cheeks. There was something peaceful about her, a gentleness that was easier to discern when she was asleep.

A muscle twitched under her eye, and her mouth formed a faint smile. He pushed the quilt carefully aside and stood up. A rich coffee aroma rose to greet him on his way down the stairs.

Line turned towards him when he entered the room. 'Have you cleaned it?' she asked.

He pulled his dressing gown together as he shook his head.

'You got it for Christmas,' Line said. 'You ought to clean it a couple of times a year.'

He smiled at her and sat down with his coffee as she poured a cup for herself. He had cleared away the documents and carried the box back to his car before going to bed.

A bank of clouds had drifted in from the sea, reaching Stavern overnight.

Line opened the fridge. 'You don't have much in here.'

Wisting nodded at one of the cupboards. 'There's probably crispbread or something.'

She checked the shelves and found half a loaf, took out two slices and placed them in the toaster. 'Are you ready to meet him again?'

'Hmm?'

'Rudolf Haglund. Are you ready to face him?'

'I think so.'

'We're ready as well.'

'You're going to follow him?'

She opened the fridge again and took out butter and a jar of strawberry jam. 'It's worth a try.'

'How many of you are there?'

'Four cars.'

'From the newspaper?'

Wisting noticed a tiny twitch at the corner of her left eye. 'Two of them,' she answered, turning towards the toaster.

'Who's the fourth?' The toast slices popped up, and Line transferred them to two plates before inserting two more slices. 'Is Tommy coming with you?'

'Yes.'

Wisting had been thankful when the relationship between his daughter and the Dane, a former convict, ended. He was not comfortable with Tommy Kvanter still being part of her life, but did not want to say anything.

'Where did you go last night? You came home after Suzanne and me.'

If Line were to assist him, she would have to know. 'I read through the documents in the Ellen case.'

'The niece of the policeman with glasses? I thought you didn't have access to the station?'

'Jonas Ravneberg was interviewed in connection with that case,' Wisting said.

'Why was that?'

'He appeared on one of the lists. The day Ellen disappeared, a red Saab 900 was spotted in the vicinity. Jonas Ravneberg had that kind of car.'

'It's still up on his farm, which means he was there when she disappeared.'

Wisting shook his head. 'He was in Sweden.'

'How do we know that?'

'The woman he was living with confirmed it.'

A sceptical expression crossed Line's face. 'Do you know her name?'

'Maud Torell.'

Line repeated the name as though savouring it. 'We ought to talk to her.' The slices popped out of the toaster. She left them and went into the hallway, returning with her laptop. 'She was the one he was living with before he moved to Fredrikstad. Do you know where she lives now?'

Wisting shook his head as she tapped the name into the machine. 'Maud Torell?' she said. 'Unusual, but I can't find it.'

'It's not certain that she's still alive. Or she could be married and have changed her name.'

'He hasn't let many people into his life. She's the person who was closest to him. She might have received the letter.'

'The letter?'

Line explained how Jonas Ravneberg had been observed with his dog beside a post box shortly before he was killed. 'It's a shot in the dark, but it might be worth something.'

Wisting crossed to the worktop to fetch himself another slice of toast.

'When are you setting off?' she asked.

He glanced at the clock. 'In an hour.'

55

The office belonging to law firm Henden, Haller and Brenner was situated in an anonymous office block in the city centre, immediately behind Stortorvet square. There was no flamboyant sign on the door, only a doorbell beside the company nameplate. A woman answered when Wisting rang. He gave his name and the door opened with a buzz.

The office was on the third floor. Inside, the office environment contrasted sharply with the shabby common areas outside: dark parquet flooring, abstract oil paintings, and a blonde secretary at reception.

'Mr Wisting?' He nodded. 'I'll announce your arrival. You can take a seat until Mr. Henden is ready.'

She accompanied him to an open recess in the corridor where two black leather sofas were separated by a smoked glass coffee table. A broad-shouldered, bearded man wearing a leather jacket was seated on one and a stout Pakistani on the other. Wisting sat beside the man in the leather jacket.

'Would you like anything?' she asked. 'Coffee? Water?'

'No, thanks.'

Wisting had begun to regret agreeing to this meeting, at least to this meeting place. He should have asked for a neutral location. His mobile phone emitted a peep, a text from Line: *Let me know as soon as the meeting is over. We need to know what sort of clothes he's wearing.*

Wisting replied *OK*.

At five minutes past twelve, a woman in a black suit appeared. 'Ali Mounzir?'

The overweight Pakistani got to his feet and followed her. Ten minutes later the secretary who had welcomed Wisting arrived. 'Sorry for keeping you waiting. Mr. Henden can see you now.'

He followed her along a corridor until she came to a halt at a frosted glass door. The light in the conference room was dim. There was a thick carpet on the floor and the walls were decorated with works of art. Fruit and carafes of water were laid on a counter along one wall. At the end of the long conference table, Rudolf Haglund sat with his arms folded. He stared at Wisting with his eyes narrowed and a smile on his lips.

Henden rose from a seat beside him and approached Wisting to shake his hand.

Rudolf Haglund got to his feet. He was shorter than Wisting remembered, but just as pale. Haglund held out his hand. Wisting took it, and they nodded briefly to each other before sitting round the table.

'Rudolf Haglund is very pleased you agreed to attend this meeting,' the lawyer said.

Rudolf Haglund nodded.

'As you know, I had no dealings with the original case and only know it from the documents, but Haglund has told me that he never found any fault with how you treated him. He considered you to be honest and upright, and I have already told you he does not believe you were the one who switched the DNA evidence.'

Rudolf Haglund nodded again.

'Nevertheless, a major injustice has been done. My office is engaged in correcting that but, as far as Haglund is concerned, this is not only about justice in his own case. He also wants the corrupt police officer who planted the false evidence to be held responsible.'

Wisting remained silent. The press had launched a

broadside against him with information supplied by Henden. If they believed another officer had been behind any switch, there must have been another reason for them letting him take the blow. Rudolf Haglund had spent years thinking about his case and Henden, the lawyer, was an excellent tactician. They must have cooked something up, and he was not happy to be part of it.

'I assume we have a shared interest in exposing the perpetrator?' Henden had been leaning over the table, and now reclined in his chair.

'Who is it?' Wisting asked.

The lawyer flung out his hand and invited his client to speak. Haglund's tiny eyes narrowed. 'I wasn't thinking of telling you that,' he said.

Wisting sat motionless.

The lawyer could not restrain an exclamation. 'But, this meeting ...' he almost stammered.

'You'll get to know who it was, but I won't tell you. I'll simply let you know how you can find out. The first days after my arrest have seared themselves onto my memory. The interviews with you and the hours in the cell. For seventeen years, I've known something went wrong, but only when Sigurd had the cigarette butts analysed again did I realise what I had been subjected to.'

A nerve twitched at the corner of the defence lawyer's mouth. He was not comfortable with his client's use of his first name.

'I've gone over everything that happened hour by hour.' He closed his eyes as if to illustrate. 'I discovered who planted the evidence against me and know exactly how it was done.'

Wisting moved slightly to signal interest.

'I lost all conception of time without a watch and without daylight, but it must have been late in the evening. They had taken out a guy from the next cell who had been shouting and screaming since he arrived, and I was the only one left. I was almost asleep when the door into the section opened. I thought it was the custody officer, but it wasn't.'

After several deaths in the cells they had introduced manual inspection of the prisoners every thirty minutes.

'The cell door opened. The man who stood there put something on the floor. He took out a pack of tobacco and rolled a cigarette. A packet of Petterøe's Blue number 3.'

'The same brand that produced the DNA result,' the lawyer said.

'When he finished, he handed me the packet and invited me to roll myself a smoke. I accepted. He gave me a light, and we stood there nattering. A strange conversation, as I recall, about nothing in particular, but I thought it was quite pleasant. Having a fag with someone who wasn't preoccupied by the case and just wanted to kill a few minutes. Then I heard the door at the end of the corridor again.

'It was the custody officer this time, and pay close attention now: the policeman picked up an ashtray and held it out in front of me and I stubbed out the little I had left of my cigarette.'

'The custody officer can confirm this,' said the lawyer.

'I doubt whether anyone would remember that,' Wisting said.

'I think he'll remember it but, strictly speaking, it's not necessary,' said Haglund.

'What do you mean?' the lawyer asked.

'On the wall outside each cell door there are forms hanging up. The custody officers had to sign every half hour when they came down to check on us.'

That had been the instruction before the routine supervision of cells had been transferred to computers.

'On the same forms, a note was made when we went for

223

interview, when we went for fresh air, to have a shower, were served food or had a smoke.'

'This was seventeen years ago,' the lawyer said.

'The custody officer was obviously surprised that any other officer on duty was down in the basement, and through the opening in the door I heard him asking the other guy to sign the form.'

Wisting leaned forward. It was quite normal for the person who had given the prisoner a cigarette to sign for that as well.

'Do these protocols still exist today?' Haglund asked.

The forms were placed in folders when the prisoner was freed or transferred to jail. The folders were retained. They had experienced complaints about treatment in security cells, sometimes years after the case was ended and sentence passed. They would be somewhere in the historical archives in the basement at the police station. This was the document that could clear Wisting's name.

56

The text message from her father arrived at quarter to one. *Short, dark hair. Pale complexion. Blue shirt with grey V-neck sweater. Dark blue jeans. Brown boots. Unknown type of outdoor jacket.*

Thirty seconds later Wisting appeared through the door. He knew they were near and must have recognised Line's car parked farther along the street. Turning up his jacket lapels, he put his hands in his pockets and walked in the opposite direction with head bowed.

Line forwarded the text to Tommy and her two colleagues from the newspaper before opening the conference call facility. She said their names one by one and the others gave their positions. Only she could see the lawyer's office. Morten P thought there was a back door and was covering that. Tommy and Harald from *VG* were covering the intersecting streets. Wisting had the conference number and access code, and she had shown him how it worked. He could connect directly if he wished.

For conference purposes she used a phone borrowed from the *VG* offices, and wondered whether she should call him on her mobile to find how the meeting had gone. Instead, she applied herself to the task in hand. Line had been on surveillance operations before, and knew how much concentration they demanded.

Ten minutes later Rudolf Haglund appeared at the door, dressed as her father had described, as well as a black leather jacket. 'He's coming out,' she said, describing the jacket.

'Okay,' Morten P acknowledged.

Haglund took a packet of cigarettes from his inside pocket, his eyes darting up and down the street. He tapped one a couple of times on the lid and placed it in his mouth. He used a lighter from his back pocket and lingeringly exhaled, checked the time and set out.

'Møllergata direction,' Line said. 'I'll follow on foot.'

Connecting the phone to earplugs, she stepped out of the car. There was rain in the air; she could pull the hood of her windcheater up without drawing attention. Rudolf Haglund crossed the street ten metres ahead. He did not turn round.

'He's heading towards Karl Johans gate,' she said softly.

'I'm on foot as well,' Harald said. 'Walking parallel along Torggata.'

Her other phone rang in her pocket. When she saw it was a call from the *VG* building she switched off and put it back.

Rudolf Haglund walked past the restaurant of the *Stortorvets Gjestgiveri*, crossed the street at Grensen, and continued eastwards. Line passed on this information in short keywords so the others could position themselves. When he arrived at Karl Johans gate, he took a right turn.

'Up Karl Johans gate,' she said.

'I'll catch him at Egertorget,' said Tommy.

Haglund was thirty metres in front of Line. He stopped outside The Scotsman pub, stubbing out his cigarette in an ashtray on an outdoor table before entering.

'Into The Scotsman,' Line reported, positioning herself at a clothes shop on the opposite side of the street.

'I'm coming from the bottom of the street,' said Harald. 'I'll wait at the 7-Eleven shop in case he comes this way later.'

'Get a hotdog?' Morten P asked.

'Affirmative.'

Line stood at a table with stacks of college sweaters on

special offer. A young assistant who was folding T-shirts at a nearby table smiled. The music playing was so loud she had to push the earplugs further into her ears.

'Where are you, Morten?'

'Parked illegally in Stortorvet.'

Her other mobile phone rang again, from the same number. She tugged out an earplug and answered. It was one of the researchers from the fact-checking department but the music drowned out everything else.

She emerged onto Karl Johans gate just as Rudolf Haglund came out of the pub and sat at one of the tables under a patio heater. He had brought a coffee and a newspaper with him. Line turned her back and watched his reflection in the shop window.

'He's bought a coffee,' she said. The mannequin in the window wore a casual shirt that would have suited Tommy.

'What did you say?' asked the woman at the newspaper office.

'Sorry,' Line said, covering the conference microphone with her hand, 'what was that?'

'You wanted the address history for Minnehallveien 28 in Stavern.'

Line fished her notepad from her shoulder bag.

'Jonas Ravneberg lived there with Maud Torell. She is actually Swedish, but moved to Norway at the end of the eighties. Ten years ago, she moved back. She has changed her name to Svedberg and now lives in Ystad, at the very south.'

'Maud Svedberg?'

'I called because I understand this is important. You can have the address and phone number right away, or I can send them by email.'

'Send me an email, please.'

Behind her, Haglund finished his coffee and pushed the cup across the table to make room for the newspaper.

A couple of years earlier, Line had tackled a series of interviews in which she had profiled murderers whose prison sentences amounted to a total of one hundred years. The subject was: what jail had done to them and how it had affected their lives subsequently. In the main, she had encountered broken individuals who, after a long spell in prison, had nothing to offer society but fresh problems.

Haglund leafed his way to another page without reading. He was really watching people in the busy pedestrian thoroughfare. Occasionally he fixed his gaze on a particular person and watched until they were lost in the crowd.

'What's he doing?' Morten P asked.

'He's just sitting watching people,' Line said but, at that moment, it dawned on her he was not simply looking. He was selecting individuals and studying them in detail. All of them young women.

57

The wind had picked up and rain clouds hung low in the sky. Wisting found a coffee bar beside the courthouse with almost an hour to kill before his meeting at the Bureau for the Investigation of Police Affairs. He bought a bread roll and a cup of the 'coffee of the day'. This was an expression he had not come across before, but this coffee was said to be from Burundi and taste of honey, lemon and nuts.

He located a corner table inside the room, where he could sit with his back to the other customers. His thoughts were in a whirl, and he felt as giddy as if he was on a slow carousel. He thought he understood Rudolf Haglund's media strategy. He was being driven to find the evidence that would not only clear himself, but also overturn Haglund's conviction.

Very likely the old folder of signed forms from the remand cells was still stored somewhere. Bjørg Karin Joakimsen had worked at the criminal proceedings office for almost forty years, and was responsible for the archives. She was the kind of person who seldom or never threw things away. It struck him that his coffee didn't taste of anything other than coffee. Slightly weaker than he was used to, but with no hint of lemon or nuts.

He had probably been sitting in the vicinity of the document when he logged onto the police computer the previous night, but paying the police station another secret visit did not seem like a good idea. No problem finding items filed in modern times, but documents stashed away in the course of the past twenty-five years simply because they 'might come in handy', were another story. Only Bjørg Karin was likely to know where they were.

He tapped in her office number and she answered in a professional and obliging manner. Most enquiries were from people who wanted to make some kind of complaint. As a rule, they were passed to her so she could ascertain the right person to help. Most often it was not even necessary to transfer the call, as she would deal with it herself.

'So good to hear your voice,' she said, and bombarded Wisting with questions about his suspension.

'I think I can find a way through all this,' Wisting said, 'but I need some help.' He explained what he was looking for.

'Those folders are stored in the historical archive,' Bjørg Karin said. 'I know I haven't thrown them away.'

58

They followed Rudolf Haglund to a restaurant in Rådhus-gata, overlooking Akershus Fortress. A chilly, raw wind blew in from the fjord and, when the first raindrops fell, Line sought shelter under the eaves of a department store.

'How long has he been there?' Morten P asked in her ear.

'Nearly ten minutes.'

'One of us should go in. Maybe he's arranged a meeting or something.'

'I'll do it,' Harald said. 'I need a piss anyway.' Harald disappeared through the restaurant door. The rain was pouring down now, and strong gusts of wind were blasting sheets of rain diagonally across the streets. Two minutes later, he re-emerged. 'He's sitting with Hulkvist.'

'Gjermund Hulkvist?' Morten P asked. 'That should've been our call. He owes us that. He said he wasn't interested in giving an interview.'

Gjermund Hulkvist, an experienced crime reporter on *Dagbladet*, had covered the country's major crime stories for years and was known for his wide network of sources.

'Now they're eating lunch,' Harald said.

'That gives us some time,' Line said. 'I'll go and pick up my car.'

The rain had soaked her through. She started the engine and switched on the heater to clear the windscreen while she wriggled out of her jacket and sweater. She changed into dry clothes from the bag on the rear seat before setting off to find a vacant parking space in a side street. This allowed for several options, depending on which route Rudolf Haglund chose when the interview was over.

She decided to call the police officer who had interviewed her in Fredrikstad to ask if there were any developments in the murder enquiry, but first she would try the unregistered number again.

She detached the microphone and keyed in the number. To her astonishment, a young girl said hello immediately. Someone was laughing in the background. She checked she had called the right number as she introduced herself, 'Who am I speaking to?'

'Who are you calling?'

'I don't really know. I'm responding to an unanswered call.'

'You've reached a phone box,' the girl said.

'Whereabouts?'

'Outside the railway station in Fredrikstad.'

That was logical, Line thought. The person behind the murder had called from a phone box. It also explained why no one had answered. 'Is there a camera there?'

'Camera?'

'CCTV, at the railway station?'

The girl hung up.

Line wiped a streak in the condensation on the windscreen with the back of her hand. The rain had chased everyone off the street. She reviewed the course of events in advance of Jonas Ravneberg's murder. At 14.17, he had received a phone call that had caused him to contact a lawyer's office and arrange a meeting. Seven hours later he was dead. There must be a connection. She still had no idea who had phoned, but the conversation had originated from a public phone box.

She called Erik Fjeld who answered at once. His voice sounded hollow; he too was sitting in a car. 'I need a photograph,' she said.

232

'Are you still on the story?'

'I'm just pulling together some loose threads.' She explained about the phone box outside the railway station. 'Could you take a photo of it?'

'I'm half an hour away.'

'Excellent. I need to know whether there is any CCTV.'

Erik Fjeld hesitated before replying. 'Okay,' he said, and she thought she could hear his car accelerate. He obviously understood the assignment was not just about an empty phone box.

59

The Norwegian Bureau for the Investigation of Police Affairs led an anonymous life in the city centre, situated in the back yard of Kirkegata number 1. The building also housed a company that dealt in telephone sales, several accounting firms and others with no need for advertising placards and window displays.

Two women stood at the vehicle entrance, smoking and sheltering from the rain. Wisting felt their eyes boring into the back of his skull as he walked towards the door. He studied the list on the entry system and rang the button marked with the bureau's title, gave his name and said he had an appointment at two o'clock.

The door opened with a buzz. 'First floor.'

He glanced over his shoulder. On the other side of the courtyard, a man stood with his camera raised. Another hung from his shoulder, and raindrops dripped from the brim of his cap. Reporter, Wisting thought, as he hurried inside. Someone must have tipped him off.

Chief Inspector Terje Nordbo met him at the door and they shook hands. Wisting had searched for his name on the internet without finding any results other than a listing fairly far down the list of competitors in the *Birkebeiner* ski race. The chief inspector opened the door into a spacious room and ushered him inside.

The walls were grey, cold and bare, with only a ticking clock and a narrow window. The desk had a computer monitor, keyboard and mouse, in addition to a pile of blank sheets of paper, a ballpoint pen and a small digital recording device; the same type his investigators used.

Terje Nordbo hung his jacket on the back of his chair before sitting. He drew the keyboard closer and rolled up his sleeves. Wisting felt strange to be across the desk from a police investigator. Slim and with cropped hair, Nordbo wore rimless glasses and a tightly knotted tie, and was probably ten years younger than Wisting.

Wisting must have several thousand hours more experience, but nevertheless felt subordinate. An internal enquiry was always unpleasant. Everything the investigators discovered would be relayed and further scrutinised by the best criminal lawyers in the country, and people who sat behind massive desks on top floors would always find something to criticise if they wanted to.

'I'm going to record our interview,' Terje Nordbo said, starting the recorder. 'Later I'll draft a resumé that you'll be given to read through and accept.'

Now I'm on the other side, Wisting thought, where many men and women had been before, where he had placed hundreds, thousands of suspects. Before the law, they were innocent until the opposite had been proven. As far as the investigators were concerned though, it was the opposite. The starting point for them was that the person in the chair was guilty. To solve a case, it was crucial to believe that, to have a firm belief that the person facing you had done what he was charged with. That was how Wisting had felt when he interviewed Rudolf Haglund seventeen years before. In the interview room he had told himself that he was now sitting beside Cecilia's killer. It was like a sports contest. If you did not believe, and believe that the game was worth winning, you lost.

'You are charged with breaking paragraphs 168 and 169, second sub-section, of the Criminal Code.'

Wisting was unprepared. He had spent days going through the Cecilia case, meaning to find who had planted the evidence, but had spent most of that time searching for an alternative killer. He was too ill prepared to face the charges against himself.

He grasped the edge of the table and felt the rough metal border. Breach of the Criminal Code paragraph 168 was as he had expected: false accusations. Usually cited against those who gave false reports, it was also applied to those who obtained false evidence. He did not know paragraph 169.

'Paragraph 169 sets a minimum punishment of one year's imprisonment,' the investigator said, as though he could read Wisting's mind. 'When an innocent party has served more than five years, the guilty person can be sentenced to a maximum term of twenty-one years. This becomes time-barred after twenty-five years.'

Suddenly the case became far more serious, the consequences more wide-ranging than he had appreciated. If he did not succeed in clearing his name he would do time.

'The background has emerged with the application made by Henden, the lawyer, to reopen the case against Rudolf Haglund,' the investigator continued. 'As the accused, you are not compelled to give a statement and, of course, you have the right to defence counsel at any stage.'

Rainwater poured down the windowpane in even, fast-flowing streams and the air in the room already felt clammy.

'Have you understood the charges and your rights?'

Wisting nodded.

'You have to answer out loud.'

'Yes.'

60

The dashboard clock showed 14.37. Rudolf Haglund had spent almost an hour in the company of the *Dagbladet* journalist. The rain grew heavier, and water cascaded along the pavement gutters.

Line had the red ring binder from the Cecilia case on her lap in the car. It was marked *Suspect* and contained the statements given by Rudolf Haglund and all their other information on him. She would use it to familiarise herself with him and as a reference book depending upon who he visited and what he got up to.

No DNA, fingerprints or other traces of Cecilia had been found at Haglund's home. Forensics had come to the conclusion that she had never been inside. The house was typical of the seventies: large living room, kitchen, bathroom, toilet, utility room, two storerooms and three bedrooms. A number of photographs had been taken in the course of the search. Each room pictured from a variety of angles, followed by close-ups of the pornographic magazines discovered in a suitcase in one of the storerooms. Every single magazine was photographed. The intention of the folder had obviously been to illustrate Haglund's sexual preferences and support a sexual motive.

She flicked back to the living room: drab hessian wallpaper on the walls, brown cord carpet on the floor, blue velvet settee and two matching armchairs, glass-topped coffee table, television set and video player on a wheeled console.

Evidence of a sad and lonely life, Line thought. About to close the folder, she was halted by something apparently insignificant. Three shelves were built on the wall behind the television and on each shelf was a line of model cars.

She switched on the interior light. Yes, it was a collection of model cars.

She had not read anywhere that Rudolf Haglund collected model cars. The closest she had come was the witness statement that Haglund had arranged contact between Jonas Ravneberg and one of the employees in the furniture shop who had inherited a box of model cars. Neither Haglund nor Ravneberg was easy to know. Perhaps this was how they had met in the first place, through a shared interest.

She checked the email on her phone and downloaded a message from the fact-checking department. Maud Svedberg lived in Lilla Norregatan in Ystad. She had adopted the name Svedberg when she married twelve years previously, but was listed as separated with no children. If she did not follow the news in the Norwegian press she might not know her former partner had been murdered. If so, Line would have to break the news. She felt she was riding two horses saddled together, Jonas Ravneberg and Rudolf Haglund.

She tapped in the number and was answered by a husky female voice. 'I'm working on a murder case and believe you knew the victim,' she said.

'A murder case?'

'A murder report. The murder victim was called Jonas Ravneberg, and I think you knew him.'

'Jonas?'

'You lived together in Norway seventeen years ago?'

'Is he dead?'

238

Line described what had happened. 'You lived together, didn't you?'

'That was years ago.' Maud Svedberg spoke so softly that Line had to concentrate to hear properly. 'I'm living a different life now. I moved back to Sweden and got married.'

'When did your relationship come to an end?'

'It was so many years ago.'

'He moved to Fredrikstad,' Line said. 'Was there any particular reason?'

'He had problems with his nerves. You work for a newspaper?'

'*Verdens Gang*,' Line confirmed. 'I'm keen to find out who he was.'

'I don't want you to write about us.'

'I don't need to. I just want to speak to someone who knew him well. It doesn't seem as though many did.'

'That was what our problem was. He kept more and more to himself. He didn't share his thoughts, or anything else, with me. Eventually there was no need to share a house either, and he moved away.'

'Have you heard anything from him?'

'I had my fiftieth birthday last summer. I am … was … two years older than him. He didn't write much but he sent me a letter. Didn't say anything about himself, just a few lines about the time we spent together.'

'Have you received anything in the post during the past few days?'

'No. He wrote his address on the back of the envelope, and I sent him a postcard from Spain when I was there in September. I thanked him for his letter and wished him well in life.'

'Can you think of any reason for anyone to kill him?'

Maud Svedberg did not have time to respond.

'*Movement*,' Morten P announced on the other line. '*Haglund coming out. Walking towards Akersgata.*'

'I've got another phone call,' Line said. 'Can I phone you back later?'

Maud Svedberg's voice was almost inaudible as she thanked Line for calling.

61

Wisting gave his statement for over an hour, without a break, as objectively as possible. He named everyone who worked on the Cecilia case and explained how responsibility was divided. Terje Nordbo listened patiently, but without making many specific notes. He would already have read through the records, and Wisting's summary would be familiar.

Regarded objectively, Wisting's handling of the case had been flawless. Starting with a report about a missing girl, he had steered it through numerous witness statements to a discovery site and an arrest. When he finished, Nordbo homed in on his evaluations, reflections and feelings about the case. He discussed the interpretation of theories, procedures and instructions and, suddenly, it felt as if nothing was straightforward any longer.

'Why were you selected to lead the investigation?'

'I was assigned by the chief superintendent, so that question really ought to be asked of him.'

'We'll do that, but have you given it any thought?'

Wisting was used to accepting the responsibility allocated to him without question. 'I was there, and I had the qualifications.'

'Didn't it bother you?'

Wisting shook his head. Nordbo pointed to the recorder. Nodding and shaking of the head were not good enough. 'Had you been in charge of such a major investigation before?' he asked.

'The Cecilia case grew into the most serious case I had ever led,' Wisting said, 'but when I was called in she was still only a missing person.'

'Only?'

'From the beginning it was obvious that Cecilia Linde had not vanished of her own accord. Most likely she had met with some kind of accident; parts of her route were hilly and bordered the sea. Just the same, I allowed for a worst case scenario.'

'Worst case scenario?'

'That she might have been the victim of criminal activity.'

'What guidelines did your superior officers give you?'

'Guidelines? I'm not sure I understand the question.'

'Did they tell you they were satisfied with the job you were doing?'

'I didn't get the impression of anything otherwise. There was continual questioning about allocation of resources, of course, but there was never any criticism of the work.'

'What were their expectations?'

It was not usual for the chief constable to tell him what his expectations were. They had the same goal: to solve the crime and bring the criminal to justice. 'Results. Naturally, they expected results.'

'How did that become obvious during the investigation?'

'I don't understand the question.'

'Did someone in particular become impatient when results did not appear?'

'Everybody was impatient,' Wisting said, 'but most of us were used to that. We're experienced and knew it could take time to build a case.'

'What about the media?'

'What about them?'

'Weren't they impatient?'

'As ever, they made demands about making a break-through and posed questions about progress.'

242

'What was your reaction to that?'

'Two reactions. Firstly, answering questions all the time inhibits progress. Secondly, media interest provokes tip-offs and information from the public.'

'Was it stressful?'

'Of course, but handling the media is part of our job.'

'I imagine the public clamour became enormous.'

'Was that a question?'

'Let me word it differently. How did it affect the investigation when you had nothing new to say?'

'My responsibility was to lead the tactical investigation and I concentrated on that. The police prosecutor at that time, Audun Vetti, dealt with the press.'

'You attended the press conferences?'

'Yes.'

'How did it feel to sit through them without fresh information?'

'It wasn't like that. The case made progress. There were daily developments, if no real breakthrough.'

Wisting studied the investigator across the desk as he leafed through his papers. Nordbo had homed in on something that was not only central to the case, but that had produced catastrophic consequences. While they were searching for Cecilia Linde, it had emerged that the police were in possession of the cassette. The day Audun Vetti confirmed this to the media, her body was dumped in a ditch.

If there was anything he could be criticised for it was that he had not succeeded in keeping the information about the cassette and the massive search quiet. The perpetrator had no choice but to get rid of her when it became common knowledge. Wisting avoided the subject.

'How did this lack of a breakthrough affect you personally?'

'That wasn't something I thought about or focused on.'

'Did it weigh you down?'

'That's quite an accurate description.'

'How did your family respond to the case?'

'I didn't say much to them.'

The investigator riffled through his notes. 'You have a pair of twins? Line and Thomas. How old were they at the time?'

'Just turned twelve.'

'Were they aware of what was going on?'

'Ingrid, my wife, spoke to them about it. I was seldom home before their bedtime.'

Eyes cast down, Wisting remembered how he had unloaded his thoughts on Ingrid and gone to bed with his head as clear as possible.

'Was it something you missed?'

'What?'

'The time away from your family. Did you miss them?'

'Of course.'

'How was your marriage?'

Wisting stared through the window. The rain washed over it, distorting the world outside. He understood that Terje Nordbo was shaping a motive, viewing Wisting's responsibility as an insupportable burden, trying to substantiate Internal Affairs' theory that he had planted false evidence to escape the pressures. 'I don't think my marriage is relevant to the case,' he said.

'I think it is.'

Their silence filled the room.

Terje Nordbo reclined in his high-backed chair and waited. Wisting had done the same many times. It was often effective; sitting in silence could become so oppressive that the suspect just opened his mouth and kept going. He looked at the window again, and a tiny rivulet of water as it ran down the glass. The contrived pause made him realise how much the interview was stressing him, that Nordbo was determined to provoke an emotional reaction or slip of the tongue.

Perhaps it was his own fault, he thought. Maybe he had unwittingly let it happen because of the lack of a break-through. Perhaps his ineffectiveness had forced someone else to take matters into his own hands.

Terje Nordbo broke the silence. 'How many interviews did you conduct with Rudolf Haglund?'

Wisting knew the answer, but understood where the investigator was going. He had persuaded Wisting to describe a case that had become almost stuck and that had weighed him down as leader of the investigation. This provided motive; now he wanted to know whether Wisting had also had the opportunity.

'Six.'

'Why did you interview him personally? Did you consider delegating?'

Wisting's mobile phone rang. Nordbo was obviously annoyed, but adopted an indulgent manner. It was Bjørg Karin from the criminal proceedings office. 'I need to take this,' he said, already on his way out.

62

Rudolf Haglund left the restaurant in Rådhusgata at 15.43 hours. He strolled into Tollbugata and down to Børsen, the Oslo Stock Exchange, past another block and into a multi-storey car park. Soon afterwards he drove out in a silver Passat. Unknown to him, he was now in the middle of an invisible net.

En route southwards along the E18 highway, with Morten P five car lengths ahead. The other three were behind, but constantly changing position so their headlights alternated in his rear view mirror.

Haglund drove at or just above the speed limit, tyres hissing on the wet asphalt. Line was first of those behind. At Liertoppen, he suddenly reduced speed and other traffic overtook. Line warned the others that she was about to go past him and they fell further back. She drove past with her gaze fixed on the road ahead. Having overtaken, she cast a glance in the mirror, through condensation and rain on her rear window, to note the position of his headlamps.

Staying in the left lane she passed Morten P. Now there were two cars in front and two behind, leaving them vulnerable if he took an exit lane.

'He's speeding up again,' Tommy said.

'I'll fall back,' Morten P replied.

In the mirror, Line watched the others manoeuvre.

'Here he comes,' Morten P said. 'I'll position myself at the rear.'

Haglund continued in a southerly direction. The motorway

bridge above the town of Drammen was congested with cars. In the heavy rain, they appeared as lights floating into the distance.

At the industrial area of Kobbervikdalen, Line's other mobile phone rang. She had to put it to her ear since the open line shared with the others monopolised her hands-free kit. It was Erik Fjeld.

'It took a bit longer than I said, but I have a picture of that phone box of yours.'

'That's great,' Line said. She had dropped her speed to take the call and saw in her rear view mirror that Haglund was edging out. 'Hold on!'

She asked for someone else to take over at the front as the silver car went past, followed by Tommy, herself becoming the security car at the back and muted the hands-free device so that she could hear what the others were saying but they could not hear her. Haglund's vehicle disappeared from her sight.

'What about the CCTV surveillance?' she asked, shifting the phone to her other ear.

'They've been bothered by a lot of vandalism, so they installed a CCTV system before the summer.'

'Do they still have the recording?'

'That was why it took so long. The police were there yesterday. It had been handed to them.'

Line gave an exclamation of annoyance, even though it was, in a way, reassuring that the police in Fredrikstad had beaten her to it.

'It's digital,' Erik Fjeld explained. 'They were only given a copy. The actual recording is still here at the railway station.'

A gust of wind caught the car, and she gripped the steering wheel with both hands. A sheet of rain swept across the road. 'Can you get us a copy?'

'The staff here wouldn't do that, since the police are already involved, but I was allowed to watch the recording.'

'And?'

'I was left on my own and managed to take a few photographs of the screen. I can send them to you, but they're not very helpful. The telephone kiosk is at the edge. All that can be seen is a man dressed in dark clothes with his back turned.'

'Does he appear in any other camera angles?'

'No, only in the one image.'

'Can you see if he arrives in a car?'

'All that can be seen is a dark shadow.'

'Okay, then. All the same, that's good work. Send me what you have. I'll find out what the police have discovered.'

As they approached the toll station on the E18 near Sande, Harald reported that Haglund was driving to the manual payment booth. Line slowed to avoid getting ahead of him when she drove through the subscription payment lane.

When she was through the toll station she called the police in Fredrikstad. She considered making a call to the news editor first, to be sure no one else was working on the story, but dropped the idea. The murder case no longer featured in the headlines and would not appear again until an arrest or some other major development happened. She was put through to the police prosecutor who had attended the press conference.

'You picked up a video from the railway station,' she said, careful not to reveal how much she knew.

'Routine,' the policeman answered tersely, obviously tired of journalists.

Line changed direction: 'Have you identified the man who phoned Jonas Ravneberg from that location?'

Silence: the information that the police had collected the video recording could have been obtained from an employee at the railway station who had tipped off the newspaper, but telephone data was more difficult. The most likely explanation for the policeman was that another officer had leaked it.

'We can put an appeal in the newspaper,' Line offered, in an effort to coax more details from him.

'I'll have to come back to you on that one,' he said.

'Does that mean you know who made the call?'

'I can't comment on that.'

Line moved the phone to her other ear. 'You can see a connection?'

'Can I come back to you?'

'*He's turning off from the motorway at Kopstadkrysset,*' Harald said.

'What did you say?' the policeman asked.

'Can I call you back?' Line broke off and switched on the multi-user connection.

'*I'm overtaking,*' Tommy reported. '*Taking the next exit.*'

'Who's following him?' she asked.

'I'm the first car,' Harald replied, 'but too close. I'll have to lose him at the next exit.'

'I'm behind,' Morten P said. 'I'll take over.'

Line moved her car into the exit lane and glanced at the red ring binder on the passenger seat. They were now in Horten. She could not recall reading anything about Rudolf Haglund having any connection with the little rural community. It was still almost an hour's drive from Larvik and his home.

'He's driving inland,' Harald said. 'I'm letting go.'

'Got him!' Morten P said, but then broke off: 'No! He's pulling into a bus stop. I'm driving past. Hold back, Line!'

It was too late. Line had already turned off and was on the secondary road. She spotted the silver Passat several hundred metres ahead on a straight stretch. As there was nowhere she could turn, she was forced to overtake. She accelerated to make sure she passed at the maximum possible speed, so that Haglund would not notice what she was driving.

Morten P took command, ordering Harald to keep his head down beside the E18, but to be ready in case Haglund turned and drove back. Line was directed into the nearest side road to take up an observation post.

Tommy took the first exit from the E18 to return towards them, continuing for another couple of kilometres to the front position.

They loitered for almost quarter of an hour until the silver Passat drove past the side road where Line was positioned. 'He's on his way,' she said, and set off. The others all acknowledged.

Haglund drove inland. There was little traffic, making him difficult to follow. He maintained a normal speed, and Line was able to remain as lead car for several kilometres. The landscape was monotonous, with huge, flat fields, and buildings became increasingly sparse, only a few solitary farms. They drove past a small lake before the road began to climb. When it flattened again, Haglund braked in the middle of the open countryside and turned onto a gravel track.

'He's turning off,' Line said, passing the side road and pulling over.

'What do we do now?' Harald asked.

Line thought quickly. If they followed him along the narrow gravel track they risked discovery. On the other hand, what was the point? Seventeen years earlier, the concluding stages of the investigation had failed to find Cecilia Linde. They were now located within an hour's radius of where she had been abducted.

'I'm going to follow him,' Line said, reversing. 'The rest of you stay where you are and keep the line open.'

The others stopped talking. The gravel crunched underneath her tyres as Line turned onto the narrow track.

'Be careful,' Tommy implored.

63

Wisting took his phone and closed the door. 'Did you find them?' he asked, picking his way down the corridor.

'I think so,' Bjørg Karin said. 'They were in a box with old copies of the Police Times. What do you want me to do with them?'

Wisting checked his watch. It was too late to ask Bjørg Karin to look through them and he would not ask anyone else. 'I'm in Oslo, but I'll be back tonight. Would it be possible for you to take them home?'

Bjørg Karin did not give an immediate response and Wisting realised he was asking a great deal. 'It's really important to me,' he added.

'If it can be of any help to you, then ...'

'Would it be okay if I come to your house for a look?'

'I'm not doing anything else this evening. When will you arrive?'

'Some time after seven.'

'Is there anything else I can do for you?'

Wisting had a number of loose threads that were only a few keystrokes away, but he was removed from both office and computer. 'Are you sitting in front of a computer?'

'Yes.'

'Can you look something up in the Population Register?'

'Just a moment.' He waited while she logged in. 'What have you got?'

'A name: Danny Flom. Apparently he has a son who will turn sixteen next week,' Wisting said. 'Can you confirm that?'

He listened as she worked on the keyboard. 'Yes,' she answered. 'Victor Hansen.'

'Isn't he called Flom?'

'He's taken that as his middle name. Victor Flom Hansen. Wait a minute, and I'll go to the family profile.'

Wisting waited. Terje Nordbo came into the corridor to fetch a jug of water.

'It looks as though he's not the biological father,' Bjørg Karin said. 'He's his wife's son. Danny Flom is listed as the adoptive father with full parental responsibility.' Wisting nodded, satisfied that this was one less complication. 'I'll see you tonight?'

'Yes, and thanks for your help.'

He put the phone back in his pocket and returned to the interview room.

'Does it suit you to continue now?' Nordbo asked tartly, pouring water for them both.

Wisting was not at all sure. Through his line of questioning, Nordbo had revealed that he was being investigated, not simply the case. The Bureau for the Investigation of Police Affairs had already made up its mind, and now it was seeking confirmation.

'You work as head of investigations; where do you think you would have been today, professionally speaking, if you had not succeeded in convicting Rudolf Haglund?'

Wisting took the measure of his adversary. His career progress had never been a driving force. He worked from one case to another, with no ambition other than to solve them. The question had no place in an objective investigation. Terje Nordbo was not interested in solving the case. He would have to do that for himself. It was a waste of time continuing. He stood up.

'What are you doing? We're not finished.'

'Maybe not you, but I am.'

64

An old warning about the danger of forest fires hung from a post, and a rusty road barrier lay in the ditch. Line's headlights shone on cascades of rain that had made the gravel track soggy. Twilight was advancing, but the ruts from Haglund's vehicle were easy to follow. Aware that her whole body was shaking, she switched on the heater, filling the car with the smell of engine oil.

The track climbed past a rocky slope before wheeling to the right with rock face on one side and sheer drop on the other. Patches of white fog appeared in front, but the track soon levelled and the landscape changed. Massive fir trees grew to the edge of the track and heavy branches swept along the side of the car where the track divided. Haglund had gone left.

Line slowed down. A sign gave a reminder about the cost of fishing permits, but said not a word about where the track led. She eased past the junction. Fifty metres further on she could make out a lake and an open area.

'He's turned off the track,' she told the others. 'Looks like a fishing spot.'

'I doubt he's going fishing,' Morten P said.

'I'm driving on. The track climbs. I'll try to find somewhere I can look down on the lake.'

The track narrowed, but snaked through a logging area where the terrain opened out, with only an occasional slender tree remaining. At a layby she pulled over and stopped. The area was overgrown with shrubs, but she could see Haglund's car and the roof of a building below her.

She rolled the side window down a crack to prevent misting and the scent of heather, juniper and moorland reached her. The rain was drumming on the roof, the wind whistling faintly. She produced binoculars from her equipment bag but could not see any movement.

'I'm going out to try for a better vantage point,' she said, pulling on her jacket.

She stepped from the car into a puddle and one of her shoes filled with ice-cold water. She swore, tramping out of the puddle while shaking off water. Then she heard a scream from somewhere behind her but far distant. The second scream was closer. She turned to see a huge black bird flying over the forested slope, flapping its wings and screeching.

When she turned back, Rudolf Haglund stood in front of her car. Rain ran down his face, dripping from the tip of his nose and chin. His tiny eyes squinted at her without blinking. She took a step back.

'I know who you are,' he said, over the sound of the rain, his button-like gaze pinned to her. 'What do you want? Why are you following me?'

That gaze, she thought, her heart hammering in her chest, so sharp it almost hurt. Those eyes took in everything. He had probably spotted her on the street in Oslo. 'I'm a journalist,' she said. 'Your case interests me.'

'Can't you leave me in peace?'

'*What's going on?*' Tommy demanded in her ear. '*Line?*'

Shaking his head, Rudolf Haglund turned and headed down the slope.

'She's not answering,' she heard Tommy say. 'We're going in.'

'Wait!' Line called out. Rudolf Haglund turned to face her.

'Line?' Tommy asked.

'Wait,' Line repeated. 'Can we talk?'

'About what?'

'About Jonas Ravneberg.'

Haglund let his gaze drift over her without making eye contact, sliding over her breasts before lingering on her hips. 'Keep away from me,' he said, continuing down the slope. 'You'd better keep away from me.'

His words sounded more like a warning than a threat.

65

It was still raining when Wisting turned off route E18, an incessant, chill, heavy rain.

He had never visited Bjørg Karin Joakimsen's home and had needed to phone Directory Enquiries for her address. She stayed at Hovland, a district built in the sixties, in a *cul de sac* secluded from the main road. An extensive property, it had a garden front and rear, but was modest in comparison with the houses that had appeared more recently. The garden seemed well maintained, but the house was in need of attention.

She had been widowed for ten years. Wisting had not known her husband but, at his funeral, had sat in the rear section of the church with other colleagues. He did not think she had met another man. He parked beside the fence. It was five past seven. He strode unhurriedly to the front door.

'Come in!' Bjørg Karin invited, shivering as she peered out.

He wiped the rain from his shoulders and entered into an aroma of coffee and fresh baking.

She accompanied him into the living room before disappearing into the kitchen. The coffee table was set with candles ready to be lit. A brown cardboard box sat on the dining table at the other end of the room. Wisting remained standing.

'Have a seat,' Bjørg Karin said, adjusting a picture hanging crookedly on the wall. Jesus Christ and a man beside a ditch.

It crossed Wisting's mind that he did not know her. They had worked together for decades, but he had no idea who she was, would not have guessed that she would hang an embroidered picture of Jesus on her living room wall. As with most of his colleagues, they were strangers outside the workplace.

Bjørg Karin poured the coffee. 'All this is so strange,' she said. 'Everything's been turned upside down.'

Wisting raised his cup. 'What are folk saying?'

'Everybody's preoccupied with the girl who's missing, Linne Kaupang, but nothing seems to be happening. I think they're scared to put a foot wrong, so don't do anything at all.'

'That's not like Nils Hammer.'

'No, but Audun Vetti's prowling round the station.' Wisting was taken aback. Audun Vetti and the rest of the administration were based at the police station in Tønsberg. 'It's Christine Thiis I feel sorry for. She's the one with responsibility for the prosecution, but he doesn't give her a chance.'

Wisting knew Audun Vetti liked to be visible and at the centre. As police prosecutor in Larvik, he had never been short of suggestions or slow to criticise and rebuke. In other words: no leader, a hindrance.

Wisting ate two buns before heading to the dining area. 'Is this it?' he asked, pointing at the box.

'Yes. I don't know how it might help you.'

Wisting took a folder from the box and leafed through. The forms were filed consecutively according to the date the prisoner had been released or transferred. These papers were from three years after Rudolf Haglund's conviction. He chose a different folder, of more recent date. Several different police officers had signed the forms.

'You can take it with you,' Bjørg Karin said.

Wisting replaced the folder. 'I'll do that,' he said, drawing the box towards him.

'I hope you find what you're looking for,' Bjørg Karin said, 'and that you'll come back to us soon. It's not the same without you.'

He thanked her and carried the box outside. The top folders were soaked by the time he got them on the back seat. He made a U-turn, waving to Bjørg Karin at the door, but soon he pulled over again, leaned across and rummaged until he found the right folder.

His fingertips were cold. He made a fist before browsing through the sheets and, in the middle of the folder, finding Rudolf Haglund's file. He had spent three days inside, and several receipt forms were stapled together.

Haglund was remanded in custody on the morning of Saturday July 29th, exactly a fortnight after Cecilia Linde had vanished. Every half hour, a name had been signed to acknowledge supervision. In a couple of places there was an additional insertion of the word *smoke*. At 14.38, Frank Robekk had written *escorted leave, casualty department*. Just before four o'clock, he was back.

At the foot of the first page the words *interview, lawyer,* were cited. One hour later he had been served food, and that same evening one of the police officers had written *interview, W. Wisting*. Three hours afterwards, he was back in his cell, and the next forty-eight hours followed this pattern: routine supervision, meetings with counsel, nourishment, and interviews. There were not many custody officers alternating on the supervision rota, and the same signatures were repeated.

On the final night, the name appeared. The page began to shake in Wisting's hands. At 01.37 hours, on the night of Tuesday the first of August, Rudolf Haglund had received a visitor in his cell. The word *smoke* was written in large, slightly sloping letters in front of a cursive signature Wisting knew extremely well.

The name was completely unexpected, but everything fell into place.

66

Rudolf Haglund disappeared into the bushes covering the slope. A gust of wind rippled the treetops and swept icily round her. Raindrops seeped through her hair and oozed down her neck.

'What's going on?' Tommy asked in her ear.

'He spotted me,' she said, holding the microphone to her mouth. 'He recognised me and knew I had followed him all the way from Oslo.'

'How ...' Harald asked.

'Was it only you, or had he noticed all of us?' Morten P asked.

Down near the water's edge, a door slammed and a car engine started. 'Just me, I think.' The headlight beam pitched forward onto the track. 'He's driving back,' she said.

Morten P was clear: 'This is how we'll tackle it. We'll pick him up and follow. You check where he's been, and then make your way home.'

Before she could protest Morten P was instructing the others to resume the surveillance operation. Jacket and trousers drenched, she sat in the car and glanced in the mirror. Her hair was plastered to her scalp and her face deathly pale.

As she turned the ignition, cold water ran down her spine inside her clothes. She shivered and held her hands stiffly on the steering wheel. At the fork in the track she turned back towards the lake. Churned by the storm, the water crashed against the mooring posts of a jetty, tossing an old rowing boat up and down. Close by there was a dam and what looked like an old sawmill.

She stepped out of the car under the roof of the shabby building. Rusty circular saws, machines with frayed belts, and a pile of offcuts spoke of past activity. In front of an extension with its door closed, a rusty axe lay in the midst of a heap of sawdust. The door was not locked.

The first room she entered was small and smelled of damp. A wooden bench ran along one wall. Two empty beer bottles stood on a table and an old newspaper lay on the floor. Water dripped from the ceiling, and weeds grew between the timber floorboards. An internal door led into an office, where an ancient filing cabinet stood in one corner and a wheeled chair lay on its side. A faded notice listing timber prices hung on the wall.

She went outside again, pulling her jacket more snugly round her. In her ear she heard that Morten P had picked up Haglund's car on the main road and the others were following.

Line ran her hand through her soaking hair and looked around. This was not a suitable place to hold a kidnap victim. Perhaps Haglund knew it from his fishing and had only used it to trap whoever was following him. Another strange looking building caught her eye between the trees on the other side of the dam: a grey concrete cube with a rusty metal door. From the outside, it measured approximately three metres by three metres, and had no windows. The door was in a recess, which showed that the walls were at least thirty centimetres thick.

The door was locked with an iron bolt and a stainless steel padlock, which she lifted and weighed in her hand. She hit the door several times with the palm of her hand and listened. All she could hear was the rain. 'Hello?' she called.

Clenching her fist, she tried again. Anyone shut inside would certainly have heard, at least if they were alive and conscious.

Reluctant to leave without seeing inside she fetched the axe, raised it above her head with both hands and let it fall, missing the padlock and striking the bolt. She raised the axe again and this time the padlock shot round the bolt ring but remained intact. On the third attempt, the lock splintered and tumbled to the ground.

Line threw down the axe, removed the bolt and pulled the door towards her. Stepping inside cautiously, she took a step to one side to let the light pour in. The room was empty apart from a thick tarpaulin by the opposite wall. She pulled it aside to reveal a stack of wooden boxes, with letters and numbers she could not read. One of the lids was removed to reveal a number of sausage-shaped packages wrapped in brown paper. She picked one up and a sticky liquid seeped onto her fingers. *Danger*, she read. *Explosives.*

Her heart thumped; this was a dynamite store. Probably from when they used explosives to clear paths through the forest. She replaced the block warily and left, pulling the metal door shut behind her and replacing what was left of the bolt and padlock.

Whatever else, Linnea Kaupang was certainly not here.

67

Line crouched forward, straining to see as the wiper scraped across the windscreen. She had never met Rudolf Haglund before, but he had obviously recognised her. How did he know who she was? He might have seen pictures of her in *VG*, or may have looked into her father's private life, but it struck her there was something familiar about him too. Had they met before? It might have been Rudolf Haglund who had come storming out of Jonas Ravneberg's house in Fredrikstad.

The idea grew more likely the longer she thought about it. He was in Ravneberg's limited circle of acquaintances and had committed murder before, but why would he kill Jonas Ravneberg? Was it something from the past? Something he had nursed through the years inside?

She went down a gear and overtook a lorry, just as she remembered Erik Fjeld's CCTV images from the railway station in Fredrikstad. She braked and turned into a layby. The lorry she had just overtaken flashed its lights and sent a deluge of water over her as it passed. On the car speaker, she heard that the others were approaching Larvik, in close pursuit of Haglund's silver Passat.

She opened her mobile phone emails, downloaded the unread messages, and opened Erik Fjeld's. The first attachment showed an empty phone box. The next photo was of a video screen, the telephone kiosk from the previous photograph. A man was standing apparently using the phone. He was dressed in black, but nothing more was visible. In the next two photographs he was heading away from the phone box. A possible resemblance to Rudolf Haglund nurtured her theory, but it was impossible to conclude anything definite.

She turned onto the road again and hung on the tail of another lorry.

The Cecilia case created a link between Haglund and Ravneberg, a connection between the present and the past, but she could not grasp what meaning the old murder case actually held for the new. She thought about asking her father's opinion. He should be finished at Internal Affairs, and she was anxious to hear how the meeting with Haglund had gone. What she herself had on Haglund in the Fredrik-stad case was so insubstantial though, that she wanted to keep it to herself. She postponed the call.

Tommy reported that Haglund had turned off the E18 and was heading towards Larvik.

Line decided to drive home to the house in Stavern for a hot bath. She had only a shower in her flat in Oslo, and missed sinking into a bathtub filled with perfumed bubbles.

'*Towards Stavern*,' Tommy corrected.

Vexed that she could no longer take part in the surveillance, she began to question its value. If Haglund had abducted Linnea Kaupang it was unlikely he would travel to Oslo for meetings and newspaper interviews. Less likely that he would journey to the other side of the Oslo fjord to kill a man. She gripped the steering wheel. If he had not already rid himself of her.

'*He can't be on his way home*,' Morten P reported. '*He's going somewhere else. Driving towards the centre. I'm letting go.*'

Line turned up the volume.

'*Following him down to Tollbodgata*,' said Tommy, who was familiar with the small town. '*Driving slowly past the Hotel Wassillioff.*'

'Not too close!' Line warned.

'He's parking. I'm driving past.'

'I'm waiting at the Statoil petrol station,' Harald explained. *'I can see him from here.'*

Line passed the Sandefjord exit road.

'He's leaving the car. Looks like he's carrying something. Walking up the street.'

'What's he carrying?'

'No idea. It might have been his wallet that he's put into his inside pocket. He's going to the right, towards the bank.'

'Verftsgata,' Tommy said. *'I can overtake him at the next intersection.'*

'I'm out,' Harald said. *'Going down slowly.'*

Concentrating on the open conversation, Line dropped her speed. An estate car drove past and indicated to move in front of her. The rear orange and red lights merged, blurring like watercolours on the wet asphalt.

'Who's got him?' she asked. 'Tommy?'

'Negative. Standing at the chemist's shop.'

'Harald?'

'I've gone into Verftsgata after him. Can't see him.'

'Morten?'

'I've just parked my car beside the church. Have we lost him?'

'Hold on a minute,' Harald said.

The scraping background noise caused by the wind disappeared. Instead they heard subdued music and Harald clearing his throat.

'I've got him,' he said. *'He's gone into a café. The Golden Peace. He's sitting at the far end of the place.'*

68

In her mind's eye Line could see Rudolf Haglund at her father's table. She disconnected the open conversation and lifted her mobile phone to call him just as it rang: a foreign number, country code 46, Sweden.

'Line here,' she said.

A woman coughed. 'You said your name was Line Wisting?' The voice was reedy and hesitant: Maud Svedberg, Jonas Ravneberg's live-in girlfriend of seventeen years ago.

'Yes, that's right.'

'We spoke earlier today,' the woman explained. 'I have your number from your call.'

'That's right.'

The woman hesitated before asking warily: 'Are you related to William Wisting? The policeman?'

'He's my father. Why do you ask?'

'No ... it's so odd.'

'What is?'

'Jonas has sent me a package.'

'A package?'

'A large, grey envelope. It must have been in the postbox when we were talking.'

'What's in it?'

'That's what's so odd. There's another package inside, with your father's name, and he writes that I must give it to him if anything happens. And, of course, something certainly has.'

Line felt her hands sweaty as they clamped on the steering wheel. 'Anything else?'

'Not much. It looks as if he scribbled it in a hurry. He writes that he's depending on me and he wants to explain everything. In the meantime I have to look after the package.'

The contents must be important, Line thought. Something crucial. She made up her mind. 'I can come and collect it.'

'I don't know ...'

Line did a mental calculation. She had not been to Ystad before, but knew it was a seaport situated southeast of Malmø. The drive from Oslo to Malmø took about six hours. If she took the ferry across from Horten to Moss instead of driving back via Oslo, she ought to make it in seven. 'I'll talk to my father, and then be on my way,' she said.

By setting off immediately, she could reach Ystad by midnight, but she needed to change her clothes and was unsure of the ferry times. 'I can be with you early tomorrow morning.'

'I could just send it in the post.'

'No, not at all,' Line said. 'I'm on my way.'

69

Wisting had a name. He knew who had fabricated the cigarette evidence, but lacked proof that would stand in court. The cigarette Haglund had been given in his cell could be explained as a friendly gesture. There were no grounds for claiming this was exactly the cigarette butt that had been exchanged for evidence item A-3, but for Wisting it was enough. Everything was understandable now, though more demanding and challenging.

He gripped the steering wheel with both hands and spread out his fingers, his thoughts swirling in a confused effort to find a way forward. Eventually a possibility began to take shape, initially as a tiny, fleeting glimpse, and then as an idea that became clearer. If he could hold things together for long enough there would be one tremendous collapse when he was done.

He could not wait to reach home. Finn Haber's number was not stored on his mobile phone, and he had to call Directory Enquiries to reach the retired forensics expert.

'Have you caught the burglar?' Haber asked.

The plaster cast still lay in Wisting's boot. He had almost forgotten the break-in. 'No,' he said. 'I think I know who it is, but I need some help.'

'Okay then, how can I help?'

'Can you find fingerprints on seventeen-year-old papers?'

'Theoretically, but it depends on the paper, how it's been stored and the print itself.'

'But can you do it?'

'I don't have the right equipment, so I'll have to improvise. With the help of moisture, the right temperature and some chemicals, yes, it should be possible. I've got what I need. I can do it.'

'*Will* you do it?'

'Whenever you like.'

'You'll be hearing from me.'

He disconnected the call and rang Sigurd Henden. Haglund's defence lawyer answered in a gruff voice. 'I hadn't expected to hear from you so soon.'

'I found a name in the old records, but it doesn't constitute proof.'

'Have you spoken to the custody officer, to see what he can remember?'

'Not yet. What I need is something more tangible. Technical evidence.'

'I don't think I can help.'

Wisting stopped for a pedestrian. 'That depends,' he said. 'Do you still have the three cigarette butts?'

'Yes. They were returned from the lab in Denmark last week.'

The pedestrian reached the other side. The tyres on Wisting's car spun on the wet asphalt as he drove on. 'Do you have the original container?'

'Of course. They're each enclosed in a paper envelope, marked with the discovery site, date and time.'

'I need the one marked A-3. You've been given permission by the public prosecutor to undertake fresh forensic investigations. Haven't you?'

'That's correct.'

'I have an expert who can examine the envelope for fingerprints,' Wisting said.

'Now? After seventeen years?'

'He says he can do it.'

269

'No one here has touched the envelopes. They are lying together in a box of evidence items and were sent on from here in the same container. I expect they used gloves at the laboratories.'

'That's fine.'

'What do you expect to find? The envelopes are handled by the police in the first place. Your seventeen-year-old fingerprints may well be on them.'

'No chance,' Wisting said, at the same instant turning into Herman Wildenveys gate. He would soon be home. 'None of the investigators had any dealings with the crime scene work, but I expect to find the prints of one person who certainly didn't have anything to do with the crime lab.'

Henden cleared his throat. 'I'll have the envelope sent by courier. You'll have it sometime this evening.'

70

Line's car was in the driveway. That put him in a good mood, as he had expected to come home to an empty house. He took the folder of custody records and let himself in. The shower was running.

'Hello?' Line called as he closed the door.

'Only me,' he replied, heading for the kitchen. The water in the shower stopped. 'Coffee?'

She gave a response he could not hear, but nevertheless set out two cups.

At the police station, he had an envelope filled with negatives stored in the fireproof safe, copies of irreplaceable photos from Ingrid's family albums. Having no such secure storage in the house he stood with the folder in his hands, scanning the room. Finally he opened a kitchen drawer and placed it there.

Line emerged from the bathroom wearing jeans and a bra, with a towel wrapped round her head.

'I made a cup for you too,' Wisting said.

'I need it. I've a few hours in the car ahead of me.'

'Are you going out again?'

'To Sweden.'

'I thought you were following Haglund.'

'We are. He's sitting inside *The Golden Peace*.'

'What's he doing there?'

'Just watching the world go by.'

Line told him about her confrontation with Rudolf Haglund near the sawmill. 'I think he may have recognised me from Fredrikstad. I wonder if he was the one who attacked me. If he was the one who killed Jonas Ravneberg. It's just a feeling. I can't see what his motive might be, except it must have something to do with the Cecilia case. That's what links those two. They knew each other at the time she was murdered, and now something has surfaced.'

Wisting observed her. She had a special talent for piecing together fragments of information and making connections. It was a flair he also discerned in skilled investigators. In the initial stages of an investigation, creative thinking could be more important than knowledge.

'What do you think?' she asked, taking a seat beside him. 'What could the motive be?'

'I've always considered there to be eight motives.'

'Eight?'

'Jealousy, revenge, money, lust, thrills, exclusion, and fanaticism. Jealousy and revenge murders are always the easiest to solve, together with murders that have a financial motive. Only seldom do we have murders where the motive is thrill-seeking. As a rule, it's serial killers who kill for the sake of it, for the thrill it engenders, and fortunately we haven't had many of them.'

'Was lust the reason Cecilia Linde was murdered?'

'I assume so, though we never found any sign that she had been sexually abused.'

'What do you mean by exclusion? What's that about?'

'That mostly happens in extremist circles. Either radical religious or political groups, motorbike gangs.'

'And fanaticism?'

'That's what we call honour killings. When honour and feelings of shame are the motivation.' Of interest to Wisting was what he could recognise in himself, jealousy, revenge and lust. Fortunately other factors were required to convert them into a murder intent. Most killers he had met were rather stunted and self-centred, and lacked the ability to empathise. Like Rudolf Haglund.

'That was only seven,' Line said. 'What's the eighth?'

'The most difficult of all is when a murder is committed to hide another crime.'

Line became pensive. Nothing he had said was new, but he could see he had triggered a thought process. Then she seemed to give herself a shake. 'How did things go for you today? What did Haglund actually tell you?'

Wisting gave her Rudolf Haglund's version, but skipped telling her about the name. Instead, he told her all the questions that had been posed by Internal Affairs, and that he had broken off the interview.

'Was that such a good idea?'

'Probably not,' he said, crossing over to the fridge. It was almost empty, but he took out butter, cheese and a jar of jam. 'What are you going to do in Sweden, by the way?'

'Running an errand for you,' she said, glancing at the clock.

'What kind of errand?'

'Collecting a package. I've spoken to Jonas Ravneberg's former girlfriend. She lives in Ystad. He sent her a package and a letter telling her the contents should be delivered to you if anything happened to him.'

Wisting had never had anything to do with Jonas Ravneberg. They had never met. The only line of contact was through Rudolf Haglund. 'To me? We ought to alert the police in Fredrikstad.'

'Why should we?'

'They can get the local police to collect the package and examine the contents.'

'And do you think that'll be faster than me driving down there to collect it?'

Wisting, knowing the bureaucracy associated with cross-border criminal justice, had to admit she had a point.

'I'm driving down there tonight,' Line said. 'I can go to the police in Fredrikstad on the return journey and hand over the parcel. Do you want to come with me? It's your name on the package.'

Wisting felt a tingle of curiosity before the practical policeman gained the upper hand. 'I've got a couple of things to attend to here,' he explained, glancing at the drawer where the folder of custody records lay.

71

At the exit road for Torp airport, she turned off the motorway and drove into a filling station, bought a hotdog and
two new windscreen wipers. After eating and changing the
wipers, she set off for Horten and the ferry. The streetlights
were off on some stretches, and moisture glinted on the
black road surface. On her left she passed the old prisoner
of war camp that had been turned into a prison. Several cars
were parked in a layby, bright lights ahead. She dropped her
speed as she passed: a police patrol car and a TV2 news van,
a uniformed police officer standing in front of a camera.

It struck her they must have found Linnea Kaupang's
mobile phone. It must have been traced to this vicinity. The
police would be holding a televised interview at the discovery site in the hope of prompting witnesses. It would soon
be nine o'clock. The news vehicle had satellite antennae on
its roof and the interview would probably be included in the
main news broadcast.

Morten P and Harald Skoglund had already covered the
story for the newspaper. They were still watching Rudolf
Haglund. She reconnected to the conference call and told
them what she had seen.

'We've reported it,' Morten P said. 'But *Dagbladet* got it
first. The police confirmed the find to them this afternoon.'

'What does that mean?'

'That they beat us to it.'

'I mean for the case. What's the significance of her phone
being found here?'

'The police think it was thrown out of a car; therefore confirmation that Linne Kaupang is the victim of a crime.'

'How's it going with Haglund?'

'He's still sitting in *The Golden Peace*.'

'What's he up to?'

'Drinking coffee and people watching. Harald's inside as well. Harald?'

'I'm sitting by the door,' Harald Skoglund said, 'developing a bellyache.'

'Is he just sitting there?'

'Yes, I don't think anyone has twigged who he is.'

Morten P took over: 'I've sent Tommy to check his house. That's safe as long as we're watching him here. With us, Tommy?'

'I'm here,' Tommy said. 'I've gone round the house. All quiet.'

'What plans do you have for the rest of the evening?' Line asked.

'That entirely depends on what Haglund has in mind,' Morten P replied. 'We don't give up so easily.'

'Keep me in the loop, then.'

Driving into the Horten tunnel it dawned on her that whoever abducted Linnea Kaupang had probably driven along this same road. Perhaps he too had been bound for Østfold.

Turning off near the ferry terminal, she drove to the booth and bought a ticket. The queue ahead had already started to move, and she was quickly waved on board. The ferry trip from Vestfold across to Østfold lasted half an hour, which Line spent reading the online newspapers. The discovery of Linnea Kaupang's mobile phone was described in them all. She did not find anything new about the murder in Fredrikstad, not even in the two locals.

It was quarter past ten when she drove ashore at Moss, and raining just as much on this side of the fjord. She entered

Maud Svedberg's address in Ystad into her GPS, and the electronic map told her she should arrive just before four o'clock. She was already tired but decided to drive for as long as possible, and then snatch a few winks of sleep somewhere. At just before half past ten, she drove over the Svinesund Bridge to enter Sweden.

Half an hour later, her eyes heavy with fatigue, she found a darkened picnic area. She locked the doors, reclined the seat and closed her eyes. The rain beating on the car roof sent her to sleep.

72

At midnight Wisting heard the courier's van arrive in front of the house and had the front door open as the driver dashed through the rain. He handed over a big white envelope and Wisting signed a receipt on a computer screen. In the kitchen, he placed the package on the table and opened it with a sharp knife. It contained another, slightly smaller envelope, already open.

Wisting emptied the contents on the table: the container for evidence item A-3. He recognised Haber's signature and cursive handwriting in the headings marked case number, seizure number, location and date. It was a different type of envelope from the evidence bags they used nowadays, but bore no signs of deterioration. Wrapped and stored, it had lain untouched for seventeen years. He pushed the box back into the envelope, placed it in a document folder and headed outside to his car.

The weather took a turn for the worse at Finn Haber's old pilot house. The wind howled through the masts and crossbeams. Choppy waves crashed against the jetty, breaking and falling back again, but welcoming light spilled from the windows into the darkness. Wisting reached the entrance porch with salt sea spray soaking his face.

Finn Haber led the way into the kitchen, unrolled a sheet of paper on the table and prepared his equipment. Wisting had envisaged fingerprint powder and brushes, but all that was laid out was a clear plastic box with a lid, a magnifying glass, a camera and a brown glass jar with a cork stopper.

Taking the padded envelope from the document folder, he placed it on the table. 'How will you tackle this?'

'Using iodine crystals,' Haber replied. He shook the brown glass jar. 'It's the oldest method and still the best. When the crystals are heated, they convert to vapour without undergoing a liquid phase. The vapour combines with amino acids from the fatty residues in the fingerprint.'

'Might it destroy the prints or the paper?'

'Iodine doesn't produce a permanent result. After a few hours, the prints are no longer visible, though they are still present. The iodine doesn't wash away the fatty oils or proteins from the surface, as silver nitrate does. If we don't succeed with iodine, we can try other methods.'

Wisting did not understand a great deal of what Haber said, but he spoke with conviction based on experience.

Haber drew on a pair of rubber gloves and, carefully removing the seventeen-year-old evidence container from its envelope, placed it on the grey paper. 'It's my envelope, to be sure,' he said.

He took a photograph before picking up the glass jar and removing the stopper, releasing an odour reminiscent of chlorine. Haber shook three or four tiny brown nuggets into the plastic box and put the jar aside. He placed the envelope marked A-3 in the box and replaced the lid. At the kitchen worktop he inserted the plug in the sink and filled the basin with warm water. 'It only takes a couple of minutes.'

He put the plastic box into the water and let it float.

Through the clear plastic Wisting could see the entire process, watching as several round fingerprints appeared, like a photograph in a chemical bath in a darkroom. He glanced across at Haber.

'It's almost magical,' Haber said, lifting the plastic box out of the water. 'The invisible becomes visible.'

He opened the lid and picked up the brown envelope. The

prints had a lilac sheen; some were more distinct than others, and some overlapped. He laid the envelope on the grey paper and picked up the camera.

'These are from more than one person,' he said, taking a picture. 'There are both loop and whorl patterns.'

Wisting peered over his shoulder.

'The loops may be mine,' Haber said, examining his own finger. 'Those are the very faintest prints, but there are several others. This has turned out better than I hoped.' He took several more pictures. 'This is just half the job. To establish whose they are, we need something to compare.'

Wisting produced the document folder from the kitchen table and pulled out his notepad. Between the hardback covers he had inserted a sheet of paper, almost like a bookmark. He laid it open on the table.

Haber leaned over, peering at the letter. Then he adjusted his glasses and took a step back. 'Are you serious?' he asked.

Wisting nodded and looked down at the letter advising him of his own suspension.

'He's the chief constable now,' Haber said.

'Acting chief constable,' Wisting corrected.

73

Wakened by her own shivering, Line started the engine to activate the heater. The dashboard clock showed she had slept for almost three hours. At some time during the night the rain had stopped, and a cloud of mist had formed around the car. She checked her phone. Morten P had texted two hours earlier: 'H has gone home. We're standing our ground.'

Her satnav told her she would reach Ystad at 06.47, too early to ring Maud Svedberg's doorbell, but giving Line time for breakfast.

She drove on through the night, wondering whether she should call Morten P. If Haglund had gone to ground for the night, they were probably taking it in turns to sleep, and she didn't want to risk waking him. She would receive a message if anything occurred. Instead she found a Swedish music channel to help her stay awake.

Although she stopped at a petrol station to use the toilet and buy a soft drink, it was only 06.34 when she arrived in Ystad.

Deviating from the satnav's directions, she continued until she reached a small harbour and from there drove around the little town. A paperboy stood in front of a yellow painted stone house with roses round the door; otherwise the streets were deserted. In the town centre she found a bakery cafeteria with its lights on and a sign that said it would open at seven o'clock. To kill the time Line toured the surrounding streets. It was an attractive town with small, pretty market squares.

When the cafeteria opened, she ordered two sandwiches, a bottle of Ramlösa mineral water and a coffee, found an open wifi network and read the online papers on her mobile phone as she ate. Her father was on the pages of *Dagbladet*, framed by a doorway, glancing over his shoulder. *Terminated interview*, said the headline. The well-known, experienced head of investigations risked a prison sentence after the revelation that crucial DNA evidence had been planted. A senior officer in the Bureau for the Investigation of Police Affairs confirmed that William Wisting left before the meeting was over, and explained that the case was not time-barred. Legislators regarded the fabrication of evidence as seriously as murder. The guilty party risked twenty-one years imprisonment.

A knot of tension twisted in her chest.

The story concluded with an advertisement for the paper edition and a lengthy interview with Rudolf Haglund on how it felt to be robbed of one's life.

A colossal white ferry arrived at the quayside just as dawn broke. In the car again she re-activated the GPS, which led her through the network of cobbled streets to Lilla Norregatan.

Maud Svedberg lived in a whitewashed, half-timbered house with a pitched, tiled roof. The street was so narrow there was no room to park. She turned into the next side street and found a parking space outside a church before returning on foot.

The woman who had cohabited with Jonas Ravneberg in Norway seventeen years earlier looked just as Line had imagined. Small and slim, her facial features were quite prominent, giving the impression that her head was too large for her body. Her eyes were pale and round, and she had a slightly timid expression. She gave a tentative smile when Line introduced herself, holding out a hand with long, slender fingers.

282

'I hope I'm not too early,' Line said.

'I'm an early riser.' Maud Svedberg ushered her into the house. They sat at a circular table in the living room. Maud Svedberg put her feet up on a stool. 'I slept badly last night,' she said. 'This business with Jonas is worrying me.' She looked older than her fifty years.

'How did the two of you meet?' Line asked.

'It was years ago,' Maud replied, without elaborating.

Line told her about the murder and what she had found out about Jonas Ravneberg.

'He was always so anxious and uncertain,' Maud said. 'That was why he had a disability pension. He was nervous in company. Couldn't manage to work. We were quite alike in that way, but something happened that last summer. Something made it impossible to live with him.'

'What was it?'

'He closed himself off. Never talked about anything, and became angry if I asked.'

'Do you know why he changed?'

'No. We lived together, but he had his own life. He inherited the farm from his parents and spent days on end there without me hearing anything from him. In the end we just drifted apart.' She sat with her hands folded on her lap. 'He took his clothes and moved to the farm. To his model cars and all the other stuff he collected.'

'Do you remember the Cecilia case?' Line asked.

'She vanished that last summer we were together.'

'Did Jonas ever talk about the case?'

'He didn't talk about anything.'

'But he knew the man who was convicted of killing her, didn't he?'

Maud Svedberg reclined against the chair back, her head moving thoughtfully from side to side.

'Rudolf Haglund,' Line said.

283

'No ...'

Line tilted her head to one side. 'Are you sure?'

Maud rose to her feet. 'We lived together for nearly two years,' she said, 'but I never really got to know him. He never introduced me to anybody, and never talked about friends, although I knew he had some. He occasionally used the phone, but didn't want me to hear.'

She crossed the room as she spoke and, opening a drawer in a bureau, withdrew a brown envelope and returned to place it on the table in front of Line. 'That's it,' she said.

Line lifted the package. It weighed next to nothing. The contents were rectangular with sharp corners, like a small hard box. 'Can I see what he wrote?'

Maud returned to the bureau, took out a sheet of white paper and handed it to Line. The script was sloping, apparently written in haste. It said no more than what Maud Svedberg had already explained: that he thought of her and would like to come to Sweden so that they could meet, and in the meantime she should look after the package. There was a great deal he wanted to say, but it would have to wait. If anything should happen to him, she should make sure the package was delivered to Chief Inspector William Wisting in Larvik.

Line handed the letter back.

'Aren't you going to open it?' Maud asked.

Line had intended to wait until she was outside in the car, but Maud Svedberg was equally curious about the contents, so she ought to open the package before she left. She tore the paper at one end and upended it over her lap. A video cassette slid out.

74

The comparison took some time. At the top of the fold in the envelope, Finn Haber had found a whorl-shaped fingerprint suitable for identification, and made a start on the laborious task of comparing it with the prints on Wisting's suspension letter. He was still crouched over the kitchen table when Wisting left around half past one.

On his way home, he drove past *The Golden Peace* and saw Suzanne clearing tables, but did not go inside. Instead, he went home and to bed before she returned. The day had been too complicated to sit up explaining into the small hours. Besides, he was exhausted.

In the morning he made himself a cup of coffee in the machine. The wind had quieted, and the rain stopped overnight, but heavy clouds still hung in the sky and the air was saturated. The phone rang; it was Line.

'I'm on my way home from Sweden,' she said. "I've collected your package from Maud Svedberg.'

Wisting stood in the middle of the kitchen, coffee cup in hand. 'Have you opened it?'

'Yes.'

'And?'

'There's a video cassette inside.'

'A film?'

'A V-8 cassette, an outdated standard from fifteen to twenty years ago. We'll need an old system to play it.'

'Where will we get hold of something like that?'

'I think Grandad has one.'

'I'll ask him. When do you expect to be home?'

'There's a ferry from Strømstad to Sandefjord at half past two. I should make that and be back sometime before six.'

'Okay. Drive carefully.'

Wisting missed the rest of what Line said. Directly in front of him on the table lay a yellow cassette recording, an AGFA cassette, exactly like the one Cecilia had used in her Walkman, but this had Wisting's name written on it with a thick, black marker pen.

He lifted it and turned it round. His name was written in bold letters on both sides. The phone rang again. This time it was Haber. 'It's confirmed. The same person has held your suspension letter and the packaging of A-3. And it's not you. I've eliminated your fingerprints.'

Wisting's bewilderment about the cassette dampened his enthusiasm, although he was glad of the confirmation. Seventeen years previously, Audun Vetti had been a young prosecutor with ambitions, a man in a hurry to move up in the world. The Cecilia case was at a standstill, and so a hindrance on his career path.

'That still proves nothing,' Finn Haber said. 'He could come up with a story to explain why his prints are on the envelope.'

'I'll make sure he doesn't get away with it,' Wisting said. 'Have you documented your findings?'

'Everything's photographed,' Haber confirmed. 'It just needs Vetti's formal registration in the fingerprint register.'

Wisting replied absentmindedly, barely absorbing what he was being told.

'Is there anything else I can do for you?'

'No, that's fine. More than fine.' Wisting thanked Haber again for his assistance and put his phone aside before taking the cassette up to his bedroom. Suzanne was sleeping soundly. Hunkering down beside the bed he placed his hand

286

on her bare shoulder and shook her gently. She woke gradually, stretching and turning slowly towards him.

'Wisting held the cassette in front of her. 'Do you know where this came from?'

Rubbing her eyes, Suzanne licked her lips to moisten her dry mouth. 'One of the customers left it on the counter yesterday,' she said, straightening the quilt. 'He asked me to give it to you. It was important, he said.'

Wisting exhaled slowly through his nose and stood up.

'Is something wrong?' she asked.

'This comes from Rudolf Haglund.'

Suzanne sat bolt upright. 'The murderer?'

Wisting nodded. 'He was in your café last night.'

'But ...' Suzanne began, shifting her gaze from Wisting to the yellow cassette. 'What's on it?'

'I don't know yet,' he answered as he headed towards the door. 'You just go back to sleep. I have to go somewhere.'

They did not have a cassette player in the house. Thomas had taken theirs with him when he left to join the army eight years earlier and neither had come home again. He would have to go to the cottage to play the tape.

The roads were still wet, and in several places there were puddles on the asphalt. Sheets of water sprayed from his front wheels as he drove through them.

The air was sharper at the coast, the sea still churning white, even though the wind had dropped.

Letting himself into the cottage, he scanned the room, but saw no sign of unwelcome guests. Line had been the last person here. She had washed the used cups and stacked the Cecilia documents tidily on the coffee table. The old portable radio sat on a shelf below the window. He lifted it onto the window ledge and inserted the cassette with the A-side facing out before pressing *play*.

First he heard some kind of rustling, as if someone was

out walking and their clothes were rubbing. Then there were two voices: two people saying hello and introducing themselves with their first names, Gjermund and Rudolf. Rudolf Haglund.

To begin with, Gjermund said most. He thanked Rudolf Haglund for coming and wondered if many others had made contact. Haglund confirmed that they had, and his companion asked if it was all right to record their conversation. It was an interview. Rudolf Haglund had given him the recording he had made of a newspaper interview.

The journalist explained they would like some new photographs, and a photographer would come. Haglund must have nodded his agreement, because the conversation continued, soon to be interrupted by a woman taking their order. Haglund wanted a well-done steak, while the reporter chose a fish course. Haglund ordered a cola and the journalist asked the waitress for a *Farris* mineral water.

Wisting knew only one journalist called Gjermund. Gjermund Hulkvist of *Dagbladet*. An experienced crime reporter with a friendly manner, who gave a great deal of himself personally to get what he was after. On the recording, he used Haglund's first name and said how grateful he was for the interview.

'You're good,' Haglund said. 'I like what you write. You stick to the facts. That was what I liked when you reported on the case seventeen years ago.'

'Nice of you to say so.'

'It wasn't simply that you kept to the facts, but you were also first to break the news.'

'That's the benefit of having a broad network of contacts,' Gjermund Hulkvist said.

'In the police?'

'Well placed.'

Wisting turned up the volume. Seventeen years ago

Gjermund Hulkvist and *Dagbladet* had revealed that the police had Cecilia Linde's tape.

A chair scraped on the floor. 'I'm not interested in an interview if the person responsible for me being convicted of a crime I didn't commit is one of your contacts in the police.' Haglund was obviously indignant.

'Not Wisting,' the journalist assured him, his voice low and intense. 'Higher up.'

'The prosecutor?' Haglund drew his chair back towards the table.

'Let's just say he's working as the chief constable these days, and that it can pay to cooperate with the press.'

The conversation continued, but Wisting was not listening. The journalist had gone as far as possible without naming his source. However, this was more than a hint about who had leaked the information about Cecilia's tape: Audun Vetti.

75

Roald Wisting was an energetic man. After retiring as a hospital doctor he accepted positions of trust in a variety of clubs and associations. It was due just as much to his busy lifestyle as Wisting's long working days that they did not see each other more than a couple of times a month. When Ingrid was alive, his father used to come for dinner every Sunday. Now they met for coffee at *The Golden Peace* from time to time.

Roald enjoyed walking and had strolled to Wisting's house with his camera over his shoulder. 'I haven't used it for years,' he said, placing the black bag on the coffee table, 'but I tested it at home before I left. I have some amusing films of Line and Thomas.'

Producing a cable, he pulled the television set away from the wall. Wisting thought of telling him about Audun Vetti, but decided to let it lie. He had no need to clear his name to his father.

'This cassette was inside it,' his father said. 'It must be from the summer before they started school. We were all in Denmark, at Legoland and Givskud Zoo.'

Wisting smiled, his father had trailed round so enthusiastically with his video camera, filming Lego cars driving in miniature towns built with little plastic bricks.

Roald squinted through his glasses, trying to locate the right access point for the camera lead. 'We ought to transfer them onto DVD discs,' he said. 'Colour and quality deteriorate over time.'

'You're right,' Wisting said. 'There are probably firms that do that kind of thing.'

'I'm sure there are ...' his father mumbled. 'Now we shall see.' He attached the lead from the TV set and found a socket to connect it to the electricity supply. 'When's Line coming?'

Wisting glanced at the clock; the ferry from Sweden should have just arrived in Sandefjord. 'In an hour or so, I think.'

'And what kind of video is it she's bringing?'

'We don't know yet, but I think it's to do with the Cecilia case.'

'I was on duty at the hospital the day you came in with the murderer. The rumour flew like a sigh of relief through the departments. I didn't have anything to do with it, but the nurses in reception talked about him for ages. A couple of them even knew him, from when he'd been a patient.'

Wisting recalled the tiny operation scars on the photograph from the time Haglund was examined by the doctor on duty. This part of his past had not been properly clarified during the investigation. 'He had moles removed?'

'That's right,' Roald said, as the memories came back. 'A number of cell changes were discovered when he came in for follow-up treatment.'

'Follow-up treatment?'

'We operated on him for prostate cancer a few years earlier.' He pointed the remote control at the TV.

'Doesn't that operation make you impotent?'

'It can do.'

The television picture flickered on the screen and a red Lego bus drove towards a bridge, stopping as the bridge opened to let a boat sail by. Wisting took out his phone and headed for the kitchen.

'What is it?' Roald asked.

'I have to check something.'

He selected the number of the retired psychiatrist who

291

had examined Rudolf Haglund. If Rudolf Haglund had lost erectile function through the treatment for prostate cancer, it shone a whole new light on the case. This was something that should have emerged in the forensic psychiatric examination. It was even stranger that Rudolf Haglund had suppressed information that could contribute to his acquittal.

The psychiatrist did not answer. Wisting left a message asking him to call back and returned to the living room. The twins appeared on the TV screen, each with an ice cream cone. Behind them, Ingrid had a broad grin on her face. 'That's only their third ice cream of the day.'

He had not seen moving images of her in the five years since she died, but it was probably her voice...

Now the children were in an Indian settlement wearing feather headbands. Wisting sat down to watch and, gradually, thoughts of Cecilia Linde, Rudolf Haglund and Audun Vetti faded as he was drawn into the children's world of gold mining, riverboats, train journeys, timber slides, and the driving school with Lego cars, and Ingrid's infectious laughter. The memories touched him. He was disappointed when the film ended.

Shortly afterwards Line arrived looking tired, with a bulging carrier bag from the tax-free shop. Her blonde hair was tousled, her clothes dishevelled and she had shadows under her eyes. At the same time she seemed pleased. She hugged them both.

Wisting put the carrier bag on the kitchen table. When he returned Line was inserting the video cassette in the camera. 'It was rewound to the beginning,' she said, closing the camera's cassette compartment. Wisting took charge by pressing the *play* button and they all watched the television screen.

Grey, black and white grains whirled before a kitchen appeared: cooker, kitchen sink. The image suddenly blurred, the screen went completely black and then fresh images of a kitchen interior appeared: a window with white curtains, a crocheted valance. Strong back light made it difficult to see anything outside.

Line perched on the edge of the nearest chair.

The screen went black again. Now: pictures of an empty room, white brick walls, grey flooring. The film was taken from above, looking down, as if someone was holding the camera with arms outstretched above him, tilting it to get the widest possible view of the room. A shadow fell towards the centre; someone was moving outside camera range.

The film jumped, and now the camera had a slightly different angle, though still viewed from the same raised position. This time someone was standing in the centre of the room: a naked woman, her head bowed, she lifted it slowly, stared into the camera. She wore a leather collar round her neck.

Wisting supported himself on the edge of the table. It was Cecilia Linde.

Her eyes were filled with fear and torment and suffering, dried tears glittering on her cheeks. She closed her eyes momentarily and, when she opened them again, her despair was even more evident. Her lips moved. At first, no sound, then: '*Please* ...'

As her bottom lip trembled, tears spilled over and ran down her cheeks. '*Please,*' she begged again.

All awareness of her naked body was gone. She stood with her arms by her side, making no attempt to cover herself. '*I'll do whatever you want. Just let me out of here.*'

'Spool it back,' Line said. 'All the way to the beginning.'

Roald did as she said. The crackling image appeared on the screen again. The picture rolled.

'Stop!'

The image froze with the camera held crookedly. Line cocked her head to study the screen: blue wall, kitchen

293

worktop with dirty glasses and plates, wall cabinet in the same colour as the walls, white enamel cooker with three rings, kitchen sink and slop sink in stainless steel.

'I've seen that kitchen before,' Line said. 'I know where Cecilia Linde was held. It was at Jonas Ravneberg's farm.'

76

Line lifted her camera bag from the passenger seat to make room for her father. As she knew the way to Jonas Ravneberg's smallholding, they took her car. Wisting sat with gritted teeth. Jonas Ravneberg had slipped through his net seventeen years earlier. Cecilia had been held in his cellar for twelve days while they searched in the wrong places and looked in the wrong direction.

'Shouldn't we phone someone?' Line asked. 'Police and ambulance? If it's him, Linnea Kaupang may have been locked in the cellar for days.'

'We'll wait till we get there,' Wisting replied.

He tried to make it all fit. Jonas Ravneberg was an anonymous figure, but had appeared peripherally in both the Cecilia and Ellen cases. Now he had been murdered himself, shortly after Rudolf Haglund was released and could produce evidence that he had been unfairly convicted. But he could not quite let go of the idea that Haglund had abducted and killed Cecilia Linde, though two perpetrators was a rare occurrence in crimes of a sexual nature.

Line dropped her speed and turned onto the dirt track. The car skidded from side to side until the tyres gained a grip and she accelerated forward. Dense trees obliterated the faint dusk light. The rutted tracks of another vehicle ran ahead of them.

'Are your colleagues still watching Haglund?' Wisting asked.

Line nodded grimly. 'I spoke to them just before I got

home. He hasn't stepped outside the house all day and his car is in the car port.'

Line shifted down a gear, shooting out of the ruts and bumping over something solid. Wisting hung on to his seatbelt as they slithered towards the ditch, but she pulled at the steering wheel, the wheels spun and the car swerved back in line. The track narrowed, bushes scraped the sides; they rounded the final bend and the smallholding appeared in front of them. A car was parked in the yard, with mud splashes round the wheel arches.

Line took her foot off the accelerator too late. A man standing beside the barn was caught in their headlights. 'Frank Robekk,' Wisting said.

They stepped from the car, leaving the engine running. Robekk raised a hand to shade his eyes and they saw he was carrying a flashlight. In the other hand he held something that looked like a gun. 'Wisting?'

'What are you doing here, Frank?'

'There's something you need to look at.' What he was carrying was a cordless drill.

'What are you doing here?' Wisting repeated.

'What we should have done seventeen years ago. Searching this place.' The barn door was barred and bolted and fresh splinters of wood lay on the ground. Frank pointed at one of two holes he had drilled, holding his flashlight to the other. 'Look inside!'

Wisting put his eye to the hole. It was dark inside, and the light from the torch spread out in a cone shape, striking the rear of a car, three or four metres inside. Covered in dust, it looked completely grey. The registration plate was missing, but the light from the torch found the lightning bolt of the circular Opel logo.

'When I read that someone called Ravneberg had been killed not long after Rudolf Haglund was released I remembered the name. From the time my niece went missing. Locating this place was easy, the rest was simply looking.'

'What is it?' Line asked.

'It's the car,' Robekk answered. 'The car he used when he abducted Cecilia Linde.'

Line bent towards the hole to take a look, but Robekk directed the light towards the shack at the far end of the yard, where the ancient Saab was parked. 'We blundered completely,' he said. 'The Saab was spotted when Ellen disappeared, but we didn't get the significance. We totally fouled up.'

Wisting scanned the yard for something to break open the barn door. 'I've got tools in my car,' Robekk said.

He fetched a crowbar from the boot and handed the flashlight to Wisting. The timber, old and dry, splintered as Robekk dug at the bolt mountings. He threw himself into twisting and turning so violently that splinters flew in all directions. There was a crack and the first bolt fell to the ground, then the second. Five minutes later all the bolts were off. Frank Robekk threw the crowbar aside and pulled open the massive, double barn door.

Wisting entered behind him. Grains of corn crunched underfoot. Minute particles of dust danced in the torchlight beam. The stench of straw and manure filled the air. The barn had a high ceiling, but the space was only wide enough to park a car. Pickaxes, spades, rakes and other tools were propped along one wall, together with two cartwheels. On the other side, dry hessian sacks were piled. A ladder led up to the hayloft.

The car was covered with a thick layer of dust, which Wisting was about to wipe away when he heard a click. A couple of powerful flashes followed and the room was filled with light. He glanced at Line who was standing just inside the door.

Frank Robekk opened the rear left-hand door of the Opel. A faded air freshener hung from the mirror. Otherwise everything was clean and tidy. The key was still in the ignition.

Wisting walked round the vehicle. It was rusty, as the witness on the tractor had described, the rust exacerbated by the years spent in the barn. Round the wheel arches, large patches had flaked off, and the bracket holding one of the side mirrors had disintegrated so much the mirror hung by a thread. He halted in front of the boot and pressed his thumb against the button. It was resistant and made a scraping noise as it slid down, clicked, and opened with a little creak.

Frank Robekk raised the lid.

A bundle of clothes lay neatly folded on the black rubber mat. A short-sleeved sweatshirt, trousers, minuscule white underpants and a grey sports bra, beside a pair of running shoes with white socks pushed inside. At several places in the cramped space, rust had eaten cracks in the metalwork that, even seventeen years ago, would have been large enough to drop a little Walkman through.

Wisting turned and looked through the barn door to the main house resting squarely on thick cellar walls.

77

His mobile rang while he was still inside the barn. It was Steinar Kvalsvik, the psychiatrist. 'You called?'

'Yes, but it can wait,' Wisting said, looking through the open barn to the farmhouse opposite. The light from Line's car headlamps brought everything into sharp relief.

'What was it about?'

'Haglund had an operation for prostate cancer. He was possibly impotent as a consequence. I think it's odd it wasn't mentioned in your report.'

'I agree. It should have been, but a psychiatric examination is based on case documents and discussions with the accused. I don't know why he held those details back, but it doesn't change anything. If anything, it's more likely to support and reinforce his motive.'

'How can that be?'

'Sexual impulses are not located between the legs. Their locus is inside the head. Moreover, sexual abuse is more often about power than lust.'

Wisting glanced at Line as he listened. She had switched off the ignition, but left the lights on. Seeing him looking, she raised her camera and preserved his image for posterity as he ran his hand through his hair. Stepping to the side she took another photograph, with the rusty Opel in the background.

'An erection is actually a complicated interaction of hormones, nerve impulses and muscles in which both physical and psychological factors play a part,' the psychiatrist continued. 'Cancer treatment often impairs the capability but not the desire.'

'Haglund was a masochist,' Wisting commented, thinking of the pornographic magazines they had found at his home.

'Sexual masochism implies enjoyment of domination, or humiliating or inflicting physical or psychological pain. In the extreme case of abducting a woman and inflicting all this on her, well, that could bring about a long-awaited gratification for him.'

Wisting shifted the phone to his other ear. He did not have time for this call now, but wanted to hear what Steinar Kvalsvik had to say. 'Do you still believe Haglund kidnapped Cecilia Linde?' he asked.

Frank Robekk was making his way to the farmhouse with the crowbar in his hand.

'I'm even more convinced. Surgery on the prostate might explain not finding any semen on her. The sphincter muscle on the bladder can be damaged by the procedure. He would then have what we call a dry orgasm. The semen instead ends up in the bladder and is later discharged when urinating.'

On the other side of the yard, Frank Robekk started to break open the front door.

'There's still something bothering me,' the psychiatrist said. 'I have a disturbing feeling.'

'Yes?'

'It's more a thought that won't let go.'

'Yes?' Wisting repeated.

'It's about this girl with the yellow bow, Linnea Kaupang. I think he may have taken her. That he's holding her somewhere.'

Wisting was already striding across the farmyard, suspicions strengthening as he went. 'Thanks for phoning,' he said. 'I'll get back.'

Frank Robekk swore as he kicked the door open.

'The cellar!' Wisting shouted, pointing to the other end of the house. 'Not inside the house. If she's here, she'll be in the cellar!'

Robekk lowered the crowbar and walked towards the trapdoor at the end of the house. The bushes on either side were pressed to the ground, and branches had been broken. It had been opened recently and set down on either side of the cellar opening. Frank Robekk jammed the crowbar under the padlock mounting.

Wisting's phone rang again. This time it was his father. 'I'm in the middle of something!'

'I've watched the rest of the film,' Roald Wisting said. 'At the end a man turns up: Rudolf Haglund.'

Wisting grasped what his father was saying, but did not have time to fully appreciate what it meant for him, for the case and for the nightmare he had been drawn into. How it removed all doubt. 'You're certain?' he asked.

'I recognised him from the newspaper. It's him all right.'

Wisting ended the call and waved Line over. 'Are you sure Tommy and your colleagues are watching Haglund?'

'Do you still believe he ...' she began.

'Phone them. Make sure they don't let him out of their sight!'

Line took out her mobile as Robekk struggled with the padlock. This entrance was better secured than the barn door. Wisting rushed back to the barn and returned with a sledgehammer. His second blow shattered the lock. The hinges squeaked as Robekk lifted one flap and laid it to one side. The stench of rot and mould rose from the darkness. Somewhere they heard water dripping. Nothing else.

When Robekk switched on his flashlight, a stone staircase glistened damply beneath them. Wisting hefted the sledge-hammer and took the first step down to a high-ceilinged room with whitewashed walls. Neither spoke. The walls were speckled with mould and an icy stillness filled the space like an invisible fog. Empty jam jars, tin cans and bottles with handwritten labels were arrayed across a table. There was a door in the middle of the opposite wall. Robekk examined it: locked. Wisting broke it open with two hammer strokes.

They entered another room. Beside the door Wisting found a switch and the electric current buzzed before an enormous ceiling lamp came on. This room was smaller than the first, and curved in a horseshoe shape. Opposite them was a door equipped with an extra iron mounting and a padlock. Beside the door was a stool and, close to the ceiling, a peephole. An old-fashioned video camera on a tripod was propped against the wall.

Handing the sledgehammer to Robekk, Wisting stepped onto the stool and looked inside.

78

A young, naked woman lay motionless on the floor in a foetal position. The same leather collar worn by Cecilia in the video footage was fastened round her neck, as though she were an animal that someone owned. Wisting pressed his forehead against the cold wall and the foul odour of urine hit him. She twisted her head to look up.

She must have heard us break through the trapdoor, Wisting thought. 'Linnea!' he shouted. She squeezed her eyes shut as Robekk landed a first blow on the door. A shudder coursed through her body. 'Linnea,' Wisting shouted again. 'It's over. This is the police.'

Robekk raised the hammer for another strike as Wisting climbed down, punishing himself for all the minutes wasted, all the hours squandered while Linnea Kaupang had been imprisoned.

Line arrived, phone in hand. 'He went into the woods,' she said.

'What do you mean?'

'Haglund,' she said. 'Tommy went to the house to make sure he was there. Haglund went into the woods behind the house carrying a large lantern.'

Wisting pictured the map in the conference room during the Cecilia case, with increasingly larger areas shaded where they had searched. Haglund's house at Dolven could not be more than a kilometre from here. Practically speaking, he and Ravneberg were neighbours. 'Did he see Tommy?'

Line shook her head. 'He's following.'

There was a final, violent crack as Robekk smashed the door open. 'She's in here,' Wisting said. 'Send for an ambulance, and phone Nils Hammer. Tell him to bring all the officers he has and get here without delay.'

Linnea Kaupang staggered to her feet, shielding her breasts with her hand.

Wisting pulled off his jacket and covered her trembling shoulders. Linnea whispered something and took a few unsteady steps. Robekk put his arm round her and led her outside but Wisting remained, surveying the room, trying to grasp the scale of the atrocities that had taken place here. It was smaller than a prison cell. Suddenly the walls closed in and he could hardly breathe.

At the door he placed one hand on the wall and felt something scratched there. No telling what kind of tool had been used, perhaps just fingers that had rubbed backwards and forwards for long enough to form two uneven letters: C and L, just as Cecilia Linde had initialled the yellow cassette that carried her last words to the world.

Immediately above were two other letters, E and R: Ellen Robekk. On the floor lay a little yellow hair slide, used to scratch some kind of final greeting. L K. He closed his eyes.

Line was shouting something from the top of the stairs. All he caught was 'Haglund'. He heard steps on the paving stones and then she called out again. 'He's here!'

79

Wisting raced after Line, down towards the river and, in the sweep of her flashlight beam, saw two men fighting, rolling on the ground. 'Tommy!' Line shouted.

It was impossible to tell which was which. One freed himself and tried to stand. The other hurled himself at his legs. The first shook one leg free and kicked out. There was a cry of pain. Line's flashlight found the face of the standing man, Haglund. He wriggled free and darted into the forest.

Wisting grabbed the flashlight and sprinted after, along a path and behind a turf house, pushing bushes aside, jumping over tussocks and tree roots, scratching himself on fir needles and twigs, paying no attention, tumbling over and scrambling to his feet again, dashing on. 'Haglund!' he shouted, but all he heard was boots on muddy ground and the sound of the river.

The path snaked through the forest until it reached a ford where the river broadened and was not so deep. Haglund had waded halfway across, the rushing waters reaching almost to his knees. He hauled himself onto a boulder, rose unsteadily to his feet and looked back.

'Haglund!' Wisting yelled again, but Rudolf Haglund jumped down to wade further across. Wisting stepped into the river to follow. Ahead of him, Haglund lost his balance, floundered in the water, struggled to his feet again, and staggered on with his arms wide.

The immense flow made the going treacherous. Wisting felt the icy water push against his legs as he picked his way forward over uneven stones that moved when he stepped on them.

Haglund had almost reached the other riverbank when he fell. Waving his arms in the air but finding nothing to hold, his back arched and he dropped backwards into deeper water.

Wisting retreated onto the riverbank and ran the flashlight downriver until he spotted Haglund's head bobbing in the water. He kept the torch beam on him steadily, watched him struggle to the other side and climb ashore. As he stood up the bank edge, earth and sand, gave way under his feet, collapsing and subsiding into the water. Haglund lunged at the branches of a tree but could not grab hold, fell backwards into the river and cracked his head on a boulder. His body was swept, face down, turning with the river's swirling movements.

Wisting ran along the bank, holding one arm up to brush aside twigs and branches while trying not to lose sight of Haglund until the current carried him back to Wisting's side of the river.

Wisting threw the flashlight away and waded out until the river suddenly deepened and the stony bed disappeared from under his feet. He made a few powerful swimming strokes to reach Haglund while the current carried them both downstream. He trod water and pulled upwards to keep his head above the surface, but the current tugged at his clothes and kept dragging him down. He caught hold of Haglund and managed to turn him face up, placing his left arm under his chin to keep his face above water.

Swimming with one arm, his mouth filled with water every time he breathed in but they were both being dragged under. He kicked out with his feet and felt the riverbed, managed somehow to grip the stony surface and hauled Rudolf Haglund with him into the shallows. Gasping for air, he heaved the weighty body onto the bank.

The current had carried them back to the grassy slope below the smallholding. Wisting collapsed onto his hands and knees, coughing and panting. Others dragged Haglund further onto the grass. He heard Line declare that Haglund was breathing and stood up. Sirens sounded in the distance.

80

Rudolf Haglund lay in the back of the ambulance with two uniformed officers attending. He stared at Wisting with those tiny black eyes of his and, when their eyes met, every feature of his face twisted. He opened his mouth, as if he wanted to say something, but nothing came out.

Wisting pushed the door shut and watched the ambulance roll slowly down the narrow farm track. It was a strange feeling, as it always was when cases built up over a long period of time reached an abrupt, long-awaited resolution. It brought a kind of unburdening, and the investigators needed time to themselves before they could move on. He would not have that with this case, not yet.

A blanket had been placed round his shoulders but still he shivered as he stood motionless, watching what was going on around him, now automatically: floodlights switched on, crime scene examiners putting on white, sterile overalls, overshoes, gloves and hats; others huddled in small groups, deep in discussion, as portable radios crackled into life and crime scene tape was unfurled.

Frank Robekk stood inside the barrier, occasionally stopping a policeman to ask something or give advice.

Line stood beside Tommy and her two newspaper colleagues. The elder of the two spoke into a mobile phone while gesticulating wildly with his arms. Line was using her camera, but already had the photographs for next day's newspaper.

Nils Hammer approached. 'They've taken her to hospital

in Tønsberg,' he said. 'Her father's been alerted. He's on his way there too.'

Wisting nodded.

'Physically, she's unharmed. He hadn't done anything to her, just watched.'

Wisting nodded again. 'I know who planted the DNA evidence,' he said, staring straight ahead as he spoke. 'How the cigarette butts were switched.'

Hammer gave him a penetrating look.

'I can prove who did it.'

'How ...'

'When I was suspended, I took a copy of the Cecilia case documents with me. I've been working at the cottage, re-examining everything to do with Rudolf Haglund.'

'Who was it?' Nils Hammer asked.

'I need some further documentation,' Wisting said, 'and just a couple of days to draw everything together.'

Hammer's phone rang. He responded with a number of brief instructions and turned to face Wisting again. 'I'll need a statement. Can you come with me to the station?'

'Not tonight.'

'Vetti won't like that. He's already arranged a press conference.'

'I'm going home for a hot bath. Then I'll sleep. It's a long time since I had a good night's sleep.'

Wisting took a quick shower and put on the same dark clothing he had used when he entered the police station. Before leaving again he searched through the cardboard boxes containing Ingrid's belongings in the garage storeroom. He found what he wanted and drove away.

Switching on the radio, he listened to the news. The newsreader described recent events as 'a dramatic development in the case of the missing Larvik girl'. Rudolf Haglund had been taken into custody, charged with the abduction of Linnea Kaupang, who had been found alive. An interview with Audun Vetti followed. The reporter pointed to the similarities with the Cecilia case.

'What about the accusations Haglund was convicted on the basis of fabricated evidence?' he asked Audun Vetti.

'Regardless of the question of guilt, the Bureau for the Investigation of Police Affairs is investigating the possibility of punishable offences with regard to the presentation of evidence in the Cecilia Linde case,' Vetti said. 'Today's arrest has no impact on that.'

He passed the exit road leading to the cottage at Værvågen and took the next side road. Less used than his usual route, water splashed out onto the verges as he drove over puddles and mud. Trees clung tightly together on both sides, and an occasional branch scraped the car roof or struck the side panels like a clenched fist. Finally the track ended at a little plateau above smooth coastal rocks.

He stepped from the car and looked at the familiar coastline silhouetted against the sea. The air tasted of salt and waves broke against the skerries. He trod carefully over the slippery hillside, using his flashlight to pick his way to the coastal path where he could follow the blue marks eastward to the Wisting family cottage. A faint light from the exterior wall cast shadows on the lawn. He could hear the thumping noise of waves against a fishing boat not far off.

The cottage was cold and dark, but he did not switch on the light or heating. He groped his way forward to the armchair beside the front window and sat under a blanket. Out in the bay he could make out the boat he had heard, under the dim illumination of a masthead light. He drew the curtains, but left a gap to see through. It was a matter of waiting.

After three hours he began to wonder if nothing was going

to happen. Perhaps Nils Hammer had not passed on the information. He rubbed his face and reached for yet another blanket from the settee and, suddenly, was wide-awake. A sharp light pierced the night, shining across the rocky coastline before vanishing. Wisting pressed his forehead against the windowpane. A car was approaching. The front headlights swept over the wild roses as it pulled up. The lights were switched off and a door slammed.

81

By the pale moonlight Wisting could see that the man walking along his path had chosen to wear dark clothing, a woollen hat pulled well down, and his jacket lapels up around his
ears. As he stepped into the light from the outdoor lamp, he
glanced back so Wisting could not see his face. A couple of
heavy thumps on the door, and then another. 'Hello?'

Wisting remained still and silent as the man moved across
the verandah. The floor timbers creaked. His silhouette was
outlined on the curtains. He stood at the window and, cup-
ping his face in his hands, peered inside. Wisting pressed
himself against the back of the chair, but knew the angle was
too oblique for him to be seen. The man's breath condensed
on the glass before he returned to the door.

Wisting braced himself, listening to the sound of metal
scraping hesitantly against metal. The lock rattled, the door
swung open and the man slipped inside like a shadow,
heading purposefully for the light switch. He took only two
steps towards the table where the Cecilia documents were
scattered before seeing Wisting.

The colour drained from Audun Vetti's bony face and his
lips tightened.

'I don't have it here,' Wisting said, standing up.

'I tried to knock …'

'The evidence isn't here, but I can prove you were the one
who made the switch. You even signed for it, when you were
down in the cells and took a cigarette end from Haglund.'

'You're mistaken,' Vetti said sharply. 'I wanted to get him

to talk, make an informal arrangement about the sentencing, so he knew what he was up against.'

'You took the remains of his cigarette to Finn Haber's lab and swapped it for the contents of the evidence bag.'

'You're fantasising, Wisting. Making up a story to shift the blame onto someone else. No one will believe you. I was never anywhere near those cigarette butts, neither when they were found nor later.'

Wisting took a step forward. 'Are you saying you've never seen the central piece of evidence?'

'As far as I was concerned, they were simply letters and numbers in a report. Points on a list of evidence. I came here because I was worried about you and wanted to know how you were. I hadn't expected to be greeted by such accusations.'

'Was that why you broke in?'

'You'd forgotten to lock the door, and obviously heard me knocking.'

'I think you came to find out what proof I had against you.'

Vetti moved towards the door. 'I have nothing to prove. I never touched the evidence.'

Wisting took another step towards him. 'Why are your fingerprints on the evidence bags then?'

Vetti stopped in his tracks, his Adam's apple wobbling up and down in his sinewy throat. He wiped his mouth with the back of his hand. 'It's not ...' he protested. 'Those bags are seventeen years old. It's not possible.'

'Not only possible, it's been done.'

Audun Vetti's eyes changed; a black glimmer appeared. 'He was guilty, regardless. You could see it too, in those tiny rat eyes of his. But you couldn't get him to admit it, and we risked him getting back out into society again.' He held up a trembling forefinger. 'Okay, I did what had to be done, but you can never prove it. There's plenty of ways to explain the fingerprints. I'll say I was in the lab going through the evidence. Picked them out, one by one. That was part of my job.'

'You just told me you had never touched the evidence bags,' Wisting said. 'That you'd never even seen them.'

Audun Vetti snorted. 'Who'll believe your version? Internal Affairs have already charged you.'

Wisting moved to the window and jerked the curtains aside. The moonlight was brighter now, and he could see Finn Haber's fishing boat at the jetty. The old skipper jumped nimbly ashore.

A faint sound from the shelf below the window was just audible, the hiss of a cassette tape running. Wisting followed Vetti's gaze to the depressed *play* and *record* buttons on the old portable radio.

'Listen. Soon I'll be officially appointed chief constable. I can resolve this. Get it to work to the advantage of us both.'

'I'm listening.'

'We needed to have a secure case,' Vetti continued. 'The media were hounding me. It was for the best for all of us. No one was damaged by it and Haglund got what he deserved.'

The timbers creaked on the verandah outside. 'You were the one who killed her,' Wisting said. Finn Haber entered and stood with his arms crossed. 'You killed Cecilia Linde,' he repeated. 'When you told Gjermund Hulkvist of *Dagbladet* about the cassette tape you delivered her death sentence.'

Pressing *stop*, he ejected the cassette and tucked it into his breast pocket.

Vetti staggered backwards, swaying like a tree about to fall. From his eyes, he knew he was going down.

82

When Nils Hammer placed a large mug of coffee in front of him, Wisting saw how the days of responsibility for Linnea's disappearance had taken their toll. He was pale and exhausted, and his eyes were bleary and fixed, greyer than usual.

'I thought Vetti was supposed to be here,' Hammer said.

Wisting could not muster the energy to answer. Christine Thiis, the assistant chief of police, appeared in the doorway with a sheaf of papers.

'Have you seen Vetti?' Hammer asked.

She sat down. 'He's ill.'

'Ill?' Hammer repeated. 'He seemed perfectly well yesterday.'

Christine Thiis shrugged, not seeming to know any more about Vetti's absence. She said, handing a sheet of paper to Wisting: 'Your suspension is lifted.'

'That's good,' Hammer said. 'Rudolf Haglund is asking for you.'

'Is he all right?' Christine Thiis asked.

'He's in a custody cell. The patrol car collected him from the hospital an hour ago.'

'Will he talk?'

'To Wisting,' Hammer replied.

The assistant chief of police looked at Wisting. 'Will you do that?'

Wisting had talked to many people who had committed serious crimes. Getting close to them, encouraging them to open up, had given him insight and understanding. Once, he had struggled to get through to a man suspected of car theft. He had asked for advice from an older colleague who told him it was impossible to teach how to elicit a confession; you had to find your own way.

Wisting had found his own way: easy, quiet and patient. He could listen without letting his emotions get in the way, put himself in the other person's shoes and demonstrate empathy. In time he had learned that, deep inside, all human beings are afraid of being alone. Afraid of loneliness, everyone craved a hearing.

Haglund held his secrets inside for seventeen years. No one was born to carry such a burden and he too must long to share his innermost thoughts. Even if it put him inside again, the need to be heard would overwhelm even that.

Wisting got to his feet. If Haglund would talk only to him, he should listen. Not for Haglund's sake, but for the people he had wounded. The people who needed to know what happened to their loved ones.

Four hours later he completed the interview and entered a silent conference room. The entire department had gathered. 'Done?' Nils Hammer asked.

Wisting pushed the interview report across to Christine Thiis.

He had persuaded Haglund to tell the whole story from the time he met Jonas Ravneberg while fishing and the two men developed a kind of reticent, tacit friendship. The interview concluded when he confessed to killing Ravneberg and breaking into his house to search for the video tape, ending up in a brawl with Line as he fled.

'He was practically living at Ravneberg's farm the summer Cecilia went missing,' Wisting said. 'Secluded and out of the way, it was exactly what he needed. Also, he had it

316

to himself since Ravneberg stayed mostly at his girlfriend's house. He repaired the roof, did joinery work in the barn and undertook the kind of tasks Ravneberg couldn't do for himself. He fished in the river, used the smokehouse and looked after a few pigs.'

'And kept Cecilia Linde captive in the cellar,' Hammer said.

'During Ravneberg's few visits, which were at specific times, he gagged her and drove her about until he could shut her in again. That was when she smuggled out the Walkman. When his car was highlighted in the media, he hid it in the barn. His intention was to get rid of it permanently but he was arrested first.'

'But Ravneberg must have found it. Why did he never say anything?'

'He discovered the car, the clothes and the video camera, and even the initials of the two girls on the cellar wall, and he got scared. Haglund had used his cellar. The year before, it was his car Haglund used when he snatched Ellen Robekk. He guessed, and eventually knew, that Haglund was going to be convicted, at least for the Cecilia case. He chose the solution he had always chosen. He left the car there and fled from his problems.'

'What happened?'

'Haglund knew the cigarette butts found by the police couldn't be his. He had smoked at the Gumserød crossroads while he waited for Cecilia, but he hadn't thrown away his cigarette. When the case was reopened, there was only one thing standing between him and a million kroner compensation claim: the video film. He tried to persuade Ravneberg to hand it over. We know how that ended.'

'That's it,' he said, getting to his feet, but he could tell they wanted more. 'Everything is in these papers. All the details.'

Hammer accompanied him to the door. 'One more thing,'

he said. 'Which one of us did it? Who planted the false evidence?'

The silence following his question was almost combustible, every eye was on him, and the name he gave was as devastating as a bomb blast. He left the conference room, closing the door behind him, and drove home without really feeling anything, neither satisfaction nor anger.

The paved courtyard in front of his home was scattered with twigs and rotten leaves. No one was waiting inside now that Suzanne was on her way out of his life. Again he would have to face going to bed alone and getting up alone in the mornings. Solitary meals. Why in the world should it be so difficult to share his life with another person? Was there no room for more than the police?

He stood for a few moments in front of the empty house, thinking about all he had endured. Not only his break with Suzanne, but also how it felt to be investigated himself. It had been degrading for him and those around him, but it had been instructive too. Its lessons would be with him the next time he sat on the safe side of the table in the interview room.

He skirted round the car, opened the boot and took out a football. With slightly more force than intended, he threw it over the hedge.

83

The double newspaper stand in the reception area of the *VG* building was almost empty. The editor had crammed as much information as possible into two lines of front-page caption. *Murderer charged again. Kept third kidnap victim alive.* Different sizes of font had been used so that *alive* was what caught the eye. The familiar photograph of Linnea Kaupang was placed so no one could be in any doubt about who was *alive*. In the main picture she had her back turned, blankets round her shoulders, on her way into an ambulance, the camera flash bright on police uniforms. Line's name was printed in small letters under the lower edge.

The editorial office hushed when she entered. Journalists who seldom lifted their eyes from their computer screens turned towards her. The news editor at one end of the room began to clap. The applause spread, followed by whistling and cheers. Joakim Frost came out from his glass office and stood with his hands by his side, smiling broadly. More from satisfaction at the circulation figures than recognition, Line suspected.

When the spontaneous ovation from her colleagues subsided, she sat down behind a desk. Frost approached her. 'I'm pleased the news about your father didn't get in the way of the journalist in you,' he said. 'Fresh newspapers come every day. Readers soon forget. What we wrote about yesterday, no one remembers tomorrow; by then there are new villains or heroes on the front page.'

He made the accusations against her father sound trivial.

'Now we need a follow-up,' Frost continued. 'Everyone's trying to get hold of Linnea Kaupang, but you were the one who rescued her from the cellar. Line, can you take Harald or Morten with you and do an interview?'

Line shook her head. 'I'm busy with another story. Morten P and Harald are busy too.'

'I don't think you quite understand,' Frost said. 'This *is* the story.'

'No, it's not! Morten P has just received confirmation that the Ministry of Justice is about to bring a summary dismissal case against a chief constable. I'm going to write about the reasons ...' She produced an old-fashioned cassette tape from her bag. '... And this will be a story that isn't based on speculation and assumption.'

84

The sky had been clear since early morning, but grey clouds had formed and it was now overcast and dark. William Wisting left his car and gazed up at the autumn sky and a large, black bird that wheeled repeatedly before landing on a mountain ledge, screeching hoarsely. A raven in the mountains had given the little smallholding the name *Ravneberg*.

Frank Robekk was already standing beside the turf house situated where the river curved past what had once been pasture. The tiny building was a small smokehouse with a hole in the roof for the smoke to escape, almost like a Sami *lavvo*. Rudolf Haglund had built it. Above the fireplace he had hung eels and fish to absorb the taste of smoke from burning juniper bushes.

Wisting opened the narrow door. The acrid smell of smoke permeated the walls. This was what Rudolf Haglund had smelled of at their first meeting in the interview room. Exactly as Cecilia had described on the tape: an unpleasant smell came from him, of smoke, but also something else.

The crime scene examiners had been busy for several hours following the directions Haglund had given Wisting during their interview. It was too cramped to hold them all. The men in white suits left to make room for Wisting and Frank Robekk.

Where the fireplace had been, a pit had been dug. Gradually, the remains of the young woman buried there had been unearthed: brittle knucklebones, a cracked skull. Fragments of fabric and remnants of a shoe had been placed in a plastic bowl.

'How long …?' Robekk asked, clearing his throat. 'How long did he hold her prisoner?'

'Seven days,' Wisting said.

The muscles in Frank Robekk's face contracted. He picked the remains of what looked like a belt buckle out of the plastic bowl.

'He used a pillow,' Wisting explained quietly.

'It would have been better if he had thrown her into a ditch,' Robekk said, brushing earth from the buckle belonging to the young girl whose uncle he had been. 'Like Cecilia. Then we would at least have known where she was.'

'That was different for him,' Wisting said, using Haglund's own words. 'Letting us find Cecilia was a diversion to stop us looking for the hiding place.'

He stepped outside, giving Robekk time on his own. An unmarked police vehicle parked beside his own car at the farmhouse and Christine Thiis and Nils Hammer trudged down the grassy slope, Hammer carrying a folded newspaper. Wisting could see part of the front page where Audun Vetti's face was splashed.

'The investigators from the Bureau for the Investigation of Police Affairs picked him up for interview this morning,' Christine Thiis said. 'The public prosecutor has charged him.'

Hammer walked towards the crime scene technicians. Christine Thiis put her hand into her coat pocket. 'You should have this back,' she said.

He accepted his badge, turning it over in his hand, noticing how worn it was at the edges, how it had come unglued at one corner. For four days, he had not been a police officer. He had not only lacked his accustomed authority, he had also been accused of breaking the law. He had always thought what made him a good detective was his ability to see more than one side of a case. This was the first time he had actually been there. On the other side.

He ran his thumb over his picture, feeling the scratches on the little plastic cover. The photograph was old. He had looked better then. His hair had been thicker and darker, and his cheeks fuller, but he was a better policeman now. His hand closed tightly round it.